C0-AZX-748

THE
CASE OF THE
FRAGMENTED
WOMAN

THE
CASE OF THE
FRAGMENTED
WOMAN

CLEO JONES

St. Martin's Press
New York

THE CASE OF THE FRAGMENTED WOMAN.
Copyright © 1986 by Cleo Jones. All rights reserved.
Printed in the United States of America. No part of this book may be used or
reproduced in any manner whatsoever without written permission except in the
case of brief quotations embodied in critical articles or reviews. For information,
address St. Martin's Press, 175 Fifth Avenue, New York, N.Y. 10010.

Design by Paolo Pepe

Library of Congress Cataloging in Publication Data

Jones, Cleo,
The case of the fragmented woman.

I. Title.
PS3560.0465C37   1986   813'.54   86-13154
ISBN 0-312-12328-0

First Edition

10 9 8 7 6 5 4 3 2 1

For Joan:
for those old days when she took my children
so I could write;
and I hers, so she could paint.
And for Marie,
A great storyteller.

I had been at the desk all morning, and I was determined to sit there until something decent came out of the typewriter. Twice, I typed:

> Once there was a woman put into a box with a smaller box inside. And all day long people in the smaller box told her what was right: a white laundry; what was wrong: germs in the toilet and ring-around-the-collar. Told her how to love her children: buy Crest toothpaste and Jiff peanut butter.
>
> Strong men cared for her: Mr. Muscle cleaned her oven; and Mr. Clean, her kitchen.
>
> Still, she felt discontent and wondered what was beyond the walls of her box.

Twice, I ripped it out, tore it up, threw it away. Bored housewives are out, passé, stale, obsolete. Besides, they're boring. I even bore myself. And certainly Sid. But then it occurred to me suddenly that perhaps I have always bored Sid.

I felt an idea for a story seeping in unbidden. I took a pen and a three-by-five card and scribbled.

Bored housewife kills husband.

Horror hit me hard. Where had that come from? I'm fond of Sid—sort of. Really I am. I tore the card into confetti, started to drop it into the wastebasket, and then on second thought burned the pieces in the ashtray. I wouldn't want my children to see that. I wouldn't want them to think their mother could think such things.

Obviously, it was time to get away from the typewriter. I considered alternatives. Make trifle for dessert tonight? The kids would appreciate that. I sighed.

Eat?

Better.

But those damn calories. Call someone for coffee?

I was debating that when the phone rang. I grabbed for it with undue haste.

"Mary?"

"Jill, hi," I said. "Do you want to go for coffee?"

"I can't. Listen, Mary, I need a favor."

I waited, listening hard, hearing something in her voice that said she needed it badly.

"Sure, Jill. If I can. What's wrong?"

"The agency that handles advertising for Richard's show is giving a promotional party to introduce a new line of bleach. Go with me, will you?"

"Richard's not going?"

"He . . . he's going from work."

"Is something wrong, Jill?"

A silence. "I just don't want to go. *He* says I have to."

"Nothing else?"

"No," Jill said in a small voice, "I just don't want to go alone."

"Well, sure I'll go. I was bored anyway."

There was another of those silences. I knew there was something I should say or something I should ask, but I couldn't think what.

"I've been thinking about Easter," Jill said in that little girl voice.

"Easter?" My mind searched for a connection.

"Remember that Easter my Daddy started raving about infidels who put rodents on holy cards, and you started shouting back, 'Rodents? Rodents?! Are you talking about rabbits?'"

"I don't do that often, Jill," I protested. "Most often I was the good little girl. Remember?" I think Jill often invests me with strengths I don't really possess.

"Yes, well . . . I was just thinking of it."

"Where shall I meet you?"

"The Sage Advertising Agency. In the Clawson building, say three-thirty. You know where it is?"

"Sure."

After I hung up the phone, I sat for a time staring out the window and growing increasingly uneasy. Jill sounded peculiarly desperate today. She was my oldest and probably closest friend. We'd grown up together. I should know what to do or say to help her, but I didn't.

I had an attack of that familiar feeling of the world being not quite right, of there being something out there that I should do to right it and yet having no idea what, except to feel this vague guilt.

Probably it's just me, I thought, getting up and walking across the scrap-covered floor, swinging my arms, kicking paper wads toward the wastebasket. After all, everything had just begun to look up for Jill and Richard. After years of poverty, he'd been hired to write for "Heart's Desires," a local soap. Hired, I might add, at a six-figure salary. Admittedly, it might be a certain readjustment, learning to be wealthy, but it was hard to imagine it as too big a problem.

Still, Richard's employer was an odd outfit. Local and ingrown. "Heart's Desires" was originated and sponsored totally by the Spine and Sunshine Corporation. Ostensibly, they sold biodegradable soaps, but rumor held that the real money was in selling five-thousand-dollar franchises that gave others the right to sell soap. The state's attorney general kept nosing about the company's owner and president, Patrick Henry O'Brian, but so far no charges.

I'd had the Spine and Sunshiners at my door, looking at me over their blue and white soap boxes with eyes every bit as round and sincere as those of the Seventh Day Adventists or the Mormon missionaries. And for some reason they please me, the Sunshiners. It seems symbolically correct for our society, proselytizers of soap and money. Still, it would be interesting to see those who exactly inspired such fervor in followers.

Beginning now to look forward to Jill's party, I went to find something to wear. But just what did one wear to a party to introduce a new bleach? White? Spots? An apron?

The Sage Agency was one of San Francisco's oldest and most prestigious firms. Their offices were decorated in dark wood, navy carpets with huge navy couches, brass and glass tables, and prints of pheasants and quail in clumps of grass. The effect was of taste, age, permanency. There were more modern, innovative agencies, but I suspected Patrick Henry O'Brian lusted after respectability.

The dark rooms were filled with brightly dressed people and a steady roar of conversation. A carved ice fish and swan centered the two white-covered refreshment tables, and waiters in black tuxedos passed through the crowd with trays of champagne-filled crystal glasses.

"Impressive," I said.

Jill shrugged. "Sure," she said in a dead voice.

We took a glass from a passing tray and headed for the refreshment table.

"I hate these things," she said.

"Me too. But maybe it beats making dessert."

"What?"

"Nothing." After all, Jill had problems of her own. "I don't see Richard," I said, eating one of the crab-stuffed cream puffs and scanning the people-stuffed room.

"There," Jill said, and her voice shrank thirty years.

"Oh," I said in a voice distressingly similar. I saw immediately. Richard was sitting on one of the dark couches with Hermoine Leanders, the star of "Heart's Desires." She's beautiful, I guess, if you like front-heavy women, and men do seem to. Hermoine has always seemed excessive to me. Too much wild red hair, too much boob, too much exaggerated gesture as she wailed out, "How ever shall I get through this? How will I live through this?" and other such lines that Richard and the other writers tumbled from her too-moist and full lips.

Today, she wore green velvet to match her eyes, and Richard was dressed in a cream velvet shirt with yards in the sleeves and a dozen gold chains. They leaned in toward each other just slightly, and their eyes veered abruptly away whenever they chanced to touch, but there was something about the set of the green and cream bodies or the electrical charge in the space between them. Something. It was impossible to look at them and not know that they were lovers.

"He's sleeping with her," Jill said, now that explanation was unnecessary.

I sighed and took another crab puff. It might well be a five or six puff day. "I am sorry, Jill," I said. "If there's any-thing. . . ." I let it fade away. Times like these I seem able only to spout clichés in some small, strained voice.

"Of course he's sleeping with her," a brittle voice said from behind me. I whirled. "It's a prerequisite of the job. Didn't you know?" The woman swayed slightly, pushed in between us, then toasted us with her nearly empty glass. She was as thin and whip-muscled as the starving jackrabbits that used to for-age the outskirts of the small Kansas town where Jill and I grew up. Jill introduced her as Anne Brant, adding that she and her husband Tom were the other writers of "Heart's Desires." There was a silence during which Anne drank and Jill watched her with little girl eyes.

"Did Tom?" Jill ventured at last.

"What?"

"Did Tom . . ."

"Oh my dear." Anne signaled another drink from a passing waiter. "Did Tom? Wrong tense. Does Tom?"

"But . . . but Richard . . ."

"Oh, Hermoine's ambidextrous." Anne laughed, a quick

chopping laugh. "Did you really think Richard was hired for his literary ability?"

"Look—" I said.

"He's a good writer!" Jill burst out angrily.

"He's also pretty."

"It's just an old soap opera! And local to boot! Richard's been published in the *Kenyon Review* and in—"

"You think Tom isn't talented?" Anne Brant laughed. "He's also unfortunately aging, bloating. Hermoine was getting bored." Anne too sounded bored. But I had to admit that for the first time that day, I wasn't. Somehow that made me distinctly uncomfortable.

"I don't believe any of this," Jill whispered. But she did, really.

"Hasn't Richard told you how we have to kill off our leading man because he won't be accommodating?"

"He . . . he only said there was trouble between Hermoine and Brad."

"Oh." Anne laughed and drank down half her glass of champagne.

"It sounds awkward to me," I said. "I mean so many of them. Don't they run into each other? Don't they get mad?"

"Of course not." Anne finished that glass and snatched another from a passing tray. She was more than a little plowed. "Everyone is terribly English and polite. They stand in lines outside her door. 'After you, old man.' 'No, no, old chap, you go first.'"

Jill stopped blinking and just stood staring with round eyes, her jaw hanging.

"I think she's joking." I whispered. Jill's mouth closed with a little pop.

"It's business, really." Anne laughed. "The golden vagina. Through these portals pass men who will have success."

"No fun?" I asked.

"Oh that," she said with a wave of a hand.

"That," I said. I figured it was probably easy to dismiss what you had plenty of—like some rich man lighting cigarettes with twenty-dollar bills. Not that Sid was deficient in that department, but he kind of looked on it like eating dinner: a right, a comfort, not something you would prepare for or even think about. But then he was a good father, and he didn't eat out. I supposed that was something.

"Doesn't Patrick Henry O'Brian mind?" Jill whispered.

"Why should he mind?" I asked.

"He's her lover."

"Jesus," I muttered.

Anne giggled. "P.H.O.? Mind?" She waved her glass. "I think he watches. Waiter. Hey, waiter." She lurched off to catch another drink.

"We were just raised wrong for all this, Jill."

"What do you think I should do?"

"Get Richard to quit the job."

She nodded again, sniffed. "He won't, you know. He says he's so tired of being poor—of having people look down on him because he's not working, just writing."

"Well." I shrugged. "Yeah. I can relate to that."

"But it hurts." Jill began to sob. "I feel like one big bruise inside."

I put my arm around her and sighed. "I guess it never really works out like you want, does it?"

She swiped at her eyes, shook her head, and a trumpet blared. Jill and I both jumped. The rest of the room quieted, and twenty buxomy girls came tap-dancing from a side room, wearing little, ruffled bib aprons and not much else.

"This must be the new bleach," Jill said.

I giggled, and several people about me including Jill looked startled, then disapproving. Obviously they took all this seriously and expected everyone else to do likewise. The girls bounced and bobbed; finally landing on a loud left foot, they swept twenty perfectly manicured hands back toward the door. Then out came the bleach.

The audience clapped and yelled like they were at a football game. The little man wearing a bottle with a red, white, and blue Sterex Bleach label tipped his plastic lid and bowed.

Even I had to admit the agency had done a masterful job of casting. Never had I seen a man who looked more like bleach. Not just the plastic bottle and cap. The body beneath looked to be shaped exactly like the bottle, as if it came from a mold. Then too, he was totally hairless. Not just clean-shaven. Hairless. Head, chin, arms. Nowhere did one single hair rear to mar that white, slick skin.

He grinned a sweet little smile with a baby's pink lips and then began to sing and dance, his plastic skirt belling to and fro.

> All good housewives, hear my song.
> Choose me, and you won't go wrong!
> Use me for I've got the might.
> Make me bleach your whites so bright.
> Stick with me; I'll treat you right.

Again the listeners cheered, then rushed up to shake Bleach's hand. I stood there thinking about the money someone got paid for writing that particular bit of mental pollution. I was depressed again. I decided it was probably a ten puff day. Then I decided it was a two or three cocktail day. I worked my way to the bar, passing Anne, who was telling someone with sputtering emphasis that Hermoine had had breast implants and syphilis. When I got to the bar, I hung around listening to two men rave about the new bleach until I finished my first drink. I grabbed another, decided my men were beginning to sound like a bad commercial, and began to circulate.

The agency was on the tenth floor. It was late in the day. Sunlight poured through wall-size windows, warming the room, fracturing in the melting ice sculptures. Booze and all, I began to feel peaceful.

And then I saw them: illuminated by the orange light, her golden hair aflame, his bald head glancing light like a mirror.

He was shorter and so stood looking up, his pale, lashless eyes adoring. Jill smiled down gently, like a queen receiving a subject. She'd always liked admiration, and God knows, she needed some now. Still there was something . . .

Nah. I shook my head. My lovely and discriminating friend? A bleach bottle?

Never, I thought. But for some reason I was sad again. I looked at the bar, the refreshment table. But deep inside, I knew it was time to go home.

2

Somewhere in there, Jill started to change. She stopped calling or coming for coffee, and if I called her, she'd say she was too busy to get together. I began to worry that I'd lost my oldest friend. For a time, it became my third most popular worry, just down from my daughter's new interest in boys and my son's in motorcycles.

Then one day in the networking group that Jill and I both belonged to, I began to see what was really happening with Jill.

Jill no longer talked at the networking group; she cried. The rest of us sat around and watched her uneasily.

"You're going to have to do something, Jill," someone would venture hesitantly.

"Leave the bastard," someone else would shout.

Jill would cry harder then, and we'd rather helplessly get up and go pat her shoulders.

We soon learned to wait until the last fifteen minutes of our alloted two hours before asking Jill how she was doing.

"Well," she would answer and then burst out sobbing.

And then one day in late spring it changed. That meeting was at Jill's. Looking back, I know I should have sensed something amiss as soon as I entered her apartment. It was immaculate, no open magazines or gothics on the coffee table, no rag on the mantel to mark where she had gotten with the dusting before boredom totally overcame her.

We held that meeting in their family room since the soap writers were using the living room. Jill's face was relaxed; her eyes dreamy. We had no more than seated ourselves when she bathed us with this beatific smile and began, "We've been wrong. Do you know that? We've been totally wrong."

We all just looked at her.

"We should accept ourselves, our femininity, our softness, our gentleness. We shouldn't fight our destinies, our natural natures. We should accept our holy role as women."

"I understand," Cecile said, and we all turned eagerly to her. Cecile's getting a Ph.D. in psychology, and we all look to her for wisdom.

"She's becoming a holy roller," Cecile snickered. This is about the quality of wisdom we usually get. But there is something about labels or authority or women—something—but like Charlie Brown with the football he just keeps kicking at, we never seem to stop expecting.

The rest of us turned back to Jill with saucer eyes.

"There's a spirit all about us," Jill whispered, her glowing eyes sliding from side to side, seeming to be indeed watching something moving about her. "If we accept it, relax, blend—" She smiled suddenly. "Have you ever noticed how beautiful the bubbles are when you do dishes?"

There was a hollow silence.

"The way they prickle on your wrists, the dishes coming out all shining. Order from disorder—that is true good." She stood up and went to the closet, moving with her old flowing grace and sureness, tranquility seeming to radiate from her. "I want to show you something."

We glanced at one another uneasily.

Jill pulled open the closet door and rolled out an upright vacuum cleaner. She pushed it toward us, smiling. Not one of us moved. "It's new," Jill said. "Remember how the old one kept breaking down?"

"Yeah," I muttered.

Jill passed her hand up and down the gray plastic handle, then ran the back of her fingers over the gleaming gray skin. Her lips moved. She touched the handle release and began to roll the vacuum back and forth on the orange carpet, her face softening, remolding to mirror some inner feeling. Back and forth, back and forth. Jill's eyes glowed. The tiny wheels left marks on the rug.

"This will never break down," Jill breathed, leaning toward us over the gray creature. "This will never fail me."

For some reason, jingles began to sing in my head. *Mr. Clean takes care of me. . . . I just love Mr. Muscle.* "Jill," I said too loudly. The other women looked at me with expressions of desperate encouragement. I found I had nothing else to say.

We seemed congealed in some thick watching silence, half turned toward Jill, half away. Only our eyes moved, flicking to her, to each other, to the great hushed Hoover crawling back and forth in the center of our circle, almost noiseless, except for the soft swish of its well-oiled wheels. I realized suddenly that I had seen the look on Jill's face before; it came flying forward out of memory. New Year's eve. Twenty years ago. "Should old—" Swish, swish. Jill's face just so—looking over Richard's shoulder one minute after midnight. And now over the Hoover shoulder.

Jill snapped the machine upright. It had a grinning, sensual expression on its chrome face.

Since then, I've had nightmares about that vacuum. I'm sleeping and someone touches my breast. I open my eyes, and there in the dead light of dawn is the Hoover bending over me. I raise my arms, and he lifts me, turns me over, and I lick the carpet with my tongue.

I've thought about asking Cecile what it means, but then again I'm afraid she'll tell me.

"Out there," Jill went on in a hushed voice, one hand still on the gray plastic handle. "All about us, it's all working smoothly —bringing food, carrying away waste, the lights are lighting, the vacuums vacuuming"—she seemed to be sinking into herself, fading from us, even from the vacuum—"washers washing, dryers drying . . ."

Cecile began to flounce with irritation, but the rest of us were mesmerized.

". . . drains draining. Who knows what makes them run?"

"Experts make them run," Cecile snapped.

Jill gave her a small secret smile. "That's what *they* tell you." She looked about at the rest of us. "But think, just ask yourselves, don't you only think they do, because *they* tell you they do?"

She waited, triumphant, for an answer, her gleaming eyes picking at each of ours in turn. "Do you want some coffee cake?" Since this was said in the same tone of voice, it took some time for any of us to respond.

Minds are funny things. Like being in a forest, a slight turning, a hesitation, couldn't it be that there are Martians in space ships, a step more and suddenly people are goose-stepping and *heiling* or Mansoning, having an altogether ecstatic time? It has always seemed to me man's duty to weigh and estimate, to worry every turning, to send his reason to leap and crash against that great wall of possibility, uncertainty, to do the best he can with his puny means. Still you can't blame man for trying to get back into the garden and regain some innocence.

I started then to hope she was sleeping with Harvey.

Hormone deficiency, hairless, whatever. It was a step up from a vacuum cleaner.

Friends are such precious commodities. I hoped Jill wasn't going mad. But hope seemed all I could do. Hope that this was just one of those jagged times we all have to pass through. I hoped something resembling the old Jill would come out the other side.

And then it seemed there was something more I could do.

It was a bright, spring morning, and I was shaking out closets and considering ways to rearrange my whole life when the doorbell rang. I answered it and found Cecile on the doorstep. This was a considerable surprise since Cecile had never before seen fit to visit. To my knowledge, she's never visited any of the group. We're all older than Cecile—all middle-aged housewives trying to break out of or into something else. And as I said, Cecile is a graduate student in psychology. It's my secret theory that she's writing her Ph.D. thesis on us.

"Mary," she said and stomped past me before I had time to say hello. "I guess you know she's gone?"

"She is?" It was early, and my mind popped as I tried to figure out who was gone and where.

"They found her car abandoned down in the Mission district. Police think she was kidnapped."

"Who?" I said, growing alarmed.

"Car was wiped clean of fingerprints."

"Jill?" I shrieked out. I had gotten so in the habit of worrying about her.

"No," Cecile said, sounding disgusted. "Hermoine Leanders. Jill probably did it."

"She did not!" I screamed.

Cecile shrugged. "She's not running on a full tank, Mary. You have to admit the pistons are pinging. All that Great Detergent in the Sky stuff."

Sometimes I lie in bed at night trying to imagine clients actually going to Cecile with problems. Maybe she'll go into experimental psychology and torture little animals.

"The thing is," she said, "we probably should go by Jill's and just see if she needs anything."

I understood now why she was here. With me, she'd have a better chance of getting in. Still, maybe she was earnestly concerned. And I did feel a sudden urgent need to check on Jill, and I cannot deny, coward that I am, that there would be something comforting about having Cecile and her head full of psychology books along.

"OK," I said. "Wait just a moment and I'll get a sweater."

We took the bus. I looked out the window, watching the old paint-shedding Victorians and the big, pink stucco apartment buildings flipping by. "I had another argument with Carolee last night," I muttered.

"Adolescent children must rebel," Cecile recited, squirming to work a notebook out of her jeans pocket.

"Um," I said. "And that motorcycle of Timmy's. It worries me." It was madness to admit such things to Cecile, but it's like an itch that must be scratched. If Cecile hadn't been there I'd probably have told it all to that little old lady with the kind face and shiny black straw hat across the aisle.

"Motorcycles," Cecile answered. "Slaying the dragon."

"Beg pardon?"

"The dragon. The archetypal mother symbol. Boys have to do that before they can get the princess."

"A dragon? A dragon!" I stared at her. "And now it's my fault he rides motorcycles. Mothers get blamed for everything! You know that, Cecile? Absolutely everything."

Cecile shrugged. "Jung," she said, digging a pencil from her back pocket and opening the little yellow notebook. The bus racketed on up Turk. A young girl sitting beneath the No Radios sign snapped on a transistor. "Drop Kick Me, Jesus, Through the Goal Posts of Life" blared out.

"Jung," I muttered.

"Uh-huh. Everybody lives a myth. What would you say yours was, Mary?"

I thought about it watching an old lady working her way slowly onto the bus behind one of those three-legged chrome canes. "Cinderella," I said. "Someday my prince will come, but I have to sweep till he gets here." I paused. The old woman sank wearily onto a green, plastic leather seat. "The thing is,

Cecile, he came, and I'm still sweeping. Still, I keep hoping—
not for a prince perhaps . . ." I scowled, thinking. "A savior
maybe."

"Save yourself," Cecile said shortly. She lives in a wonderfully simple world. "Cinderella isn't a myth. Jung probably
wouldn't mind though." Cecile probably had a direct pipeline
to him. "Jill doesn't talk much does she?"

I blinked. "Jill? No."

Cecile licked the lead of her pencil and wrote *Jill* at the top of
the first page of her notebook and then beneath it: *1. Doesn't talk
much.*

It occured to me that in all that warm supporting a networking group is supposed to do, I may have overlooked the fact
that I didn't much like Cecile.

We walked two blocks over to the large, exclusive apartment
complex where Jill now lived. She answered our buzz, told us
to come up, and was waiting in the open door of her apartment
as we came down the long hall, the deep carpet sucking away
the sound of our feet.

"Oh, Mary, Cecile, how nice of you to drop by," Jill cried,
happily leading us into her pale, quiet living room. Richard,
Tom, and Anne were already seated on the couch before the
TV.

"Any word about Hermoine?" I found I was whispering.

"See," Jill said, waving at her glass collection. "Not one single fingerprint." I stared stupidly down into all those glittering
little animals. "That's not easy to do because when you pick
them up to dust them, you almost always leave marks." She
smiled brightly at us. "I have a secret method. I'll be glad to tell
it to you if you want to know."

"Time warp. We just got stuck in the Glass Menagerie,"
Cecile muttered.

"Later," I said quickly.

Jill nodded. "All right. I've also got a marvelous new way for
getting tea stains out of tablecloths. I'll give you that too." She
led us over to the writers, who looked politely irritated at this

interruption of their important work of planning just what Hermoine/Madaline couldn't live through next, that is, if she lived through this disappearance.

"Oh hi, Mary," Richard muttered in respect for the nearly twenty years we'd known one another.

"Richard," I said and sat down on the pale couch at a right angle to theirs. Cecile slumped down beside me, shoved her hands in her jean pockets, and stared accusingly across at the three writers.

"Any word about Hermoine?" I asked casually.

Richard frowned.

"This is so nice," Jill cried happily. "I'm so glad you all dropped by. I've got a cake in the oven and a fresh pot of coffee on."

"Naturally," Cecile muttered.

Tom and Anne, who are Jack Spratt and his wife reversed—her thin; him, fat; and her complexion as red as his is dead white—were staring, steadily, stonily toward the TV. Obviously, they were fighting. Jill stood just behind them, beaming down, one hand laid gently over the other.

Cecile ground her jean-clad bottom on the damask couch.

"Any word of Hermoine?" I asked again, too brightly.

"No," Richard snapped, reaching toward the TV controls.

"She'll turn up," Tom muttered.

"If she doesn't, it'll sure play hell with our chances of getting the show on a national network." Richard turned on the set, and Hermoine's tortured face jumped out at us.

Both Cecile and I started. "There she is!" we cried out, my voice relieved after all, Cecile's decidedly grumpy.

Richard and Tom looked crossly at us.

"Taped," Richard said. "The show's taped. We have Hermoine for a couple of weeks yet."

"She'll turn up," Tom said again.

"I'd better see to that coffee for you," Jill said brightly. "But actually, you know, I don't think she will."

Richard shot around. "What?!"

"Jill," I cried, trying to stop her.

"She's a disruption; she creates disorder," Jill said, shaking her head sadly. "I just don't think she'll be allowed."

"Jill," Richard shrieked.

"Please don't yell, Richard. It isn't my choice, you know."

"Yup," Cecile muttered, writing wildly in her little notebook. "Like dust and dirty laundry, poor ol' Hermoine must be tidied away."

Jill made an apologetic little motion with one hand and went off to the kitchen.

The room was hushed then except for the TV sound. The off-white drapes were closed, and light crept beneath them, spreading like shadow on the thick white rug. The air smelled faintly of rose air freshener.

Richard, resplendent in lavender velvet shirt and fourteen gold chains, leaned in toward the set as Hermoine's face filled the twenty-nine-inch screen. She did look good with that heavy red hair and the green eyes that look constantly hungry. But there was a slight green cast to her skin. There was a color malfunction in the set.

Hermoine (Madaline in the soap) waved her arms, gritted her teeth, and wailed, *Oh, how ever shall I bear this?* Her magnificent breasts beneath the fragile pink gown rose and fell with her agitated pant.

Richard and Tom's eyes misted; their jaws sagged.

"*Oh, oh, oh,*" Madaline wailed, arching her back, tearing at her heavy red hair. Her large nipples pointed through the soft cloth. Mournful background music swelled.

Richard and Tom's hands slid unconsciously along their thighs.

"*Aug—*" Now a strap fell over one shoulder—lace inched over one full breast. Madaline is so full-busted she seems, like a ship's figurehead, to be leaning into the wind.

Richard and Tom strained forward. They knew the scene would dissolve before public taste could be offended. Still, their eyes watched unblinking as lace slipped inexorably down that soft incline.

"*A-a-a-a-a,*" Madaline screamed on.

So close. So close. Richard and Tom passed thumbs over fingertips. I watched, sensing that both were reliving the feel of that breast, that nipple. I was resentful and moved all at the same time. Soft sighs rose throughout the pale room.

"*E-e-e-e.*"

Jill came from the kitchen with quick, busy little steps and started to dust her glass animals, then glanced toward the TV. She stiffened. "Oh dear, just look at that."

The men ignored her.

She scurried over and bent to peer into Madaline's vast, screaming mouth. "Just look at that."

"Jill," I whispered. "Jill, come sit here by me."

She gave me a vague smile. "No time, Mary. No time to sit."

Richard and Tom hissed irritation and leaned to see around her.

"How did that get so smudged?" Jill polished at the big green breast, her dustcloth a perfect censor's patch.

Richard and Tom gritted their teeth in concert, and the breast faded into a small, dancing bleach bottle. Now Jill's face softened. Gently, she Windexed the bottle's tiny underwear-clad legs; polished the little red, white, and blue label; the small red cap. Jill stroked her rag along his little plastic handle and hummed as he sang, "*All good housewives hear my song—*"

"Jill," I shouted this time. "Could we have coffee or something?"

"It's on," she breathed. Cecile began to write furiously.

Richard looked off out the window and smoothed his blond, wavy hair. Jill told me once that she thinks when he makes love to her he thinks of Hermoine, but I'd bet he, like Narcissus, never stops admiring his own beauty in the pools of his mind.

Hermoine's face reformed beneath Jill's fingers, and she backed off. Richard and Tom leaned eagerly in.

"*Brad, are you the father of my daughter's baby?*" Madaline demanded.

The camera dollied to a bed with a man covered to the waist with a sheet. He had magnificent green shoulders and a square, handsome face, working now on remorse. I'd seen him at the bleach party, but he certainly looked better undressed. Cecile, Anne, and I leaned with the men.

"*Yes,*" Brad said.

The camera flew back to Madaline to catch her oversized looks of horror, anger.

Jill went out and after a moment trotted back on tiny feet, carrying a silver tray. "Coffee's ready," she called out brightly.

Both Tom and Richard raised a hand for silence. She plopped the tray on the table before them, then resumed polishing her collection of glass animals.

"*How could you?*" Madaline screamed. "*How could you?! You were her psychiatrist!*"

"*Madaline, please listen!*"

"*After all that's happened to her! The man she loved turning out to be her father's hit-and-run killer! Then being raped, and that jury finding her attacker innocent! And now this! Now this! How could you?!*"

Jill ran a finger across the mantel. It came away clean.

"*I've had to have her committed,*" Madaline screamed, her full, sensual face flushing greener. "*My baby!*" She ran at the naked man, fists flailing. He sat beneath her pounding hands, eyes closed, face working. Suddenly he reached up and toppled her onto the bed beneath him. There was a ten-second close-up of his rather fine back and shoulders. After a moment, Madaline's perfectly manicured hands creeped up and across that back, and everything faded into a box of Sunshine Soap.

"Well," Richard said, then stopped, cleared his throat. "Well—rather powerful, don't you think? Too bad we have to get rid of Brad."

"Yeah," Tom agreed. "Too bad."

"Listen," Jill said.

We all stilled.

"Just listen to all the hushed sounds of order. The purr of elevators and machines, of people coming up, trash going down, dishes being washed, garbage consumed. Pulsing like a giant heartbeat. Doesn't it make you feel . . ." She thought about it. "Comforted?" She frowned slightly. "No, safe."

"Anal," Cecile muttered.

I glared. "It makes *me* feel safe," I said too loudly.

Richard gave me one of his slight smiles.

"But you're not drinking your coffee," Jill cried. She set down her dustcloth and hurried to fill the cups. "It'll get cold."

"You know," Anne said, "If Hermoine doesn't turn up, we won't have to get rid of Brad."

"She'll turn up." Tom tried not to look uneasy, but he was. Tension hung in the pale room like fog.

Richard frowned. "How are we gonna get rid of Brad anyway?"

"His shoulders brought the ratings up two points," Anne said.

"Suicide," Tom said.

"Maybe murder."

"Jeez, Richard, we had the hit-and-run just last year."

"So her husband jumped from the damn bridge two years ago."

"Actually she's killed off five husbands and lovers in the last two years," Anne said. "Let's have him go to Arizona."

The two men glared.

"Jill," Richard said. "What do you think? Would you kill him?"

Jill looked fondly down at Richard's fine-boned face, touched his blond Shakespearean waves. "Oh no," she said softly, happily. "No, I'd kill her."

We all sat for a moment in a ringing silence, listening again to Jill's words and thinking of Hermoine missing, her car abandoned.

The phone rang, and Jill trotted off to answer it.

"She'll turn up," Tom whispered. Everyone turned to stare at him.

"She'll turn up."

3

Hermoine went on bellowing at Brad, *"I trusted you! Dr. Morton says this pregnancy may push her right over the edge."*

"She looks so like you, Madaline. I only did it because—because she looks like you." Brad's voice throbbed anguish. *"All these years I've had to look at you across crowded rooms. I've had to watch you with Stanley and then with your husband. I've had to watch you with other men, touching them, smiling at them, while inside I've been dying that it isn't me you touch. I ache to hold you. You! No one else. Only you!"*

And despite my worry about Jill, or maybe because of it, I felt myself sliding into it. In a world where all people say to you day after day is, "Where's my gray socks?" or "Isn't there any milk?" it does tap your fantasy to have a handsome psychiatrist whispering desperately, "All these years I've wanted you, only you."

"I don't believe this mush," Cecile sneered.

"Hush!" Richard growled.

And so we sat there, faces flickering blue-white, watching Hermoine register horror at Bradley's confessions until Jill came back with a plate of sliced cake. She plunked it on the coffee table before Richard, smiled at us all, then reached out and switched the TV channel.

"Jill!" Richard screamed, echoed closely by Tom and Anne.

"He says to watch this," Jill said firmly.

We all stared at her as she stood smiling back at some broadly smiling master of ceremonies.

"Who's *he*?" Richard said uneasily. I'd seen him with this

expression once or twice before, but mostly Richard tries to overlook the possibility that his wife is going mad.

"He," she said. "You know." She bent and gracefully began pouring coffee.

"The head tidier," Cecile volunteered in her flat voice. "The ultimate cleaner. The Great Detergent in the Sky." She began writing again.

Jill lifted her head and looked at Cecile. "Why yes," she said after a moment, her eyes brightening. "Yes, that might be right."

I sighed.

"Turn back the TV," Richard said angrily.

"No," Jill remonstrated, pushing a coffee cup into his limp hands. "*He* says we have to watch this."

"Switch it back, I said!" Richard gritted. Tom lit a cigarette and blew smoke from between his teeth. Anne ran a hand of chewed nails through her red hair. Embarrassed, I looked away.

"Listen, bastard!" Cecile screamed. "This is her house too! And she can damn well watch anything she wants!"

The room fell into a sudden shocked silence. We all stared at Cecile, then thought better of it and turned to stare at the TV. I was beginning to like ol' Cecile after all.

The program was some sort of quiz show. A vast, glittering red staircase covered with brightly wrapped gift boxes ran up center stage. Contestants clambered about among the boxes, ultimately choosing one. They could choose as many times as they wished and stop at any time, but if they chose one containing the "dunce hat"—a sort of witch's hat hung with signs, toys, and noisemakers—they lost everything.

"This is local," Richard said scornfully. "One of Prescott's brainchildren."

"Running them live," Tom added. "Cheaper, and besides he thinks there's more suspense that way. People watch 'cause their neighbor might be on."

Jill placed a cake plate in my hands. "Can you manage? Do

you need a TV tray?" I shook my head. A thin woman chose a box with *the* hat.

"*Oh,*" screamed the master of ceremonies, jerking out *the* hat and slapping it on the woman's head. Buzzers went off; the audience groaned. "*What a pity, Mrs. Groden! I guess you lose that new living room set and the twelve-place setting of Haviland china!*"

The woman, close to tears, wandered off stage; Jill delivered the rest of the cake. We all sipped and watched in uncomfortable silence as the careless wife is accused of her husband's ring-around-the-collar.

"Look at that," Cecile said. "The thing is, why aren't we all crazy?"

I alone grinned.

Some dreadfully obese little woman with two raisin eyes peering from beneath a dark Dutch cut was chosen as the next contestant. "*All right now, Mrs. Aznar,*" the man with the keyboard smile yelled. "*You choose a box! Any box!*"

The woman waddled up the stairs, hesitated, then touched a box. A svelte blond in something like a bunny suit picked it up and undulated down the red staircase, Mrs. Aznar stumbling after. The blond smiled with glycerined teeth at the master of ceremonies, and with a flourish set the box on the table before him.

"*So,*" he said, bending, peering under the lid. "*Let's see. Oh, Mrs. Aznar,*" he said sadly, reaching in, "*Oh, I am so sorry!*"

The little eyes stared steadily at him from beneath the square of hair.

"*There just seems to be an old oar in here.*" He slid it out and shoved it into her plump hands.

"*Oh,*" she said.

He peeked again then bellowed, "*Wait! There is something else down here . . . a little piece of paper. . . .*" He retrieved it, read it. "*Mrs. Aznar,*" he cried, then waited dramatically. She stared at him, twisting her hands. "*Mrs. Aznar, you'll have to have some place to use that oar.*"

Mrs. Aznar licked her lips.

"*So,*" he screamed, "*we're flying you to Venice, Italy!*"

"*Oh,*" she cried. "*Oh!*" She began jumping up and down, her great breasts oscillating.

"*Two weeks in the Venice Hilton!*"

She did an odd cheerleader-type jump: back arched, legs flying apart; squealing, "*Oh Venice! Venice! I'm coming! I'm coming!*"

"Jesus," Cecile cried. "Talk about prostitution."

"More cake?" Jill said.

"Imagine hoping to bump 'Heart's Desires' with that," Richard sneered. "Please, Jill, can't we turn it back?"

Jill smiled and shook her head; the little fat woman climbed the stairs and touched her next box. The blond bunny carried it down and again our happy M.C. peeped.

"Jeez, Jill," Cecile muttered, "I don't think I can take it again."

"*Oh, Mrs. Aznar,*" the M.C. cried, snatching the lid away, flinging it over his shoulder, "*I'm sorry, but*"—he shoved both hands into the box—"*you've got the hat!*" He jerked it out by the brim for all to see. The buzzers started, then the groans. The camera zoomed in. And suddenly, as if someone had flipped a switch, there was absolute silence—then screams. Framed for an instant in the big color screen was the hat with all its signs, colored ribbons, and plastic toys dangling from the brim. But this time it didn't seem to be empty. There, staring from behind a rubber hamburger and a plastic rattle, was a face. A human face. A head had been fastened into the hat and its red hair and severed muscles quivered right along with the colored ribbons and rubber spiders.

"Oh, my God!" Richard gasped, shooting forward on the couch. "It's Hermoine! My God! It's Hermoine!"

"Actually," Jill corrected, "it's only her head."

4

There was a silence so deep it numbed the ears of us trying to hear beyond it. We all sat there staring at that blank screen. Then someone began to babble behind it. "... *terrible tragedy here at station KXVU ... head of an unidentified woman ...*"

"That was Hermoine, wasn't it?" Richard asked. "I'm sure that was Hermoine."

"Jesus," Tom said in an odd voice. "Well, I guess that's all she wrote."

"Was it Hermoine?" Richard repeated.

"Yea," Cecile said, slumped on her spine, eyeing the ceiling. "That was Hermoine. She finally turned up."

Richard was trying to light a cigarette, but his hands trembled so the match kept going out. "Brandy," he croaked. "Jill, bring the brandy."

"Richard, it's hardly noon yet," she said, coming around the couch to sit beside Richard and pat his shoulder.

I stared at her; she was still smiling tranquilly.

Tom cleared his throat and looked around at the others with those tiny eyes in that great expanse of white face. "Well," he suggested hopefully, "maybe she could commit suicide."

I was disoriented. "Suicide?"

"Off screen?!" Richard sneered. "Off screen? That's brilliant Tom! Just brilliant!"

Anne's thin mouth curved in a satisfied smile; her eyes watched some inner scene. "She'll be murdered, just as she was in real life. Well, maybe not the head-in-the-box thing. That's corny. Hard to motivate. But murdered someway, somehow. The viewers will eat it up."

Tom and Richard stared at her, their eyes widening, focusing, beginning to glow. "Of course," Richard said in an awed voice. "Like the time they had the real funeral for Grandpa on 'As the World Turns.'"

"And remember how our ratings soared when Hermoine's husband jumped off the Golden Gate Bridge."

"I didn't know she'd ever been married," Cecile said, staring morosely at one kneecap.

Richard looked at her in disgust. "On the program! On the program! We have people do real things in real places. The viewers love it."

"I see," Cecile said. "Jump from a familiar bridge. Interesting." She gave a shrug and wrote in her little yellow tablet.

Richard frowned. "But who would have killed her?"

"Man, I'd say," Cecile said, still writing. "Castration complex."

My eyes flew to her face. No, she wasn't kidding. I was horrified to find a giggle rising in my throat. All these symbols. Severed heads in boxes on boxes! Freud would freak. Art, in this case, must copy life.

"Brad would be the obvious killer," Tom said.

"No," Anne put in quickly. "No, we'll need his shoulders now."

Tom watched her through narrowed eyes, searching for hidden motives. Sauce for the gander, and he looked like one, too.

They went on intently nominating and rejecting killers; they were hardly aware any longer that, beneath all this, there was a real woman dead.

"This may be the best thing that could have happened to the show," Anne said suddenly, then hearing herself she added quickly, "poor Hermoine."

The phone began to ring: producers, directors, the press. The TV was blurting, *"The body* [meaning the head] *has been identified as that of famed beauty and TV star Hermoine Leanders, forty-five, star of the local show, 'Heart's Desires.' Ladies and gentlemen, ladies and gentlemen! A bulletin has just come into our Chan-*

nel 3 newsroom. Patrick Henry O'Brian, millionaire entrepreneur and fiancé of the slain woman, has just offered a reward of twenty thousand dollars for any information leading to the arrest and conviction of her killer. Repeat: millionaire Patrick Henry O'Brian . . ."

Twenty thousand dollars. I felt my eyes glaze. I could hire a cleaning woman for years. Well, not that I would rip off a sister that way. Still the temptation . . . a dishwasher perhaps.

I have a recurring dream that I am somewhere in a great hall, maybe on a TV quiz program. God or Monty Hall or someone like that cries in a great, deep, stentorious voice, "Mary, Mary Sable! We are going to give you your heart's desire."

And suddenly before me is this huge box. I pull one of the red ribbons, and it falls open. There, inside, is a dishwasher.

"No," I scream. "No! Please! No! That's not my heart's desire. I want bigger things—peace—love—better things—finer things—No!"

But I lied. My heart's desire *is* a dishwasher. I used to peace march; I graduated Phi Beta Kappa; and now my heart's desire is a dishwasher.

Twenty thousand dollars. I noticed a similar avaricious gleam in Cecile's eyes.

"*The Chronicle,*" Anne called from the phone. "They want a statement."

"Tell them . . ." Richard paused, thinking.

Jill stood. "More coffee, anyone?"

I looked at her happy smile, and my mind finally closed on the fact that it was she who'd made us watch that program. How. . . ? My eyes flew to the phone in Anne's hand.

I stiffened, leaned forward. How could I have been thinking about money—dishwashers, cleaning women. Jill was my oldest friend. We'd grown up next door to each other. We'd left the small town and come to San Francisco together to seek our fortunes, so to speak. When I picture Jill back then, it is almost always in a long, black skirt she had and a sheer white blouse; ruffled arms raised against a blue sky, she is turning in endless ecstatic circles of worship to whatever was the current enthusiasm.

The big one was Richard, of course. Such a love affair. It still singes the corners of my mind to think of it.

Jill was what society would label a very feminine woman, which was in in those days. She had golden curls, big blue eyes, and those dainty little hands and feet; beyond that, she was given to wearing flowing white chiffon and pink ribbons. You felt she just screamed out for a flowered swing to complete the picture.

And Richard was blond, handsome, a writer, going to write the great American . . . I think he took one look at Jill and had fifty pages of his very own *Love Story* reeled off before he had walked across the bar and climbed up onto the vacant stool at her left; I was on the right.

"Hello," he said.

Jill gave him a level look, then turned toward me. We were proper young ladies, for all that we were adventuring in a bar, which wasn't done as much in those days.

"I've searched for you all my life," he said in this mellow voice, "and now you won't even talk to me."

Richard always was a little corny on dialogue. You can hear it in "Heart's Desires" with Hermoine always bellowing, "Dear God, how shall I bear this?" But the thing is, Jill had searched all her life for someone to say, "I've searched for you all my life." They had matched fantasies, and they just waltzed right off into them like Fred Astaire and Ginger Rogers meeting in one of those old movies and immediately beginning to spin in stylized dance: eyes and bodies clinging in an ethereal manner that was nevertheless God damned sexy.

And so they married. So young, so sure that they had nowhere to go but up, when of course they had nowhere to go but down. Like that old story of the lovers who achieved ecstasy and then killed themselves to save the moment, to never know disillusionment, saying something about letting the servants live life for them. Perhaps I have more of the servant mentality. Sid and I sort of liked each other when we got married, and we both are determined now to do the best we can for the kids, so I guess, in a way, we've a better marriage than Jill and Richard. Still, Jill has her memories, doesn't she?

And for a while, it *was* good. They had this garret, and Jill dropped the white dress for a black jersey and jeans; she got odd jobs and served spaghetti and cheap red wine to Richard's writer friends who sat on the bed, which was all the furniture Richard and Jill could afford. The writers talked about how they would never compromise their artistic integrity, and after the friends left, Jill and Richard made love in the crumbs and wine stains, and Jill cried because it was so perfect, and she was so happy.

And so amidst this perfection they forgot the mundane, and Jill forgot her diaphragm.

Two kids in three years.

And now it was Richard who held the part-time jobs. The garret filled with crying and the smell of urine, and the friends stopped coming. Richard got a full-time job, and they rented a little house. Richard wrote evenings and yelled at Jill to keep those damn kids quiet and couldn't she keep the place any neater?

Jesus, Jesus.

I had Carolee by then, so Jill and I began to sit together in playgrounds and ask each other what it all meant.

I carried along Thermoses of rum and Coke and proffered neat ideas like survival, like throwing all the socks in a drawer and letting people match them as they needed them.

Jill kept mumbling how she didn't think mothers were supposed to sit in playgrounds and drink.

"Hum," I would answer, refilling the red plastic cups, but I missed the fact that she was looking for a new vision to fit herself to, a new fantasy to live.

Years trudged by, with Jill struggling to be the perfect housewife and hating it, and then Richard was hired for "Heart's Desires." In a few years the show became a local success, rumored to be headed for the national networks.

About then, suddenly, from nowhere, Jill stopped struggling to be a perfect housewife and became one. She became the perfect mother, the ideal wife, the good woman. Still, I don't think the script called for her killing the bad woman.

The apartment had filled with the steady ringing of telephone and door bells. People kept filing in, excitement hidden behind sober faces—mostly reporters, several with huge, gray TV tape cameras propped on one shoulder. They milled about steadily, dark forms in the pale room, smoking, asking questions. Jill scurried in and about them like a timid woods creature, emptying ashtrays, offering coffee.

Richard, Tom, and Anne were standing now, giving interviews, staring somberly at their feet, murmuring things like, "A terrible tragedy, a great loss to the show, ah, to the world."

Harvey, sans his plastic bleach bottle, came in. Jill darted across the room to help him off with his coat. They whispered together, then moved into the kitchen. At last, I saw an opportunity to ask Jill about that phone call. I jumped up, blocking a big, gray NBC camera trained on Richard. The cameraman yelled; I ducked, veering toward the kitchen. Cecile started after me, tripping over microphone wires in the big saddle oxfords she'd found in the Goodwill.

"Who are you?" one young reporter shouted excitedly at me as I passed.

I stopped and looked back.

"Who are you?" he asked again.

"Mary Sable, a friend of Richard Taylor's wife."

"Are you connected with the program? Did you know the dead woman?" His words rolled over each other.

"No, I'm a housewife."

His face fell; he turned away without another word and ran right smack into Cecile, who proceeded to inform him loftily that *she* was a psychologist and that the killer was definitely a man. The reporter wrote madly, stopping only once to ask how castration was spelled.

When Cecile finally finished her "interview" she came to join me. "We've got to talk to Jill," I said. "We've got to find out how she knew to watch that program."

Cecile nodded. "Yea. That's right."

We moved on with great casualness, smiling, nodding at all the milling people (none of whom noticed), pushing through the swinging door into Jill's huge, rust-colored kitchen. This room had the feel of a cave—dim, cool, all in brown and tans, with copper ladles, pans, and jello molds hanging from the ceiling beams like stalactites. It was all supposed to look Colonial or something. Jill and Harvey were at the chintz-curtained window staring out at the city, his hand slowly stroking her pale hair as if she were a kitten.

"Jill," I whispered urgently.

She turned and smiled, her eyes slightly unfocused. "Come in, sit down." She seized the coffee pot. "A cup of coffee?" My nerves were already jangling from adrenalin and caffeine, but I knew Jill would never relax until everyone was served. Cecile threw her notebook on the antique oak table and plopped down on a delicate chair. Jill poured coffee. After a moment I took the chair across the table from Cecile.

"Jill." I hesitated, clearing my throat. Jill had grown difficult in her new strangeness. She rarely answered any question directly. It would be best to be subtle, approach her casually, trick an answer from her. "Say, Jill . . ."

Jill set a bone china coffee cup before me. Harvey sat down between Cecile and me. "Well, Mary, how are you?" he said, patting at my arm with his soft pink hand. "Terrible business this."

"Um. Ah, Jill . . ."

She poured coffee in my cup.

"Why was it that you decided to watch that program?" Well, that wasn't too subtle.

"'Surprise of Your Life'?" Jill said cheerfully.

I started. "Well, yes. Yes it was."

"That's the name of the show," Cecile muttered.

"Oh," I said.

I circled mentally, seeking some way to slide in so Jill wouldn't notice. There was a silence in the cool kitchen. The late afternoon sun came in through the window and shot pink needles of light from all that polished copper. Cecile slurped her coffee and asked, "You got any more of that cake, Jill?"

Jill looked gratified and went off to get it. I glared at Cecile, who didn't notice.

"Are you particularly fond of that program, Jill?"

Jill, coming back with the cake, shrugged.

"Someone on the phone tell you to watch it?" Cecile said loudly.

I sighed.

Jill set the cake before Cecile and sat down across from Harvey. "I'm so glad you like my cake, Cecile."

"Yugh," Cecile muttered, taking up her fork, slicing off the point of the wedge, and poking it into her mouth. Jill bent a little forward and watched Cecile's pumping cheeks intently. "I could give you the recipe. Mary, would you like some more?"

"Jill, please listen. You could be in trouble. How did you know to watch that program?"

"'Surprise of Your Life'?"

"Yes," I screamed. "Yes! 'Surprise of Your Life'!"

Cecile looked at me, bushy eyebrows raised. "Hey, cool it, Mare."

I clenched my teeth until my jaws ached.

Jill patted at my arm. "Dear Mary, such a dear friend. I just know such things, Mary. They just . . ." She gave a little shrug. "Just come to me. Do you know it has been three months since a single one of my machines has broken down?"

"The Great Detergent in the Sky bit," Cecile said through a mouthful of cake.

I had an almost irresistible urge to get up, take one of those copper ladles, and pong Cecile on the head with it. She stopped eating long enough to jot something in her notebook. Harvey turned his sweet smile in that soft baby face toward each of us in turn. I found myself briefly entertaining the thought that it was me who was mad.

I looked at Jill sitting there in her kitchen, the orange light outlining the pretty face that had hardly begun to sag or age. "Jill," I tried again slowly. "Think. They might well hang this killing on you."

Jill looked at me blankly.

"You made that statement about how you'd kill Hermoine. You—you knew to watch that program."

"Would you like more cake?" Jill cried, jumping up.

Cecile shrugged. "Why not?"

Harvey's pale blue eyes sought mine. "Do you really think they could implicate Jill in this?" He sounded worried.

I nodded.

He thought for a moment, his delicate translucent hands turning the delicate translucent cup round and round in its saucer. "We'll have to help her somehow," he said softly. "Maybe if we were to all keep our eyes and ears open we could find something, some evidence that would help clear her."

I looked at him. I couldn't find Tim's right tennis shoe and I'd been looking for weeks. How was I going to find a killer? "We wouldn't know how to go about it, Harvey."

"We'll just keep watching, listening. It can't hurt. The Brants are giving an anniversary party tomorrow. Everyone from 'Heart's Desires' will be there. You could come to that, couldn't you?"

"Well yes—but . . ."

"I'll come," Cecile said. "There's the reward, and besides, maybe I can get a thesis out of it."

"Please, Mary." Harvey covered my hand with his small one.

"Well sure, I'll come. But I doubt it'll help."

"Good. Jill, will you arrange for Anne Brant to invite Mary and Cecile?"

Jill turned with the cake tray in her hand. "Oh yes. Won't that be nice."

5

While we ate cake in the kitchen, pandemonium reigned in the living room, a steady swimming-pool roar of noise with an occasional shout surfacing from it.

"Sir, can you tell us—"

"Is it true there was trouble between—"

"Did Patrick Henry O'Brian—"

Then suddenly all was swallowed up in a great gulp of silence. The four of us in the kitchen sat up straight and looked at each other.

"What's happened?" Harvey whispered.

Cecile shot from her chair and stumped to the door. After a moment, she came back and sat down. "Police are here," she said and then took another bite of cake.

Harvey and I turned as if magnetically drawn toward Jill.

She smiled happily. "They'll probably want coffee." She got up and began to set out fresh cups.

"What are you going to tell them, Jill?" I whispered.

"About what?"

"How to get spots out of tea towels," Cecile said.

"About Hermoine—and why you wanted to watch that program."

"Well the truth, of course," Jill said. "I certainly wouldn't lie."

"Who was on the phone?" I blurted.

"I don't know. They wouldn't say."

"Man or woman?"

"I couldn't tell."

"Well, what'd they say exactly?"

"'Hello, is Richard there?'"

"They asked for Richard?"

"Yes."

"Why didn't you call him."

"Well, because he was watching his soap opera. He never likes to be disturbed in the middle of 'Heart's Desires.' You know that, Mary."

"OK, OK. So what'd they say then?"

"I don't remember exactly."

"Generally."

"Something about how I had to turn the channel so that

Richard could get answers or an answer to a question that was troubling him."

"They said that? Troubling Richard?"

"Um. And I guess he did. He had been wondering where Hermoine was."

"Yeah," I said. I wondered if the message could mean something else, and if so, what?

I chewed on my lower lip, then noticed that Harvey sitting across the table was doing the same. "She didn't kill her," I whispered. "I know her. She couldn't."

"I know that," Harvey said gently.

But for just an instant, I found myself wondering. . . .

The police cleared out all the press and sightseers, and then just like on "Murder She Wrote" or "All My Children" or "Dallas" they took everyone, one at a time, into the family room for interrogation. Being definitely a lesser character, I was one of the last to be led away. I felt scared and guilty, and I hadn't even known the damn woman. But I did know Jill, and I didn't want to give them the Jill I knew but a tidier, more compact model—Meg from *Little Women* or Beaver Cleaver's mother, anyone, but my "Stepford Wife" friend. I followed the uniformed officer through Jill's new long apartment on feet growing heavier with each step, trying desperately to fish what I should say from the mire inside my head. The telephone call? Would anyone have told them about that? Surely they would have. But then, what if they hadn't? Was it better for Jill if I mentioned it? Probably. But I just wasn't sure. The uniformed policeman left me in the hall and went back to the living room. I stood there for a while debating, then slowly, silently pushed the door open.

There were two of them. Plainclothesmen. One tall, in a gray suit; the other shorter, in blue. They stood with their backs to the door, gazing up at one of those movie-screen-size, pencil-thin, back-projection TVs set high on the far wall. It was filled with Hermoine's face, three feet wide. I stared, feeling haunted. Even dead, the damn woman was everywhere. I realized then that they were playing old tapes of the series.

"Nice-looking woman," the tall policeman said.

"Yup," the other replied. "Her. Joan Collins. Sometimes these old heaters are all right."

My head snapped up. Rage cleared my mind. I stepped into the room and slammed the door. "Gentlemen," I said, drawing Queen Mary from my depths. "You wanted to see me?" I asked with her regal voice.

"Who's this?" the older, shorter, fatter, obnoxious one asked, coming toward me.

His partner consulted a clipboard. "Mary Sable, old friend of the Richard Taylors."

"Ah yes." He kept on coming until his chin was five inches from my nose. He meant to intimidate me, which he did, but I was damned if I'd let him know it. There was such a lot of him. Huge shoulders in a navy suit coat that didn't hang right. Close-cropped gray hair, a red face, and a redder neck that bulged over his frayed shirt collar. He had ring-around-the-collar, and I voted that he was divorced rather than blame that old scapegoat, the inept wife. Old heaters considered, what woman would want to stay married to him? But I had to admit that muscles, fat, and mean manner did combine to give him a certain force.

"And you are?" I inquired with a faint smile.

"Smith. Detective Lieutenant Sam Smith. Sit down, Ms. Sable."

"I'm fine," I said right into his bulbous nose. "Thank you very much for your concern."

He glared, hesitated, then flipped open a small notebook, stepping back as he did so. After a moment, he sat on one of Jill's brown leather couches.

I felt a little foolish then, towering over him, so I sat too.

"You work, Ms. Sable?"

I didn't miss a beat. "I'm a writer."

His pen hesitated, and he looked up at me hard. "Soap operas?"

"No. Short stories. Novels," I said grandly, feeling not the least bit guilty at not adding that my output tended to be about two pages of each.

"Me too," he said, and I thought I heard just a hint of shyness.

"Oh?" I said. I noticed for the first time that he had rather nice eyes, green with spider lashes. My heart skipped just once. I couldn't believe it. He probably beat his ex-wife. The one I wasn't sure he had. But I was sure he voted Republican and believed in capital punishment. I grew up believing men were supposed to be strong, silent, in charge. Then I married one, and now I wonder why he doesn't talk to me or consult my wishes. Would I never learn? But then yearning seeps from deep pools reason can't fathom.

"So, you're a friend of the Taylors?" he asked.

"Yes."

"Known them long?"

"Who's this?" the detective who'd hovered in the background suddenly demanded.

I turned, confused, wondering if this was some sort of out-of-sync good cop–bad cop routine.

"Don't know," Sam Smith replied. "You know, Ms. Sable?"

I frowned. "Pardon?"

He gestured toward the screen. Both men studied the fragile young woman twisting shyly up there. She had apricot-colored hair, slightly mismatched eyes, and a mouth that hung open in a manner that should have made her look stupid but instead made her seem innocently sensual. She pulsed, trembled, palpitated like a trapped bird, rousing protectiveness in the breast of every male viewer.

The detective hit the sound button on the remote board, and Brad boomed, *"This isn't real love, you know. It's only neurotic dependence."*

I giggled, and Smith grinned. Damn, he wasn't all bad.

We watched for a moment as a six-inch tear tracked down a pale cheek as yet unmarked by time.

"That's the daughter," I said, relieved. I was willing to tell them about the show all day long. "She's in a mental institution. She slept with Brad, who's her mother's lover. He's also her psychiatrist. The daughter's, that is."

Both men stared at me.

"She got a name?" Smith grunted.

"Young heater," I purred.

"Cute."

"I thought you'd think so."

There was silence. Smith glared. And won.

"Polly Purger," I muttered.

"She get along with Leanders?"

"I've no idea."

"So now about Mrs. Taylor . . ."

I stiffened.

"I understand the two of you are old friends."

"Yes," I said cautiously. "Jill and I came west together."

The other cop, the one I'd decided was the good one, turned the TV sound off again. On the screen, Polly was running in slow motion, her pale hair and filmy gown undulating slowly about her, and now a young man ran toward her in the same romantic cadence.

"That's the boyfriend that died," I said in a bright, high voice. "Motorcycle accident. Last year. She's remembering him. She does that a lot. She's mourning. That's really why she made it with her shrink. It was her idea, really. He tried to resist. But you know men." I gave a false laugh.

Smith stared at me as if I were an idiot.

I didn't mind. Enough of this and maybe he'd forget to ask about Jill. "It was a good plot, her coming on to him week after week. Him resisting." More, I willed. Remember more. But I don't watch "Heart's Desires" regularly. And sometimes I daydream during Inez's recitation of the latest soap plots. Could I maybe work in some of "General Hospital?" Like the plot to freeze the whole town. Best not. I'm a pretty bad liar.

Smith snorted. "Whadda you women see in those soaps anyway?"

"I dunno," I said. He was sneering, but so what? I was set to discuss vociferously any subject but Jill. "Escape maybe. Housewives there—in the soaps—their toilets never overflow, and their children are either upstairs asleep or sitting quietly in little, ironed, ruffled dresses or suits. Of course soap parents lose their kids a lot. Sons or daughters that no one knew existed before are always turning up from here or there. But soap wives' toasters work and their houses stay tidy. Their problems have grandeur. Dignity."

"I hear that's true about your friend."

"What?"

"That her machines never break down."

Damn. I looked at him with rounded eyes. "Oh? Which friend is that?" Obviously Cecile had talked her fool head off. "Surely everyone's machines break down sooner or later. If you buy good products, I suppose . . ."

"Your buddy the shrink says she's real looney tunes."

"Well, she isn't," I snapped. The queen was suddenly back. I noted with horror that for all the traffic in this room there were still tiny wheel marks in the orange shag. Casually, I wiped out one with my foot.

"The two of you pretty good friends?"

"Yes, we are. And Cecile's a psychologist. She thinks everyone's mad but thee and me." I gave him a look that said she'd have serious reservations about thee.

"Who's that?" the good cop asked.

"Kindly old Aunt Kate," I answered through my teeth. "She keeps house for Madaline."

"In fact, you two grew up together."

"Yes," I hissed. "We did."

"And her husband's having an affair with Leanders." He gestured with a big hand to the TV where Aunt Kate was putting a roast in the oven, but I knew who he meant.

"Not unless he's a necrophiliac."

Smith looked at me through green slits. "He *was* having an affair with the *deceased*."

"Richard? No, I don't think so. Richard's most devoted."

Smith flipped back a few pages in his notebook and read aloud. "'Jill Taylor is in a serious depression since the advent of her husband's affair.' Question: 'Do you think she's capable of committing this crime?' Answer: 'Possible. Though I feel strongly that it is a man. Castration complex. I'd be happy to help you with this case. I could work up a personality profile of the killer.'"

Looking at me, Smith smiled this smug little smile that bunched his cheeks up like withered apples.

I gritted my teeth. Cecile, our Benedict Arnold buddy, our fellow support-your-sister sister. "Jill won't even swat flies!" I snapped. "She doesn't set mouse traps. She—she—"

"But her husband was having an affair with Hermoine Leanders?"

"How would I know?"

"I hear it was hashed out regularly in your woman's group."

"Networking."

"Whatever."

"She couldn't even step on a roach, back in the days when she had roaches."

"Who's this?" the good cop said.

Smith and I both spun around angrily.

"Pauline. Madaline's sister. She's on a life-support system. Someone's going to pull her plug." A huge electrical plug reared on the screen. A hand reached toward it, jerked away.

"But Mrs. Taylor's husband was sleeping with the deceased?" Smith roared.

"So was everyone!" I shouted back.

Hermoine was back, hanging over us, huge and beautiful, like the snakes we beheaded as kids that just kept twisting and slithering. Smith was interested now. He leaned closer, pen poised. "How's that? Who's everyone?"

"Everyone," I said.

"Such as?"

"Such as Tom Brant. And his wife was plenty pissed, too.

She went around telling everyone that Hermoine had breast implants and syphilis. And they were firing Brad, their leading man, because he wouldn't. And then there's Patrick Henry O'Brian. Lots of people had good reason to kill her. Lots!"

"But it was your friend who made them turn the channel on the TV set this morning?"

"Who told you that?"

He smiled. "It was Jill Taylor who made everyone watch that box show, wasn't it?"

I looked away and whispered, "Yes." I felt flat, defeated. Jill might well be the first from our graduating class to hang.

"Anything else you can tell us, Ms. Sable?"

"No."

"You sure?"

"Yes."

"Well, just remember that the withholding of evidence is a crime."

I lifted my eyes for one quick, sullen glance.

"OK, Perkins, go look up this Brad character. Taylor or Brant will give you the right name and address. I'll get Tom Brant back in here for another go-through." He said that still watching me.

Perkins went out.

"You've been most"—he paused—"helpful, Ms. Sable."

I got to my feet and headed toward the door.

"So," he said, "most likely we'll be meeting again."

There was something in his voice that stopped me, made me look back. His expression told me he wasn't going to mind that meeting a bit. He was crumpled and rumpled—clothes and skin both—and had only those eyes to recommend him, which in itself wouldn't have been so bad, but I doubted that being an old heater was a step up from unpaid maid. And still something in me fluttered. Being desired is perhaps woman's greatest aphrodisiac, and damn well her greatest downfall.

I blushed once and moved blindly toward the door.

6

"And that's about what happened," I said. "They had Jill down to police headquarters for hours yesterday asking her why she insisted everyone watch that program. She told them about the phone call, but she also keeps saying she knows things. Harvey called this morning. He doesn't think they believe her about the phone call. He said they asked him all kinds of questions about her. He's worried. And this can't be good for Jill. Particularly not now."

The rest of the network group looked at me, thinking. We were meeting in Jo Anne's living room, which is like her, so soft and fussy you seem to sink into it. The chairs are flowered; the curtains are lace; and there must be ten or more tiny stiletto-legged tables covered with crocheted doilies and little china shepherdesses or china ladies with baskets in their fragile hands or holes in their delicate heads for flowers. We meet here often, much more frequently than in any of the rest of our homes. Portia and I agree that it is an odd place for a network group to meet, but Jo Anne likes cooking and tidying and having people in, and we like Jo Anne, so why make waves?

There is one thing, though. Jo Anne has this plaster Jesus on the wall, eyes turned up, plaster thorns and nails all over. Jo Anne isn't still Catholic; she just hates to throw things out. But it's kind of symbolic. Well, of course plaster Jesuses are symbolic, but I mean of something more. Now when I finally get it together to join a network group, to try to get something for myself, I've got to do it looking at him bleeding bright plaster blood at me. Interesting that the world's greatest martyr should be male.

"That's terrible," Jo Anne said, folding her plump little hands and aiming comfort at me. Jo Anne affects you like a feather bed. "And I think it was terrible of you, Cecile, to tell things from group."

"This is a murder investigation for Christ's sake."

"Well, it still wasn't nice."

"Yes, well," Portia said shortly, "but that's not the point, is it? The point is that Hermoine Leanders is dead, and Jill could be blamed." Yes, Portia is well named. She faces life.

"With Cecile's help," I muttered.

"It would probably have come out anyway," Portia said. "Let's see if we can think of some way to help Jill."

We fell silent, thinking, worrying, and yet an air of suppressed excitement seemed to hang in Jo Anne's crowded little rose and gray room. We are, most of us, fortyish housewives, and not much ever really happens to us. Boredom is our daily bread, and this was rather like living the soap opera for a change.

Inez giggled suddenly. "That Harvey is weird." Inez is thin and pop-eyed with a little round head, a regular bedpost of a woman. "Really weird." She scrounged around in her chair and began one of her boogie-woogie monologues—nervous, running faster and faster until her words fairly tumbled over each other. "I mean she had that beautiful Richard. I mean that man— well, what he does to my bones—and he writes 'Heart's Desires' besides. True, it's only on that little local station that Patrick Henry O'Brian owns, but well—I like it better than 'General Hospital,' and that won an Emmy. I wonder why Hermoine was killed? Maybe it was to keep her from the arms of her true love just like when they kidnapped poor Hope."

"Who's Hope?" Cecile asked, frowning.

"'Days of Our Lives,'" we all answered in unison.

Cecile looked around at us, her eyes getting big.

"Maybe it was an accident," Inez said. "Like when Betsy was burned."

"Betsy?" said Cecile.

"'As the World Turns,'" said we.

"Looks like murder to me," I said.

"Like the Salem Slasher," Inez said dreamily. "Or the Salem Strangler."

"I'm not even going to ask," Cecile said, her face speaking volumes. "But I do hope you ladies remember we're talking real life here."

"Oh, yes indeed," Inez said. "Say, Mary, does Richard ever tell you what's going to happen next on 'Heart's Desires'? Is the daughter going to be all right? Will someone unplug the sister?"

"He doesn't say," I said.

"Well, have you ever met Hermoine or Brad or any of the stars?"

"Briefly, at the bleach party."

"It was so clever of them to set 'Heart's Desires' in San Francisco, don't you think? I mean you do get tired of Salem or Henderson or Oakdale and all those other little places. I just love it when Brad takes Madaline real places, like the time he took her to the Japanese Tea Garden. I think Richard is just a genius. If I had a man like that I wouldn't touch Harvey with a ten-foot pole. I like my bleach in the laundry. I guess Jill *is* having an affair with Harvey, isn't she?"

"I think so," Portia said. "Once, when we were having a few gin and tonics, I started speculating about Harvey, about why he looked the way he did, so small and hairless and pear-shaped, and Jill told me that it was a hormone deficiency. She just happened to add that his testicles hadn't descended. Now that's rather personal information just to *have*. I looked at her, and she blushed purple and said she'd heard it somewhere."

"No," I said quickly. "Maybe she heard gossip or something, but Harvey says they aren't lovers at all. Well, he just happened to mention that the police asked and that he said no. He sounded sort of sad, but he said he knew that Jill was a real lady and that he knew she wouldn't want to be unfaithful to Richard. That's just the way Harvey put it—'unfaithful to Richard.' Personally, I wish she had Harvey instead of Richard. Harvey is so concerned and caring. He asked Cecile and me to go to this party, said that the three of us should see if we can hear anything that might help clear Jill." I laughed. "Not that we will, of course. But still, it's touching to see a man who's concerned."

Portia straightened abruptly. "That's it," she said, sounding excited.

"Pardon?"

"Mary, you're Jill's oldest friend in the city. It wouldn't seem strange if you were to be around now when she needs help. And you could just sort of watch people."

"Oh really, Portia."

"And you are always saying how you want to get out—to escape."

True. I am always saying that.

"And you've always wanted to be a writer. This could be your book. Especially if you—or all of us, our group—found the killer. We could do it. And we'd save Jill."

"Listen," Cecile said, snatching up a cookie in angry emphasis, "Jill quit our group six months ago when she started doing this perfect housewife bit. I think she let us down, and I for one feel no responsibility for her."

I glared at Cecile. "Well I do."

"But you feel responsible for everything, Mary. You probably feel world hunger is your fault."

I took a deep breath and pulled back to let Portia handle it. She's considerably cooler than me. "I feel we failed Jill when she was here, Cecile," Portia said in her slow, rich voice. Portia is tall and thin with big, thoughtful eyes and long, graceful hands. We all kind of look up to her. Though networking groups are generally supposed to be leaderless, they rarely are. Portia is in effect our leader. "Jill was freaking out when she was here. Probably nothing we could have done would have

changed it, but still I wish we could have done something."
Portia turned back to me, "Mary, what do you say?"

"Portia, what do I know about solving murders?"

"You're bright, and after all those years as a wife and mother,
all those years of watching others, anticipating needs, you
should know people."

"Look," Jo Anne said brightly, "I could run across and do
some housework at your house every day." I think she knew
she was offering an almost irresistible incentive. I hate housework, its treadmill quality; I find it hard to believe that the
purpose of life is a clean kitchen.

"I don't know . . ." I said, frowning.

"I guess I'll help too," Cecile said, fanning a hand of cookies,
and dealing one into her mouth. "Be good for you, Mary.
Frankly, your assertiveness skills stink."

Portia sighed. "We'll all help in any way we can."

"I don't know, Porsh—"

Cecile hissed disgust.

"For Jill."

"Well . . ." I hesitated. "Well, I'll think about it."

7

Thinking about it, I left Jo Anne's and walked across the lawn
to our house. Could I? A shiver of excitement slid up my spine.
Maybe I could. After all, my life isn't over. I'm only forty
years old. Maybe I am ten pounds overweight, but my auburn
hair doesn't have a trace of gray yet, and the butcher winks
every time I go by for one of his forty-nine-cent-a-pound special chickens.

Definitely there was life left; definitely, I could. Cecile was right: assert. I ran up our front steps, excitement swelling in me.

My kids were already home. Carolee, the oldest, came at me. "Mother!" No one but an adolescent can make the word *mother* sound quite that way. "Mother! My blue blouse isn't ironed, and I've got to wear it tonight."

My image of myself as Sherlock Holmes or a writer or anything but an inept mother faded immediately. "I'll iron it now," I said in the voice that I meant to sound patient but that somehow sounded dead.

"And Bobby Prescott came home with me, and the crumby kitchen floor hadn't even been swept."

"So?" I shouted, grabbing the broom and shaking it at her. "So?! So here's the broom. Kids used to work fourteen hours a day in the mills, and you can't even sweep a floor?!"

She sighed like a locomotive. "If I did, someone would only mess it up again." Ha! She'd noticed. "Besides I've got school and drama practice and baby-sitting."

See! See! She has important things to do! And she makes money! I hate her, and I want to hit her; at the same time, I love her and want her to be happy, and I am miserable and guilty because I didn't iron the damn blouse or sweep the damn floor, so I return to an old complaint. "You leave your cereal bowls all over the house. I've asked and asked you."

She gives me the look that says I am infinitely petty, and I am. But then that's the choice—constant petty nagging, or doing it all yourself and watching your life drip away in dirty cereal bowls, or leaving it undone and being blamed. All negatives. No happy choices.

Sid came home, and I found myself again trying to tell him about the argument, about my feelings. He didn't answer; my words hung between us like some foul smell. He looked at me with this look he gets: blank face, estimating eyes. I knew what he was thinking (or do I only think I know?). I should have swept the floor. I'm the wife, the mother. It's my job. He does his job. He doesn't care for it, but he does it. Life for Sid is surface and pattern, people behaving as they should. And he does.

"What *did* you do today?" he murmured.

I stiffened, shot a glance at him, muttered, "Bathrooms. This morning. Ironing. Some."

"This afternoon?"

"Woman's group."

His brows lifted just a millimeter, and he was silent.

Sid feels my taking time for woman's groups or writing is unwifely. But never does he put this in words so that I might defend myself against the charge. If I should try to talk about it, he'd deny that he felt that way.

Sid controls by a glance, a twist of a lip, a raised brow. Never would he sink so low as to openly quarrel.

"Carolee could sweep the floor," I muttered sullenly, feeling like a competing child rather than the mother.

"Carolee has school," he said softly.

I fell silent, angry and ashamed and lonely. I turned round and round inside. I wanted to catch the bus across town to talk to Portia. To bitch, make bitter jokes, tap the misery pressing inside. But I had just left the group, and besides it was time to start dinner, so I went into the kitchen and made meatloaf.

I chopped onions and peppers viciously and pounded them into the ground beef. Then I stopped and stared at my greasy hands. Was it possible that I could find Hermoine's killer? Slowly I peeled meat from my fingers. Was it possible that I could save Jill and get out of the box too? I walked to the cupboard and stared dreamily at the spices. Was it possible that I could write the story and could even perhaps find life in Hermoine's death? Was it possible that I was out of basil?

8

Later that week I was getting the family off, handmaidening their busy lives, when Cecile called.

"Listen," she said, not bothering with any traditional salutes. "I got it all figured out."

"You have?" I dragged the phone over to the stove to stir the scrambled eggs.

"Did you know that the vast majority of murders are committed by loved ones?"

"Loved ones," I muttered. Sun drifted through the plant-filled windows, casting green shadows over the cracked yellow tile.

"That means Patrick Henry O'Brian, right?"

"Well, statistically," I said uneasily, salting the eggs.

"I say that makes P.H.O. our man," Cecile finished, in a voice as definite as the one my sixth grade teacher used to say two and two makes four. I blinked into the lemony light, waiting, certain that Cecile would now outline some masterful plan for slipping past P.H.O.'s bodyguards, wrestling him to the Rhya carpet, trussing him like the Thanksgiving turkey (probably using panty hose), then packing him round to the nearest S.F.P.D. station.

"I don't know, Cecile."

"Well, we gotta go down this morning and talk to him."

I looked about the kitchen. Such a lovely morning. It occurred to me that maybe I didn't want to do this after all. But then Jo Anne and Inez had cleaned yesterday, and Jo Anne was coming again today. That rather created a moral obligation greater than shooting your own horse. "They'll never let us in to see him, Cecile."

"Then we'll dress up as scrubwomen and sneak in."

"Scrubwomen!"

"Hey, there's no clean socks," Tim bellowed, padding into the kitchen in bare feet.

I covered the phone receiver with my palm. "Down in the dryer. Bring the whole load up, will you?"

"I don't have my shoes on."

I sighed. "Look, Cecile, I can't talk now. I've got to get the kids off."

"Ah hell, Mary. Tell them to get themselves off. You're always—"

"Right," I said quickly. I had heard it before. It's one of Cecile's regular lectures, and she may be right. "I'll call you later," I said and laid the phone in its cradle.

I stirred the scrambled eggs and told Tim to watch them while I ran down for the laundry. I came back to burned eggs and the familiar swelling irritation. I swallowed down on it and started new eggs.

"The eggs burned," I said calmly.

"I'm sorry. I was looking for my homework."

"I see." I slid scrambled eggs on plates and even managed a smile. I know what they say about honesty, spontaneity, but then isn't much of that just laying your own reality without concern for anyone else's?

I called the kids for breakfast; they came in and sat down at the table. Tiny scrubwomen crept about in the dark of my mind.

"Is there any butter, Mom?"

It would never work. You would need credentials, a badge, something to question someone as important as Patrick Henry O'Brian. We were going to make such awful fools of ourselves.

"Mom! Where's the butter?"

I got the butter, then let myself just enjoy for a moment the sight of my three children eating in the sun-drenched kitchen. Carolee, early morning disdainful; Tim, ungainly in his changing fifteen-year-old body; and Kelly, my eleven-year-old baby, dreaming with a bow of milk on her upper lip.

"Did you hear?" Carolee asked importantly. "That woman. The one in Richard's soap opera. She was murdered. Her head was right on the TV."

Dark eyes rounding, Kelly looked at her sister.

Somehow I hadn't had the heart to talk about the killing to the children. When they were small I used to drive them everywhere rather than warn them against strangers. I willed them a good world and tried to create that world with silences, blackouts.

"I heard," I said shortly.

"Sure she has," Tim said. "Jeez, it's been on the news and in all the papers. Richard was on TV last night, Mom. While you and Dad were at Grandma's."

"Oh?" I said and set a stack of toast on the table.

"What do you think he used to saw her head off with?"

"Tim!"

"Jeez, Tim," Carolee sneered, "you really gross me out."

Kelly, who felt for every hurt creature, just looked at them with bigger, darker eyes.

"Maybe a Chinese cleaver like Mom's."

"Sick time."

"Or a saw. It wouldn't be easy to get a head off all the way."

"Tim!" I shrieked. "That's enough!"

Sidney came into the kitchen, giving me a slightly accusing look. One wasn't supposed to yell at one's children. One was supposed to be a calm and reasoning adult. He went around the table touching each of the children's heads. Sid cares for his children deeply; it is an endearing trait. I handed him a cup of coffee, and for a moment we both stood watching the children eat.

I see us this way, Sid and me, standing, side by side, our

eyes on the children. We are a child-oriented family. I love Sid's caring for the children; at the same time I resent his inability to turn and look at me. I suspect that I mean little more to him than an inefficient maid. He sat down to eat, and Tim immediately began to fill him in on all the gory details of Hermoine's killing. Sid muttered something about not being hungry, catching something at the school cafeteria, something about being late (though he was in fact early), and left in a bundling rush.

I saw the children off and then started the dishes, thinking about Cecile's plan. The scrubwoman thing would never work. Sid's blue suit should go to the cleaners, and I really needed to go to the grocery store, and I had to get together something to wear to Tom and Anne's party tonight, and . . .

I should never have started this Hermoine thing. Through my window, I saw Jo Anne coming across the lawn with a mop under her arm. I winced with guilt and washed faster so that she wouldn't have to do dishes, too. No, I should never have started this.

Jo Anne came in, and I went to call Cecile back.

Cecile and I decided to present ourselves at Patrick Henry O'Brian's office and inform his secretary that we had information about Hermoine's killer. Cecile's idea of course. She planned to give him her castration theory gratis, since happily even she doubted it was worth twenty thousand dollars. From there we would move with off-handed subtlety into some masterful interrogation worthy of a James Bond, a Peter Wimsey, a Columbo, that would lay bare all Mr. O'Brian's internal motivations, frustrations, jealousies, and knowledge of the heinous misdeed. But somehow I kept seeing this as Cecile blurting loudly, "Hey listen, buddy! We want the truth. Did you ice her?"

O'Brian's secretary listened to our claim with a supercilious smile, then took a card from a stack on her desk and handed it to me. The printed message read:

Information as to the killer or killers of Miss Hermoine Leanders should be sent to Post Office Box 463, San Francisco, California. All information will be duly processed and the informant contacted.
Thank you.

Patrick Henry O'Brian

We argued with the secretary for a while. She kept looking at us as if we were lunatics, which may have been fairly accurate. Finally we wandered away, discouraged.

"We'll write that box," Cecile said. "Say we know who the killer is and that we have to talk to O'Brian in person."

"No, wait," I muttered. "I just thought of something. Isn't Portia's husband connected with the firm that handles O'Brian's P.R.?"

Cecile looked surprised. "Is he?"

"Yeah, I think. Remember, Jill brought Portia to the group. I'm sure she said they had met because their husbands both had business connections with O'Brian. We can ask Portia tomorrow. She wants to get together to talk about tonight's party."

"I know. I was asked."

It was getting late, so I made a flying dash into a grocery store and grabbed a few things; Cecile helped me carry them home, informing me all the while that Sid and the children should be doing the shopping, that I was a patsy, a formless amoeba who should stand up for herself (can amoeba stand?). I walked along, barely listening, reflecting on how Sid and his family thought me too unwomanly and Cecile thought me too womanly. Wasn't there anyone who liked me just as I was?

I left Cecile on the sidewalk outside our house, and had just inserted the key in the front door when some inner sixth sense alerted me that something was wrong. I stiffened, listened. Someone or something moved inside the house. It was too early for the children to be home. I opened the door cautiously, an inch at a time. Across the crack of revealed living room moved a strange man, dressed in army surplus and glasses, with hair and beard to mid-chest. I stared for a moment, open-mouthed, unbelieving, then shut the door silently and shot back down the steps. I caught Cecile halfway down the block.

"Cecile, Cecile," I panted. "There's a strange man in my house."

She turned around looking pleased. "Really?"

I nodded still trying to get my breath.

"Hey. . ." Now she began to look excited. "Maybe this is the break we've been waiting for," she said solemnly, just like some TV detective. "Maybe the killer has found out we're investigating him."

I frowned. "You know, somehow I doubt that, Cecile."

"You would. You have to sell yourself and anything connected with you short. The killer could easily know we're after him."

"Let's go to Jo Anne's and call the police."

"Police!" she said scornfully. "Police! Ha! We're going to do this ourselves, remember? No men."

"We could ask for a policewoman," I suggested hopefully.

She whirled and began making intricate little circles in the air with her hands. "I know karate," she said with regal hauteur, then whipped back around.

"You would," I muttered. My babies would be orphans, I thought. Now there was a good traditional response. Maybe Sid would marry again. Someone who cooked desserts. As we passed Jo Anne's house, I darted inside.

"Quick! A weapon! Something," I whispered dramatically. "There's a man in my living room. Maybe even the killer—" Not that I believed it was the killer, but Jo Anne deserved some little reward for all that housework.

Jo Anne began to tremble. "What do you want? What do you want?" She trotted into her kitchen and began running circles on the brightly polished linoleum. "I don't have a gun. What do you want?"

I followed her. "It doesn't matter. Anything."

She snatched up her rolling pin and shoved it at me.

A rolling pin?! Cecile was going to be slamming away with her fists of fury, and I'm going to stand there with a rolling pin?

"I'll take this," I said, grabbing her biggest butcher knife from the rack.

"Oh, good idea," she quavered, waving the rolling pin wildly. She hesitated, then asked feebly, "Shall I come too?"

"No," I said. After all, she shouldn't have to clean and capture both.

Cecile was waiting at my door. I had the key.

"Where'd you go?" she whispered. I showed her the knife. She looked pained. I opened the door and stealthily pushed it in a few inches.

We could see him wandering rather aimlessly about the living room, beyond the entrance hall. He stopped and began to fiddle with Sid's pipes.

Why would he do that? I tightened my grip on the knife. It kept sliding in the sweat on my palm. Suddenly Cecile shoved the door wide and galloped into the room. She stopped in the middle of the green rug, pointed the sides of her lethal hands at him, looked sidelong from under grim, furred brows just like Bruce Lee in all those movies. "Ha," she shouted, or "Aaah," or something like that. I came in slicing air with my shaking knife and stood beside her.

"Hey," the man cried. "No!" He jumped back against the wall, raising his hands. Blood pounded through me. The air seemed to brighten about him. Every whorl of his dark, frosted hair stood out plainly. I felt disoriented, strangely powerful, then suddenly there was a snap, and I sagged with relief. I could never have stabbed him; I have trouble cutting up a chicken.

"Don't move," Cecile said, shifting around on the balls of her feet, her solid, blue-jean-clad rump sticking out behind.

"Mary?" the man said uncertainly.

I stared, catching a ghost there beneath the hair. Now the pale blue eyes behind the round, gold-framed glasses seemed familiar.

"Roger?" I whispered, lowering the knife. "Roger, is that you?"

"Yeah. Hey, it's been a while, huh?"

"A while. It must be twenty years. What are you doing here?"

"Ah, shit," Cecile said, "is this more of your domestic crap?"

"I went by and got a key from Sid. I was at the folks, but you know Mom."

Indeed I did. Sid and Roger's mother was the Phyllis Schlafly of mothers-in-law. She knew just how we all should live. She tripped about on her tiny pony feet, busily writing the date in the dust atop my refrigerator, then pointing it out to Sid on her next visit. But I was just one of Mother Sable's minor failures. Roger was the big one we'd heard about for twenty years. And now he was back.

"The commune trip's finished. Time to reconnect with people. I want to be a healer."

"Whatta ya mean a healer?" Cecile said, watching him through narrowed eyes.

"A healer. Sid said it'd be OK if Storm came too. I'm going to get her tomorrow."

"Storm?"

"My kid. You probably think of her as Margaret. But when I had her a couple years back, I had it changed legally. Ruth was plenty pissed."

"I bet," I said.

"Ruth won't let her come. I'll have to kidnap her."

"Kidnap!" I cried.

"You mean that laying-on-hands stuff," Cecile said, two inches from Roger's face.

"I mean that laying-on-hands stuff," Roger said with great dignity.

"Where will Storm sleep?" I asked.

"That stuff's a lot of crap," Cecile said. "Nobody gets healed by laying on hands."

"I guess we could put a roll-away bed in Carolee's room."

"I saw an old Indian healer pull a cancer right out of a woman."

"No you didn't," Cecile puffed.

I began mentally shifting beds. Roger would have to have the guest bedroom. Carolee would hate having someone in her room.

"There was a bunch of us saw that mass come right out."

"Mass hysteria."

Roger laughed, and Cecile smiled.

Maybe with Kelly. But that didn't seem fair. Kelly often got dumped on because she was easygoing. With Carolee then. And take the consequences—weather the Storm, so to speak.

"We're solving a murder," Cecile said in an unfamiliar, cute voice.

I jumped and shot back from bed arrangements. "Cecile!"

"We need his help, Mary. We know the killer's probably a man. We need protection."

I stared. So what the hell happened to fists of fury and no policemen and solving it ourselves. Cecile had dissolved into ruffles at the first sight of Roger. I had a sudden vision of our whole sex as doomed.

"We're splitting the reward. You could have a share. I'm writing a thesis on it too," she added proudly. "You could help with that."

Roger considered. "I don't believe in violence."

"No, no," Cecile said hastily. "Of course no violence."

"Well." He stroked his long beard and looked thoughtful. I watched, wondering who it was he reminded me of. Probably just the old, younger, clean-shaven Roger, but still—then it hit me. He looked just like the pictures of Jesus that had hung in my childhood Sunday school. Except for the glasses, of course. He had all that hair and beard, but mostly it was the eyes. They were the wrong color, but never before had I seen such a Jesus-look of sadness and suffering in a man's eyes. I found myself softening inside. I was even beginning to understand Cecile's silly behavior. Portia says the only men who see and understand women are gurus and pimps. I felt suddenly light and happy. Perhaps my guru had come.

"Well," Roger said with a little smile, "I could use the money—set me up in a place of my own, get us out of Mary's space." He gave this warm, sweet smile.

"No, Roger, you're welcome here." I realized that this time I really meant it.

9

Cecile stayed and fluttered and debated for over an hour. Three seperate times, she told Roger about the Brant's party and invited him to go with us. Each time, he smiled gently and accepted. It was late when she left. I showed Roger to his room and then hurried into the kitchen to fix supper. Soon after, the children came home and stood about the kitchen talking about their day. Roger came wandering into the kitchen, wearing only a pair of cut-off jeans slit up the sides, his wide shoulders dark with sun. All that dark, frosted hair sprang every which way.

The kids were thunderstruck.

"This is your Uncle Roger."

"Hi," they said, Kelly blinking up at him in that shy way of hers.

He gave them his mournful smile, and his sad eyes drifted about the kitchen.

Sid arrived home and fixed himself a martini, a process that Roger watched so sadly I feared he might weep.

"Not good for you, Sid."

"You don't drink anymore, Roger?"

"I want to quit," Roger said. "Well, maybe just one."

Sid poured, and Roger began another recounting of the sorrowful saga of his brief stay at the Sables.

Sid listened with that same closed face he wore for my complaints about his family. It was eerie watching from the outside for a change, Roger going on, his voice rising defensively, obviously growing increasingly uneasy, and not quite sure why.

It seemed that Roger had been prepared to cure Carol, our sister-in-law, of uterine cancer, a proposal that sent Mother Sable to her bed. I giggled for three minutes straight at that one. Roger and Sid both watched me.

When I finally quieted, Roger murmured, "You know she keeps calling you Carol."

I grinned. "Some sort of Freudian wish slip, don't you think?"

Roger grinned, but Sid said coldly, "You make mistakes too, Mary. You've been known to forget things."

"Yeah," I muttered. "Sure." I grabbed up the roast chicken and hurried it into the dining room. It was time to change the subject before Sid and I were into another of our cold times. Not that normal was any too terribly warm.

Roger brought sprouts and nuts and ate them quietly, sadly, while the rest of us filled our plates with chicken and salad, potatoes and vegetables. Our eyes kept returning to that little pile. It was like having the legendary starving children of China right there at our table.

Kelly watched, her dark eyes round and pleading. "Wouldn't you like some of Mom's chicken, Uncle Roger? It's really good."

Roger put down his fork and stared at the chicken.

I turned the platter so the serving fork faced him.

"It was alive too, you know. It had feelings."

Kelly's eyes got bigger.

"Why do we feel we have the right to rip off the life chain to fill our needs?"

Sid cleared his throat and gave Roger a look.

"How would we like it if some species with a superior intelligence came in on a space ship and put us all in dairies and feeder lots and slaughtering houses."

Kelly stared down at her plate.

"That's enough, Roger," Sid snapped.

Roger shrugged and fell silent.

Kelly swallowed and lay down her fork.

I got up and went into the kitchen to fix her some eggs. I was irritated with Roger, and yet there was something to what he said. I supposed his caring mechanisms were more developed than most, including mine. I scrambled eggs and thought again of those sad eyes.

I was glad he was going with us to the Brants'.

Cecile was glad too.

I left the dishes and went to find something special to wear.

So there we were on our way to the Brants'. Me in the blue-gray crepe that made me look thinner, Roger in one of Sid's suits, which was just a little short at the wrists and ankles and a little tight across the shoulders, and Cecile wearing an off-the-shoulder silver lamé dress with a full ballerina skirt. It was exactly what we would have worn to a prom back in high school. She got it from the Goodwill. I rather imagine it was someone's enchanted-evening keepsake they'd finally decided to throw out.

The Brant apartment was dim, lit only by small lights set at the base of a number of statues. Pre-Colombian, Anne Brant informed us, taking our coats, the skin of her face quivering oddly as she examined Cecile's dress, then brightening as she viewed Roger.

Tom Brant was touring guests past the statues, reciting a brief history and the extreme age and value of each. As I moved through the dark to stop at each lighted exhibit, I found myself remembering the times as a child I had visited the local amusement park's house of horrors.

The statues were three-breasted women, or misshapen animals, or fat little men with stubby legs, lips and eyelids like garden slugs, and pencil-thin penises. I found myself thinking that they resembled Tom Brant. (Except the penises, of course. But then, who knows?)

I found the statues unappealing, but this was either bad taste on my part or a case of the emperor's new clothes since everyone else seemed to think them incredibly fine.

After the tour, Tom Brant deposited us in the darkness and went back for a new group. I looked about at the stone babies peering out from their puddles of light, at the people stirring the red-black shadow, and wondered how one went about finding a killer.

Anne Brant came by with an armload of coats and asked if I wouldn't mind just running them into the bedroom.

I carried my load of coats away through the room filled with darkness, smoke, stereo music, and conversation hum. I filed in and about clumps of people remembering suddenly how I always look forward to such parties and always hate them once I arrive. I'm always sure that I will meet wonderful, fascinating people who will wrench my horizons wide, who will utter deep profundities that will arrest my entire being, things that will cause my very soul to pause and whisper, "Oh yes." Then I am at the party, I approach someone I carefully select as a possibility. We stand facing, appropriately dressed, light lying on the surface of our cocktails, a veritable ad for gracious living. My selection smiles wisely—for indeed I choose faces creased, lined, or arranged into what for me are wise expressions—and says, "And what do you do?"

"Housewife."

And almost invariably their eyes slide, seeking who next they might move on to. But perhaps not, perhaps we talk, dredge our minds for interesting inanities to prove our charm, for subtle ways to drop hints of our cleverness, success, or superiority. We create shining cardboard persons and peer anxiously through the eye slits to see how the other is accepting it. I grow stiff with the falseness of it and begin to clam up, swearing I

won't play such ego games; they must either accept me as I am
or just ignore me, and then they ignore me, and I resent being
ignored. I go home morbid, heavy; I chastise myself for days
and wonder if it is me or the world. I tell myself that I create
the walls of my own prison; I tell myself I will never, never go
to another party. Then slowly the boredom of my days seeps
through my resolve, and I begin to look forward to the next. I
know how long and slowly a true friendship, true communication, must be nourished, cultivated, but there just is something
in me.

I threw the coats on the bed and looked about at all the mirrors. The room, even the ceilings, were lined with them. Peculiar. I thought how Sherlock Holmes would pick a piece of lint
from the red carpet, a lipstick from the crystal-topped dresser,
and deduce all sorts of miraculous things. I looked about the
room and deduced nothing. I thought of poor Jo Anne cleaning
and cleaning, my house as well as hers. I thought about how
the police had questioned Jill for hours this morning. I had to
find some clue. I actually considered riffling Anne's big old
Chinese chest, but a lifetime of inhibitions couldn't be over-
come by one networking-group assignment. I sighed and went
back into the living room.

Jill, Richard, and Harvey had arrived. Jill and Harvey wandered over to me. "Found out anything?" Harvey whispered.

"I just got here. Had to do my chores first."

They smiled and nodded as if what I had said made perfect
sense, then wandered on.

I noticed Polly, the ingenue lead from "Heart's Desires"
(who plays Hermoine's pregnant and mad daughter), outlined
in the glow from the three-breasted woman. Polly was wearing
apricot satin that looked like those slips we used to wear twenty
years ago, and she wriggled constantly inside it. Her skin and
the long hair covering her new breasts exactly matched the satin
of her dress. Tom Brant materialized from the darkness and
handed her one of the two drinks he held. They both bent their
heads, sipped, and looked at each other from the tops of their

eyes. I stopped in shadow to watch. Just a little before me Anne too watched.

Polly twisted a hand in her hair and slid around faster inside the satin. Tom's eyes slipped to her body. Occasionally through the surrounding hum of conversation I caught snatches of Polly and Tom's voices. "Hermoine—poor—so sad—" But obviously the real communication was going on between that writhing peach body and the fat-lidded pre-Columbian eyes.

I moved a little to the side so I could see Anne's expression. Anne was wearing red, which somehow managed to complement her red hair and complexion, and her pale eyes had darkened with fury. She looked rather wild and elemental and, yes, even dangerous.

A pity if it had been Anne who had done Hermoine in, only to find Polly waiting in the wings ready to understudy every one of Hermoine's roles. The noise in the room quieted slightly, and suddenly I heard Tom's voice saying plainly, "Well, Brad did it of course. He is obvious . . ." Again, sound washed up and over his voice.

This is it, I thought, stiffening. I moved forward, going to stand below the three-breasted woman on the mantel and pretending to admire it. I was so close I could hear Polly moving about in her satin casing, smell her carnation perfume.

Tom cleared his throat. "Brad, of course. Jealous."

I turned slightly sideways and moved out of the direct light so I could watch them from the sides of my eyes and still appear to be gazing at the three-breasted woman. Tom rubbed the palm of his hand on the point of Polly's shoulder. She pushed up into his hand like a stroked kitten.

"The mental institution," Tom murmured. "And there you are in those long, shadowy halls, those bizarre faces peer at you . . ."

The three-breasted woman smiled fatuously. Nothing, I thought. That damn show again.

Tom's voice throbbed on, "And the killer—maybe Brad—is coming after you just as he did Hermoine. His feet ring on the polished tile. Light glints from the straight-edged razor in his hand. You run."

"Oh," Polly whispered, her eyes rounding. "Yes."

"And run."

"Yes. Yes! I can do it! I can do it!"

"Through halls and rooms of grotesque people and great looming shock machines. 'Help!' you cry. 'Crazy,' they say. 'Paranoid.'"

"Yes," Polly crooned. "Yes, and then a young intern who's loved me desperately from afar . . . he saves me. I know this guy from my method acting class. You should see the shoulders on *him*."

Tom frowned. "A young intern?"

I grinned back at the three-breasted woman. No, Polly could never step into Hermoine's shoes.

"Well, really Tom," she continued, "I haven't wanted to complain. But do you really think anybody believed that any man could honestly prefer Hermoine to me? I mean she was *old*."

Tom looked pained so Polly wriggled at him. Anne came forward now and the red and peach faced each other with honeyed smiles, like two costumed lady wrestlers. "No," Anne said sweetly. "Brad didn't kill her. Why, you could have killed her, Polly dear. You were jealous . . ." She hesitated. "And crazy."

"Actually." Brad moved from where he'd been listening at the other end of the mantel. "Actually," he flicked a speck from his perfect sport coat, "it could be you who stalks me, Polly."

She glared, but Brad glided on. "A marvelous dramatic opportunity, wouldn't you say? And I'm quite sure our viewers could forgive murder by a madwoman once said madwoman was cured, wouldn't you say?"

"Murder, maybe," Tom muttered. "But matricide?"

Roger drifted past, stopping just to whisper, "This is all so false."

False, I mouthed, and watched him out of sight before I returned to my work.

The big people were all in the mental institution now, gliding up and down the long halls, leering, killing people on the shock machines, counting ratings, and I was getting absolutely nowhere.

"False," I whispered to myself and considered a waitressing job, so I could buy Jo Anne ten new china shepherdesses to make up for all that cleaning. Richard had joined them now, and they were all sorting suspects, nominating perfect killers. I circled the stars in the reddish gloom, listening, but no one seemed in the least concerned with the real crime. I smiled to myself. Maybe our women's group should follow their example and simply elect a guilty party, hence ridding the world of the most expendable person.

Anne noticed me. "Oh, Mary dear, would you mind terribly helping pass a few hors d'oeuvres?"

"Not terribly," I said sweetly while I made a silent but fervent endorsement of Anne's candidacy. I wandered off into the brightly lit kitchen and pulled open the refrigerator. Perfectly defrosted. Doubtless she had a cleaning lady. I pulled out a plate of deviled eggs, thinking about the book I might write about the murder, imagining being rich and famous, watching myself on a talk show, watching Johnny Carson saying "Tell us about yourself." I plunked the eggs on the table. All those faces looking at me, smiling, smiling. My hands gripped the back of the kitchen chair. I felt rather disoriented. For a moment it seemed the eggs were smiling, and then I realized that indeed they were. Anne had made a little smiling face with pimento and olive on each of the small yellow mounds. Very creative. I turned back to the refrigerator and took out the next plate. "God knows what this one's supposed to be," I muttered. Sitting in the center of a pale green lettuce ruffle totally covered in aspic was something that looked like an oversize pickled pig's foot.

And then suddenly it seemed to come at my eyes, and I knew what it was. Carefully, I set the plate on the table and looked about the too-bright kitchen. All that white and light was suddenly harsh, glaring, assailing. I found myself remembering some story about a writer who could only work with his feet in a basin of ice water. Why that story? Why now? Because my feet were so terribly cold. I stared down at them. Act! Do something! I closed my eyes. Time lapsed, slid. I opened them. The thing was still on the table.

Society has rules for how to behave when a favorite aunt dies, or when the mailman breaks his leg on your front walk, or when you spill wine on your hostess's damask tablecloth, but I know of no rule for how to behave when you find a human foot in your hostess's refrigerator. So I just stayed there with it in the kitchen, considering screaming or crying or fainting, and swallowing back my stomach, which seemed to be trying to cram itself up into my throat.

My mind snatched at flying thoughts.

Did this mean Anne or Tom or both were guilty?

No. Surely if you killed someone you wouldn't put their foot in your own refrigerator.

Would you?

Unless you were mad. I remembered Tom's voice ushering us through those empty ringing asylum halls, and the cold began rising from my feet like mercury in a thermometer. I jerked about to face the door.

There, hanging on the back of the door, was a small ruffled apron. I went over and took it down. Some monstrous thought was rising from the swamps of my mind, though as yet I couldn't quite determine its features. On the white-white kitchen walls, little Jo Annes seemed to be vacuuming, dusting, washing things at a frenetic pace. A mist of perspiration broke out on my cold skin. The foot was a clue. My first clue. No mere piece of lint this. Still, what did it mean? What did I do with it? I looked at myself mirrored against the dark window. I put the apron on, took up the egg tray and smiled; from the black window, Betty Crocker smiled back. Then slowly the smiles died. Something about that dark woman there arrested my every sense. "Last chance," she whispered. "Last chance or you'll be forever behind this tray—forever serving."

Slowly, I set the tray back on the table. I removed some of the eggs. I wrapped the lettuce about the foot. Taking great care to touch only the lettuce, I placed the foot exactly in the center of the four circles of smiling faces. I would get out from behind the tray. I would!

The foot was a clue, and I was going to use it. Confronted with it, surely the guilty person would notice and react. Or would everyone? Probably not. It was quite dark in the living room. I lifted the tray in hands that felt cold, unreal; I pushed through the swinging door. Noise and reddish-black, smoke-laced air closed about me. I pushed the tray into its dead center and followed after. Even in the darkness, Hermoine's foot seemed to pulse and glow as if it were radioactive. I threaded between dim forms, watching their faces etched in pre-Columbian light. I walked round and round. My shoulders began to ache with the weight of the tray. No one noticed. No one at all noticed my tray. Absolutely no one. My hands and feet seemed to be moving back toward me now, and my head was working a little better. I grew more courageous. I walked right up to "Desires"'s director and poked the tray at him. Without a glance in my direction he slid off an egg and went on telling a pretty girl about his bunions.

I moved on.

Who can say why? Or what? Evil? Housewife's revenge? I don't know, but as I moved off into that dim haze, the tray before me, I began to feel more there, more alive than I had in years. The little clay men grinned at me, and I grinned back, beginning to appreciate them standing there in their tiny auras of light and mystery and age. The stuffy, smoke-filled air became a presence stroking my body. I passed through it slowly, a new person in a new world, a moon-walker. I saw things I would have never ordinarily noticed at all: the wart below Polly's ear, the weariness behind Brad's suave expression. I approached cameramen, producers, actors; I felt sly, set apart. I alone of all these people knew of this foot. I . . . and the killer. Now I began to present my tray with catchy little slogans like, "Choosy hostesses serve . . ." "Hermoine always did have her foot in her mouth." People took my eggs and looked at me as if I was weird, which I guess if you think about it, I was.

I pushed into the circle of writers and stars. They ignored me, though a couple seized eggs from the silver tray. They were into finding the killer in earnest now. They didn't want a stranger. They mentioned and rejected character after character. Kindly old Aunt Kate was too kindly. Madaline's sister, Pauline, was out because she was totally paralyzed from being shot and then later hit with a car. She lay in the hospital and pleaded day after day with the other various "Heart's Desires" characters to pull the plug on her respirator. Pulling respirator plugs is very big on the soaps right now. Slowly, I passed the tray about the circle, carefully watching faces through the dimness. "Perhaps Pauline's illness could be psychosomatic," I suggested happily. "She could get out of bed in the dead of night, unhook herself from all her machines like Frankenstein's monster, then creep away on her evil missions, trailing tubes and plugs."

There was a moment while their shadowed faces actually considered it, then Richard informed me with elegant disgust that the A.M.A. would never allow it. I shrugged and pointed the tray at him. He grabbed an egg and muttered, "Who's going to pull Pauline's plug now? Hermoine was supposed to do it. Who'll do it now?"

"Dear Hermoine," I purred. "I feel as if her sweet soul were right here with us tonight."

They stared at me blankly. Anne, quick to cue, returned. "A great lady, a marvelous actress. It's just so dear of you to help, Mary." Her eyes brushed the tray. "Shouldn't that have a serving fork or something?"

"I can pull the plug," Polly said haughtily.

"Well," Brad said, "perhaps, but actually it would be interesting to have a psychiatrist do it."

And so they argued on as to who would be privileged to pull poor Pauline's plug, as well as who must do the unpleasant chore of snuffing Hermoine's life when their two weeks of tape ran out. Like an accusing finger I pointed Hermoine's big toe at first one, then another, and still not so much as an eyelash flickered.

So I left their little island of three-breasted-woman light and moved back into the reddish smoke fog. Voices and music from the stereo blended into a senseless roar. Frowning, I walked through it as through the heavy atmosphere of a dream. Nothing. Not so much as a brow twitch, a muscle twinge. No one had even noticed. No one. It was unreal.

And yet, didn't the foot almost have to mean the killer was here? Could it have been put in the refrigerator earlier?

And for God's sake, why?

A false lead?

A grisly joke?

I decided to show Cecile the foot and see if she had any suggestions. Cecile had gathered a small circle of listeners, including Roger, and was holding forth on women's psychology. She had fastened her hands in the voluminous folds of her silver skirt, and as she talked she swung it too and fro, sparking the light from a small, ten-titted dog.

"Cecile," I said, sort of poking her with the edge of the tray.

"Penis envy, penis envy," she cried excitedly, half-glancing over her shoulder at me. "A male concept." She reached back and snatched an egg off my tray. "Freud said all women should be masochists—helpless, obedient. We're beyond that."

"Cecile, I need to talk to you."

"Really?" a tall, thin man sneered. "Seems to me a lot of women are reembracing the tradional role. Look at Phyllis Schafly. Look at . . ."

"Cecile," I whispered, trying to move into the group beside her.

Almost imperceptibly, she stiffened her shoulders and slid toward Roger so I couldn't get in. "So some women are still stuck in the last century." She snatched another egg.

I stood there with my tray, feeling cold anger and rejection sliding around inside. I remembered Cecile talking in the women's group about how she had no respect for her mother, who was always cooking and serving, while her father had ideas and was interesting to talk to. Cecile, for all her militant feminism, still tended to treat women as mother, men as father. "Have another egg," I invited sweetly.

She did.

Roger smiled spacily at me, and I realized he'd done a fair amount of grass in the last hour or two.

"Egg?" I murmured.

"Are they fertile?" he burped.

"I don't know," I replied. "But they certainly *look* happy."

He and Cecile both took one.

Just then Jill and Harvey came up. "Oh," Jill said, looking down at my tray. "Isn't that pretty, all those precious little yellow faces. And is that Hermoine's foot, do you think?"

I looked at her, all angelic in powder blue crepe, and sighed. Well, someone had at last noticed. The one person here I would have willed not to notice. "Yes, Jill," I muttered. "I rather think it is."

"What?!" Cecile whipped about. "Hermoine's what?!" Her eyes, wild as a spooked horse's, shot to the tray. Her face went through a series of strange bucklings and eruptings, then slowly her mouth opened and a stuck-pig scream pierced the party noise.

There was a short, high-hung silence. Someone shut off the stereo. Then pandemonium. Everyone converged on us, crying, "What is it?!"

"That—that—" Cecile squeaked, waving at the tray. People craned to see. "Those. Those! I ate those eggs."

"It's the eggs."

"Is she ill?"

"She's sick from the eggs."

"There's nothing in the world wrong with those eggs," Anne yelled over the uproar. "I made them myself."

"My God," someone else cried in an awed voice. "Look! Isn't that a human foot!" People shoved. Something jabbed my side. The tray listed. The foot skated on its jellied sole.

"It is!"

"No!"

"No! Look for yourself! It is!"

"I feel faint!"

Someone began weeping; someone else laughed hysterically. Roger, grinning all the while, began this odd speech about how "You folks think it's fine to eat some poor little lamb, but just the look of a human foot . . ."

"Call the police," Anne cried, glaring at me.

"No," Richard said, a smug little smile on his fine lips. "I mean yes—the police—of course. Call the police. And you'd better call the press too. They'll have to know."

Tom and Anne's faces swiveled toward him. For just an instant the three of them were perfectly still amid the uproar, their eyes speaking to each other. Then Anne turned and bathed me with a glowing smile. "Yes, and the press." Tom hurried away to call.

"Oh," Cecile moaned and began shoving wildly at the wall of people surrounding her. "Lemme out! Lemme out!" The crowd stirred. The high dog table tottered. The ten-titted dog swayed. Anne screamed.

"What is it?!"

"What now?"

The dog toppled, shattering at Cecile's feet, shooting ancient tits every which way. Cecile suddenly jerked forward and upchucked smiling faces all over them.

I stood there in the midst of it all, the tray cutting into me, staring down at Cecile's wide, silver-clad shoulders, and something in me gripped, ground. Perhaps the fingers of my soul had dug back into reality, but suddenly, I was deeply and miserably ashamed.

10

The police came.

Lots of them.

Scads.

Hordes.

With and without uniforms. Solemn and officious.

The lights came on to reveal lipstick-red walls and carpet and black lacquered furniture. The police crept about scooping up minuscule things and sticking them in baggies, dusting the silver tray for fingerprints, and I knew damn well whose prints they were going to find.

I waited while Lieutenant Smith circled the room, talking to people and occasionally glancing in my direction. Sid teaches school. He's told me often that he does that to kids he's going to reprimand—keeps them waiting. He says it destroys resistance, breaks their spirit. Actually, come to think of it, he does it to me too.

I can't remember a time when I'd felt more like a naughty little kid. I guess passing a human foot at a cocktail party is a pretty big social gaffe. Everyone in the room was silent, looking pointedly anywhere but at me. Only Roger hung around, grinning hugely at me like a proud parent. I mean, let's face it. This was probably the farthest you could get from something his mother would do.

Finally, Smith came and took me away into a side room papered in a dark pinstripe and furnished with tapestry-covered couches that George Washington or Abraham Lincoln or someone of that ilk had probably sat on. My knees were shaking so hard by then I couldn't stand. I sat.

Smith toured the room inspecting the gold sconces, the carved marble fireplaces, the porcelain parrots perched on a dark inlayed table. Finally, he inspected me.

"So we meet again," he said.

I glanced at him and then quickly away, knowing from the look on his face it wasn't the pleasurable occasion he'd envisioned.

"Wanna tell me about it, Ms. Sable?"

Of course I didn't want to tell him about it. I wanted to go home. I wanted out of this. I wanted my mother. "It was in the refrigerator," I whispered. "I didn't notice what it was."

"You didn't notice what it was."

"No."

"It's got five toes, a heel, all the standard paraphernalia. How could you not notice what it was?"

"It was dark."

"In the kitchen?"

I just grabbed it out without looking at it."

He circled a few more times. "Did you know this Hermoine Leanders, Ms. Sable?"

"No."

"Not at all?"

"No. I never met her."

Two more circles.

"So tell me again why you passed the plate." I looked at him then. The bright green eyes were fixed on me hard. I knew I'd sit here until I told the truth, and maybe long past that if he didn't believe me.

I sighed. "I wanted to see how people would react."

"What?"

"I . . . we . . . Jill didn't. . . . I thought someone might react to it."

"Someone, meaning the killer?"

"Yes."

"You takin' up detective work now, Ms. Sable? In between the dishes and the dusting?"

I shrugged and stuck my nose in the air. "We know Jill didn't do it."

"We?"

"Me."

He thought about it for a moment and then slowly began to laugh. "God, lady. I seen some people do some ding-a-ling things in my time." He was roaring now, coughing and slapping at his thigh. "But stickin' a foot on a plate 'n' packin' it around to see how folks are gonna take to it—now that has to be the Guinness record for some kind of whacko. That's some detectin'. Ol' Dick Tracy's probably turnin' in his grave."

"Is he dead?"

He roared harder.

"All right," he said, quieting finally and beginning to circle the room again. "So you say you found the foot in the refrigerator."

"Yes."

"What were you doing in the refrigerator?"

"Anne Brant asked me to pass hors d'oeuvres."

"And you put it on a tray to see if anyone would react?"

"Yes."

"Did they?"

I hesitated just a beat. "No."

He studied me for a moment and then turned abruptly away. "OK. That'll do for now. I've got your address. If I need anything else, I'll get in touch." He hesitated and then took a card from his pocket. "And if you think of anything, you call me."

I nodded, and then stood there reading the name on the card and looking for courage.

"And after this, leave the detectin' to people who know what they're doing."

"Yes, sir." Fat chance, I'd leave it to him. If he didn't hang Jill, I was probably second choice now. "Sure, I will. Say . . ." I looked at him and even batted my lashes twice, feeling like the fool of the ages.

He looked back, his eyes brightening, then narrowing. "Yes-s-s?" he said suspiciously.

"So a . . ."

He started across the room toward me.

"How," I finished in a rush, "did the killer get the head into the Channel 3 studio?"

He stopped and stared. "I just got through tellin' you no—"

"I know. I know. I was just curious. I mean, I know they've got security. That couldn't be easy."

Those green eyes were mean now.

"Ah, you wouldn't know." I laughed.

"Wouldn't I?"

"Would you?" I tried for a smile, but the muscles of my face kept slipping around, and it probably looked more like some sort of fit.

He circled the room twice and ended close enough to breathe into my face. I didn't flinch. He thought hard. I figured this was the modern mating ritual. What have you got that I want, what have I got that you want. I figured, too, that if I held out and didn't faint, he'd talk. Cops love to—talk, that is. In college, I worked in a diner that served a lot of cops. They were always telling us about their cases. Once they informed the whole diner that the rapist/killer who was terrorizing the town was a dentist who also did abortions in his office. It turned out to be a janitor who worked at city hall. Being wrong didn't phase them, but I never again went to the dentist without getting this odd feeling in the pit of my stomach. Actually, I had it standing there before Smith, trying to look all sweet and shy.

Smith sniffed once and then said, "At night, workers can get in with plastic security cards. One of the technicians had her wallet lifted while she was eating in a local sushi bar. It was mailed back to her. Only the pass was missing."

I nodded, biting my lip and thinking hard. "She see the thief?"

"Nope. The place was small and crowded. She was talking to a friend. Her purse was hung over the back of her chair. Asking to be robbed, actually."

I nodded again and wondered if there was anything else I should ask. Instinct told me he wasn't going to give more without some return. "So," I said. "So thanks. Thanks a lot. I know you've got to get on with your investigation, so I'll call." I waved the card in his face and darted for the door. "Thanks again." I wasn't fond of myself right then, but then we had to use what weapons we had, didn't we? I went back into the living room. Everyone turned to stare at me. Every single one of the Brants' guests, celebrity or no. At last I was seen, and it was far from how I pictured. I was miserable.

"I was just telling everyone," Harvey called, "that you didn't even notice the foot."

"No," I muttered. "It was just in the refrigerator."

Silence. And then slowly, people began to turn away. Time to get out of here, I thought. I looked about for Cecile and Roger. He was at the punch table sipping white wine from a cut-glass cup and staring out across the room. I made my way to him and whispered, "Where's Cecile?"

"She left."

"Are you ready to go?"

"Um." He sighed. "I suppose." His earlier high spirits had vanished, leaving again the mournful Roger.

"What's wrong?" I whispered.

"That," he said, pointing with his bearded chin.

I looked but saw nothing but well-dressed people, some gazing dourly back at me. "What?"

"Just look at that. A beautiful vessel like that, and she's filling it with all that processed shit."

This time I managed to follow the chin.

"Polly Purger?"

"Peanuts. Saturated fat. Salt." He shook his head sadly at the excesses of this world and took another swallow of wine. It occurred to me that Roger's values might be a little skewed. Passing feet was keen, but peanuts were one of the seven deadly sins. But then again I supposed mine were nothing to write home about.

"Let's go," I said.

"Don't you think I should talk to her about the peanuts?"

"Nah, let it go. One night's peanuts won't kill her."

"It's bad for the baby."

I froze, looked into his face drooping with concern, then turned to stare across the room where Polly was quivering up at some stranger. "What baby?" I said.

"The one she's carrying."

"She's thin as a rail," I objected, but looking for it now, I thought maybe there was a trace of that blooming look some women get in early pregnancy. "Who told you she was pregnant?"

He smiled slightly. "No one. I knew it the minute I looked in her eyes. Haven't you heard of iriology? There's not a disease you can't diagnose just by looking in people's eyes."

"Really?" I said, studying Polly again. She could be, I supposed. Early though. Two, maybe three months at most. "Have some more wine," I said. "I'll tell her about the salt."

Roger obviously wasn't pleased with that plan, but I shot away before he had time to argue.

I made my way across the room to where Jill and Harvey stood gazing wistfully; she at Richard, who drank steadily and quietly in a far corner of the room, and Harvey at her.

"Is Polly Purger seeing someone?" I whispered. "I mean a steady, significant other?"

For a moment, both glanced toward Polly, then their eyes clicked back to place.

"No." Jill said, shrugging. "Richard's been drinking a lot since Hermoine . . ." Her voice trailed away.

"Has he?" I looked at him, wondering if that was significant.

"Police give you a hard time?" Harvey asked. I saw that he was genuinely concerned. He's such a sweet man. He's the wise and kindly middle-age male that the soap magazines all say female viewers covet on their soaps. But Harvey just doesn't look the part. Jill would be better off with him, really. But then maybe it's only in fantasies that women want good men.

"Not too bad, all in all." I shrugged, laughed. "Detective Smith isn't such a nice man." Harvey patted at me with his small hand. "But what I wanted to ask you and Jill is, is it possible that Polly could be pregnant?"

"Anything's possible, I guess," Harvey said. "She dates."

Jill smiled her dreamy smile and, with eyes still fixed on Richard, murmured, "I saw her once with Patrick Henry O'Brian."

"P.H.O.?" Harvey breathed. "I didn't know that."

"Really?" I said. "But what about Hermoine?"

"It was at Maxwell's Plum. I was there with Richard. It was such a wonderful evening. We had Brandy Alexanders and swordfish."

"You're sure it was them?"

"Oh, yes. Richard tried to pretend it wasn't. Well, Patrick Henry hardly ever goes out, and he doesn't like to be recognized when he does. He was wearing mirrored sunglasses and a hat. But who else do you know that has a limp and body-guards?"

"I didn't know he did."

"Oh yes," Harvey said. "He never goes out without them. Bodyguards, that is."

"But how did Hermoine feel about them seeing each other?"

"Hermoine?" Jill said. "She had Richard. Well, not that night, of course." She smiled to herself, a faint, secret little smile. "Not that night."

"It was never an exclusive relationship," Harvey added. "They both saw other people."

Everyone, it seemed, saw other people. One needed a score-card to keep track. Polly began to make her way to the ladies' room. I excused myself, left Jill and Harvey to return to their gazing, and followed her.

The Brants' bathroom is about the size of my living room, and all done in mirrors and black marble. It has a separate lav-atory and a huge powder room that looks as if it belongs in an expensive bordello. Polly Purger stood before the largest mirror pinching out strands of hair to arrange in stylish disarray. I went up beside her and began to put on lipstick.

She glanced sidelong at me and giggled. "That foot thing you did was far out, lady. You got you some sense of humor. Like that 'metal' dude got the cow's tongue sewn in his mouth. Far out. I dig it."

"Yeah. Far out," I agreed, wondering how one went about sewing in a cow's tongue, then wondering why I wondered about such things.

"Where'd you get it anyway?"

"Fridge."

"Weird."

"Indeed." Cow tongues weren't?

"I'd be punk if I didn't have this part in 'Heart's.' I got to have an image for the fans, you know. Thin and long hair. That's how the fans want young female leads. Beautiful too," she added, turning this way and that to get different views of herself in the mirror.

I put away my lipstick, cast a quick glance at her, then plunged. "You should cut down on the peanuts, you know."

"Nah, I don't gain weight."

"But salt can be bad for the baby."

She froze, one strand of apricot hair held above her head, her eyes fixed on mine in the mirror. Slowly she lowered the hair and stroked it until it was almost smooth. Certainly not the effect she'd been working for. "How'd you know?" she whispered, and for the first time, she sounded frightened of me.

"Iriology."

"What's that?"

"You can diagnose illnesses—body conditions—from the state of the eye's iris."

"Really?" she breathed. "That's heavy."

"Yeah."

"Well, like I wouldn't want them to know yet. What with Hermoine out of the picture they're really counting on me. This could freak them."

"But you're supposed to be pregnant in the story."

"Yeah, but they've about decided that I should miscarry and get out of the hospital, too. I mean, like I'm it for them now."

"Sure," I said, wondering if I asked if she'd tell me who the father was. Somehow I doubted it, and besides it seemed incredibly rude to ask. All this dissembling and prying into people's private lives felt wrong to me. But I suspected one must sacrifice principle for power. Besides, it was for Jill.

"Still it's heavy. The way you could tell. Can you, like, do Tarot?"

I shrugged. "No big thing."

"Hey," she breathed. "Would you do me?"

"Sure. Sometime. I don't have the cards with me now, of course."

"I do," she cried, jerking open her little heart-shaped, sequin-covered purse. "I always carry them."

"Heavy," I muttered.

"What?"

"Great," I said. "Great."

"Here."

I took the deck and flipped through it slowly. The cards were beautiful. The images were romanticized, mysterious, sensual, even a little frightening. Queens and kings, knights and pages. Penticles that were in fact coins, rods topped with flowering heads, lovers, swords carried in hands or piercing hearts or bodies, even one card labeled *Death* and bearing an armored skeleton's head. I supposed one could find an answer to anything within, but I'd no idea how to look, no idea how life's master plan, should there in fact be one, revealed itself herein. Did invisible fingers pick out just the right card, or did forces within ourselves cause them to leap into place? It would have helped to know. It would have also helped to know what the cards meant, once picked. I smiled wisely and said, "Nice deck."

"They've been burned," she whispered.

"Burned?"

"To ward off evil spirits."

"Oh good. Yes, that's . . . certainly good."

She flung herself down at a round table covered with a black cloth appliquéd with one graceful, pink, art deco flower. Slowly I sat down in the café chair across from her and began to shuffle the cards.

"Don't you want me to shuffle? After all it is *my* reading."

"Yes. Oh yes. Indeed I do. I always shuffle first to . . . to get the feel of the spirits."

I passed her the deck, and she shuffled, her face tight with concentration.

"I don't use the traditional method," I said, my mind roiling, searching. "I use the Sable method."

"I never heard of it."

"Not too many people have. It was handed down by my grandmother. She was Russian. And psychic. Very psychic."

"Oh." Polly sounded impressed, and I decided that the Russian grandmother was probably a good touch.

I took the cards and turned them slowly, studying the flower and butterfly that a high priestess held in one hand, the Empress's staff knobbed at the top, phallic surely. Carefully, I kept the faces turned from Polly just in case she knew what they meant. "Yes. Ah yes," I kept muttering in a slow, mysterious, and, I hoped, all-knowing voice. "Yes. Ah, now here, I see new life, growth, change."

"Yeah," Polly said eagerly. "That'd be the show. What else?"

I turned a few more cards. "New opportunities."

"Same thing. Go on."

"And here . . ." I gave a long dramatic pause. She squirmed in her chair. "I see . . . I see . . ." I fluttered my eyes up into my skull as if seeking answers from elsewhere. "A man. He . . . yes, I see that he's very powerful. Older. Dark. Strong. Rich."

She nodded emphatically. "Yes! That's him."

It sounded to me like standard fortune telling. I decided it was time for a little personalization. I frowned and stared at the card I had just turned up, noting uneasily that it was a man hanging upside down by one foot; "The Hanged Man" was printed beneath. I never thought of myself as superstitious, but I couldn't help wondering if even now the damned cards weren't telling me something. "There's something here. . . . It doesn't quite come to me."

She leaned forward eagerly. "Yes?"

"I can't quite . . ."

"Go on."

"He . . . he seems damaged . . . hurt somehow."

She gasped.

"I have it! His leg." I put one finger on the foot bound by the rope. "He limps."

"Patrick Henry!" she cried out.

"Patrick Henry?" I asked innocently.

"Never mind. Just see if he's going to marry me."

I turned the cards for some time on that one. At last, I decided to gamble. I tried hesitantly, "He wants the baby."

"Well, I know that," she snapped. "But will he marry me now?"

I pondered that one and turned a bunch more cards. "I see an impediment."

"A what?"

"Something stands in the way of your marriage," I droned. "A woman. Yes, I see a woman. She's . . . yes . . . a red-headed woman."

Polly nodded violently, her apricot hair snapping. "Yes, yes. But the old bitch is gone now. So is he gonna marry me?"

I turned more cards. "I see a younger man here."

"Oh, there's scads. But they don't count. Is he gonna marry me?"

"He has . . . hesitations."

"But he wants an heir," she objected angrily, as if they were my hesitations.

"Yes, I do see that. He wants an heir." Really, this fortune telling wasn't so hard. You just made a blank and let the subject fill it.

"And now that the woman is gone . . . yes, I see here that she's gone." I looked from under my lashes at Polly's face. "There seems to be violence here."

Polly shivered and nodded.

"Yes, but now he will marry you." What the hay? I felt like I owed her something.

Her mobile little face brightened as dramatically as sun bursting through heavy storm clouds. "I'll be set then," she murmured.

"Oh, yes. For life."

She stood abruptly, patted my shoulder once, snatched up her cards, and then was gone.

I sat for some time, staring at the one pink flower against its black background and thinking.

11

All in all, that had worked out well. Polly had motive. Millions' worth. And now that Hermoine was out of the picture, Polly could step in, both in the show and with the wealthy beau. People had certainly killed for less. And anyone on the show would know the studios well enough to know about security cards and their use.

I was pleased with myself. I had an urge to pop back into that aged and venerable anti-chamber and go "naa, naa, naa" at Sam Smith. I bet he didn't know about Polly's pregnancy, and I wasn't about to tell him either. And Cecile. I liked the idea of the killer being a woman, since Cecile kept insisting it was a man. Still, Polly was only a suspect, and I'd made only one small step. But success inspired me. I was here and had the opportunity. I would interrogate the other suspects.

Brad Preston and his wife Wendy stood apart from the rest of the crowd, looking out a window at the orange-pricked skyline. I walked back and forth behind him, feeling suddenly shy and noticing again the width of those shoulders, the excellent fit of the tweed jacket, the perfect way his dark, styled hair layered on his neck. He lifted a hand and laid it on his wife's red-striped taffeta waist. She looked up at him and smiled. It was like a real-life Heloise and Abelard, Tristan and Isolde, Bo and Hope. Seemingly, Brad was the rare caring and faithful husband, both in and out of the soap. Could such a man really kill and decapitate Hermoine? Still, he stood to lose his extremely lucrative job if Hermoine lived. I decided that there was nothing for it but just to push right in, pretend to be a fan (pretend?), and probably make a complete fool of myself. I went back to Roger and the wine for courage before the attack. Two glasses later, I made my approach.

Brad turned at my greeting and smiled kindly. He nodded and even looked gratified when I did my fan spiel. He seemed genuinely real, unconceited, sweet. Wendy looked on, smiling patiently, less striking physically but equally nice.

"It's just so dreadful about Hermoine," I tried next.

Brad shrugged his massive shoulders and stared off into the smoke hanging in the center of the room. "How did you come to have that foot?" he asked softly.

I shriveled inside, self-confidence fading fast. "Accident," I muttered. "I do feel just awful about it. It was in the refrigerator. I just . . ." My voice trailed off.

He watched me with probing eyes, a slight smile turning the corners of those perfect lips. "There are no accidents," he said.

"Oh no?" I was swamped with panic. He knew. Whatever must he think of me?

"No." He smiled patiently down at me. "It may have seemed so, but it wasn't."

"Oh?"

"Her's was a bad spirit. She will progress and amend these evils in her next life. It's best that she's free now to get on with it."

"Well perhaps, but . . ." I let that one float away, too. But what? I'll miss her dreadfully? Hardly. I watched "General Hospital" at that hour.

We listened to the muted conversation of the others standing about the room.

"You look tired," Brad said softly after a moment. "And sad."

I shrugged. I'd an odd and sudden urge to put my face on those endless shoulders and weep. "Well, that foot thing, you know . . ."

Yes, that . . ." He looked at Wendy, and after a moment they both gave each other these conspiratorial little smiles, then Brad turned back to me.

"Do you find it odd that it was us you came to now in your need?"

"Oh listen . . . I . . ."

"It does seem more than chance, don't you think?"

I did indeed. "Oh no . . . no," I sputtered.

"Don't you think something led you here?"

"Maybe," I said cautiously, stepping back a little.

Again, Brad and Wendy studied me with a kindly, proud-parent look.

Smith came out and shouted, "Get that Taylor woman in here." Someone's told him Jill spotted the foot, I thought, my heart dropping like a stone.

Jill floated across the room in her pale blue gown, and everyone turned to watch her.

"She'll be all right," Brad said, looking at me. "Hers is a developed soul."

I nodded, and then Brad's voice fell to a murmur I barely heard. "I'm a walk-in, you know."

"What?"

"You're not really surprised are you?"

I smiled, searching for the right response. I supposed it was some theatrical term.

"You knew when you came over here didn't you?"

"Actually, I . . ." I waited for the next word to expose itself.

"Maybe you didn't know you knew, but you knew," Brad said with a little chuckle.

"Just what is a walk-in?" I asked hesitantly.

They looked intently into my face, and I sensed I was being judged as to my worthiness to receive an answer, so I tried hard to look open, innocent, and guileless, which, feeling as guilty as I was, wasn't easy. But somehow I seemed to pass. Brad lifted a hand and touched my shoulder, and it began to tingle as if he'd held a stun gun. "You need to read Ruth Montgomery's book," he said.

"Oh?"

"*Strangers Among Us.* After I read it, I knew."

"Knew?"

"That I was a walk-in."

I was beginning to lose patience. "Could you please tell me what a walk-in is?"

"Usually spirits are reincarnated," Brad went on in that gentle, urbane manner, the quintessential soap opera doctor. "But a few special spirits come back and take over full-grown bodies to lead and help others."

"How nice," I said, since absolutely nothing else offered itself.

"Benjamin Franklin was a walk-in. Abraham Lincoln. The next revolution will be spiritual, Mary, and we walk-ins will cause it. We will lead the world away from crime and war." Brad went on—and on, describing this perfect new world of white light in which there would be no evil thoughts since everyone would read minds.

I tried to look like I believed him; I hoped he couldn't read my mind. One part of me even wanted to believe. His vision was seductive—such orderly worlds in which good is rewarded and evil swept away like so many dust puffs. I wondered if he could be Jill's secret caller.

Now Brad began the story of how he'd become a walk-in. Three years before he'd been a down-and-out failure. For over a year he'd had nothing but walk-on parts in small stage plays. Wendy worked as a waitress, and their marriage was misery. Rather than committing the evil of suicide, Brad (that Brad) had walked out, leaving his shell body to this new, developed spirit who spoke to me now with Brad's old, finely sculpted lips. A year later, Wendy followed, leaving her body for Wendy Two. Shortly after, Brad got the "Heart's Desires" job. It was ordained, predestined. Brad must become known so that he might carry the message to the world.

"I knew Hermoine could never fire me," he finished. "Hers was an infinitely inferior spirit. That was probably why she was killed."

I stiffened.

"Not," he added quickly, "that we walk-ins are capable of violence. We've put that past us in long-ago incarnations. I imagine Hermoine was killed by an Atlantean, don't you?"

"Someone from Georgia?" I asked, frowning.

"No." He laughed. "The island. Those spirits in their incarnations seek to perpetuate the evil of that island continent. I tried to talk Hermoine into walking out, but she was not advanced enough to even consider it. She laughed." He looked at me a little hungrily, and I understood that he coveted my body, just not in the traditional sense.

I made erasing motions with my hands and took two more steps back. "Well, it's certainly been interesting talking to you." Suddenly, I wanted out of there. Tarot, walk-ins, walk-ons, walkouts. Hell, the Great Detergent was beginning to look good.

12

Next morning the atmosphere was damp and electric. Rain and thunder turned the world outside both green and gray, sullen and vivid. And my inner world reflected the outer. One minute I'd think about myself passing that damn foot, and inner organs

I hadn't even known I'd had would wince. The next minute I'd think about Polly and Brad, and I'd start getting excited again about the progress of our investigation and start thinking again that maybe we could do it.

I fried eggs for the children and gazed into the yellow congealing eyes, thinking about deviled eggs and then almost immediately about Polly's baby. Polly's and Patrick Henry's.

"So how was the party, Mom?"

I jerked about from the stove. "Why do you ask?"

"Huh?"

"Nothing. Nothing. It was . . . boring." I managed something that I hoped looked like a smile.

All three children watched me, puzzled.

Roger drifted into the kitchen dressed in cut-off jeans, gray-threaded hair curling over tanned and freckled shoulders. I swallowed and turned back to the stove.

He clapped me on the shoulder. "Weird night, huh?"

I cast my eyes toward the children and muttered, "Boring."

"Oh. Right. Right. Boring."

"Eggs?" I offered quickly.

"Are they fertile?"

"I don't know."

"There's all the difference," he said. "You should get fertile eggs." He looked at the children. "For their sakes."

Like Jiff and Crest, I supposed. Roger was going on about all the wonderful things that little ol' sperm squiggling about in that yolk could do for you, and the kids were spellbound. They'd never eat another plain barren egg, that was for sure.

"You're going to be late," I called out, too brightly. "You can all talk to Uncle Roger later. Hurry." I entered into the general melee, finding books, shoving lunch bags into hands. When I got back to the kitchen, Roger had collapsed at the kitchen table.

"Coffee?" I asked, pouring myself a cup.

"Never."

I sat down across from him, sipped, smiled.

He watched me morosely. "I guess I will have an egg," he said. "Boiled. Three minutes."

A finger of irritation moved up my spine. I quelled it; he was a guest and Sid's brother, and besides, I wanted to hear all about him, his life, his healing. I got up and fixed the egg, placing it before him. He cracked it open and then sat looking down into the yellow eye for some time and scratching his bare, freckled chest. Then at last, with a little sigh, he ate.

I lifted my coffee cup.

He glanced up and asked gently, "Have you any idea what that stuff is doing to your stomach?"

I arranged a careful smile. "I'll go down to the health food store later today, Roger, and stock up."

He nodded. "That'd be nice." He rose from his chair and meandered around the kitchen, touching the plants, staring out the window, finally ending up peering into the garbage can under the sink. "You should separate this garbage. Recycle it."

"My networking group says that's a rip-off. That men sit at their fifty-thousand-dollar corporation desks polluting right and left, and we're supposed to rush around washing cans."

He raised up and looked at me. "You belong to a networking group?"

I nodded warily.

"I really believe in the women's movement," he said, straddling a chair. "Hell, look at my mother."

I nodded sympathy.

So we did Mother Sable for a while, Roger and I, each watching the other's face, gauging expressions for evidence of offense, irritation, distaste.

"Well, it's petty of me to mention it," I said deprecatingly, then went on to tell avidly of that picture Mother Sable had on her living room wall, the one of Sid and a girl he'd dated once or twice who later became Miss California. "'That's Sid's old girl,' Mother Sable is always telling people. 'She went on to become Miss California.'

"And our wedding pictures are in the drawer in her bedroom," I finished, horrified to actually feel tears in my eyes. "God," I said, swallowing. "Isn't that awful, after all these years to still feel hurt over such a silly little thing."

Roger smiled his soft defeated smile and touched my arm. "It is good to feel, to cry when you hurt."

I stared at him. To think that I ever should hear that from a Sable! He was indeed a miracle. I smiled shyly, noticing that his shoulders were nearly as wide as Brad's rating-raisers.

"You know what my mother did once?" Roger asked, his voice dispassionate, tired.

I shook my head, eager to hear.

"I was dating this girl. We were kids, just eighteen or so. And yeah, we were getting it on. Mother called up the girl's folks. 'Pardon me,' she said. 'But I have reason to believe that my son is seducing your daughter.'"

"No!" I gasped, but I believed she had. It was just her style. "What did the parents do?"

He shrugged those tanned freckled shoulders. "Said they knew it; said they thought I was a nice boy, and that they hoped she roped me. Pressure." He shook his head slowly. "I married her."

I jerked slightly with surprise. "Was that Ruth?"

He smiled at my reaction. "No. Maisey. Lasted six weeks. Never been a divorce in the Sable family, my mother kept reminding me. I was the first—and the second."

I sighed.

He grinned. "Imagine Mother trying to get me to marry Ruth. When I did, Mother sent me this nice little note of congratulations saying if I went through with it she'd kill herself." He looked at me intently for a moment. "Too bad she didn't."

We both broke out laughing.

Dreadful. But my, I was enjoying it. Revenge for all those years. Conscience made me add quickly, "She really can't help it, Roger. She thinks she's doing what's right." God, how many times had I said that to myself. "She's the victim, really, but she does feel like the oppressor."

We sat in silence, thinking.

Roger turned and gazed out the window. "It's this society," he said. "Everybody trying to set up these images of themselves, three feet taller than they really are. If we didn't shut ourselves in all those carefully groomed containers, if we just floated free, maybe we could touch, mingle, love."

I was very still, rigid with the intensity of my listening.

"It's been years since I left Ruth, Mary. I lived in communes those years. That's a beautiful trip, like a huge, gentle, non-guilt-tripping family. They really share. But it's time now for me to join that bigger family. The family of man. I want to heal." The kitchen was very quiet. For a moment I could believe that this man was truly a saint. I noticed again how much he looked like all those pictures of Jesus. I suddenly heard myself telling Cecile I was waiting for a savior and shivered. I felt I was leaning toward him and over-corrected until I was sitting in an awkward, too-straight posture. Slowly, those sad blue eyes moved to mine; a muscle in the corner of his mouth twitched slightly.

I snatched up my coffee cup and drank. I was going to have to be careful. The Sables would never forgive adultery. And Sid would be particularly irritated if it was his brother I erred with. And I didn't want to hurt my children. Still, I was awfully glad that Roger had come to stay.

"Well," he said, standing, "I've got to go get Storm. Hope you and Cecile can get along without me for a couple of days."

I smiled and was horrified to feel myself blushing.

"Be careful," he said, smiling back.

I nodded, and he wandered toward the door, stopping once and turning back to say, "You really should recycle that garbage, Mary. The family of man. It's going to be your children's world someday, you know."

I nodded again and then jumped up and hurried over to snatch a can from the trash.

Roger gave me the sweetest, the most incredibly loving smile, and I just stood there rooted to the spot, a dirty tomato sauce can in one hand, a stupid grin on my face.

13

"It was an act of hostility," Cecile kept shrieking. "It was."

The rest of the women studied the cats twining silently through Jo Anne's forest of tiny tables. Everyone kept her face carefully blank.

"Mary was just trying to help," Portia soothed. "She was just working on her assignment."

"I tell you it was a hostile act!" Cecile screamed.

"Cecile—" Portia began.

"No," I interrupted quickly. "No. Maybe that's right. It seemed to make sense at the time, but, looking back, it seems horrible—hideous. Everyone was so upset. And the police . . ."

"Oh jeez," Inez breathed. "Whatever did you tell them?"

"That I'd picked up the tray and hadn't noticed. But Smith wouldn't accept that. Finally, I sort of told him we . . . me, just me . . ." I was investigating."

"Oh jeez," Inez said again. "What'd he say?"

"He laughed."

"Laughed?"

"A lot."

"Men," several women muttered.

"Then he asked how well I knew Hermoine and did I have some reason to hate her. I think I'm a suspect now, too."

"All that's very well," Cecile said, her face severe, "but what I think we need to talk about is your hostility toward me."

I looked at her, sitting there so square, so firm, implacable as a log.

Jo Anne seized a platter of cookies and waved it at Cecile, attempting to divert or placate her. Cecile snatched one, but she still sat waiting with marvelous hauteur for my defense.

"Maybe," I said. "Maybe a little. Yes, Cecile, maybe I do feel a little hostile toward you. I mean, Cecile, you come around and you eat my food, but then when someone interesting comes along you turn your back to me. You did that last night. I think you treat me like you did your mother."

"You think everybody's looking for a mother," Cecile shouted, biting into her cookie. "That's just your paranoia speaking."

"Aren't they?" I smiled. "It feels that way to me, Cecile. The whole world wants a mother to be there: caring, taking care of, comforting, asking nothing in return; at the same time the whole world world seems to put us down for being mothers." Jo Anne and Portia looked at me, interested; the idea seemed to have touched a nerve.

"Paranoia," Cecile repeated, taking another cookie. Her eyes narrowed, estimating. "Or maybe it's projection."

Portia shot me an I-told-you-so look. We'd talked before about how Cecile demands you let it all hang out, but that the minute you do she staples a label on it.

I smiled slightly, gave a nod, and fell silent.

"All I can say," Cecile finished, "is that that was really a sick thing to do."

There was a pause during which Inez squirmed, Cecile folded her arms and looked self righteous, Jo Anne wildly wielded the cookie platter, and I studied the sad face of the plaster Jesus.

"Well," Portia said, too brightly. "So much for that. Now let's see how we're doing on the case. Mary, did you find out anything with the foot?"

"No one noticed," I said, shaking my head in disbelief. "Not one person."

"Jill did," Cecile said flatly.

Again there was silence. Cecile reached for another cookie.

Quickly, Jo Anne snatched the platter from beneath her fingers and set it on one of the tiny tables beyond Cecile's reach.

"Yes," Portia sighed. "Well, besides Jill . . ."

"Wait," Jo Anne said. She got up, went to her desk, and came back with a pen and small notebook. "I'll take notes."

"A page for each suspect," Portia suggested. "Mary, who do you see as suspects?"

"Well, Brad and his wife and Polly and Anne all had motives." Jo Anne put each of their names at the top of a page. I told them about Polly's pregnancy.

"Oh, Mary," Portia said. "That was sharp. See, we told you you could do it."

I blushed, feeling inordinately pleased.

"Psychological principle," Cecile said. "Victims make good observers."

Portia sighed. "Thank you for sharing, Cecile. So what about Brad?"

"Well, Brad stood to lose either his job or Wendy, his wife. Wendy stood to lose Brad."

"You served her the foot?"

"Yes. Nothing. She's a quiet little woman. Wore candy-striped taffeta and spent the whole evening looking out the window."

"Should I write that down?" Jo Anne asked.

"What?"

"'Candy-striped taffeta.'"

Portia glanced at her. "I think not."

"But I don't think Brad could have done it," I said, frowning slightly.

"Why?"

"He's a walk-in."

"A what?"

I explained in detail, passing around the paperback book I'd gone out that morning to buy. If nothing else, I was getting an eclectic education from all this.

"Walk-ins," Jo Anne breathed. "Books about them and everything. And I'd never even heard of them."

"Bunch a' kooks," Cecile said.

We all looked at her, intimidated as always by her monumental security.

"You don't think there's a possibility that there's anything to it?" Jo Anne whispered.

"Not bloody likely."

Portia frowned. "It's a question of is it inside or outside, I suppose."

"Inside," Cecile said. "Nuts. All of them."

"But," Jo Anne objected, "psychics find killers. And . . . and . . ."

"And Roger knew Polly was pregnant," I finished.

"Lucky guess," Cecile said.

"Whatever," I cut in quickly. Jo Anne was just sitting there, now looking like a kid who'd just been told there's no Santa Claus. "The thing is, Brad doesn't believe in violence. He doesn't even allow himself bad thoughts because, he says, the group mind will pick it up and it'll impede his progression. His killing Hermoine would be like the Pope committing rape."

"That's exactly who would do it," Cecile snapped.

"The Pope?" Jo Anne squeaked with horror.

"No, Brad." Cecile snorted. "People who don't integrate their anger repress it, and then it gets expressed in inappropriate behavior. Like the perfect boy scout, Sunday-school-teacher types who turn out to be killers. It's all shut down there in that pressure cooker, getting hotter and hotter, swelling. And then *whap*, the lid blows, and he takes her head."

Somehow I couldn't quite see Brad in the role of crazed killer, yet there was something in what Cecile said that made me uneasy.

"I'll bet you ten he's impotent," Cecile finished. "And if he is, he's our man."

Jo Anne looked for a long time with sad, spaniel eyes and then slowly wrote. We could see every letter as she traced it into the notebook. *IMPOTENT.*

"Of course you'll have to find out," Cecile finished in her prison matron voice.

"Find out?" I gasped. "How do you expect me to do that?!"

"We've faith in you, Mary. Victims make good observers." Portia mouthed the words as Cecile spoke them.

I grinned and covered it by saying quickly, "We should have a page for Patrick Henry O'Brian. Cecile and I have tried to get in to see him, but no luck. Doesn't Keith's firm handle his P.R., Portia?"

"Keith's biggest account." Portia looked definitely uncomfortable. A murder investigation was one thing, but one's livelihood was another. "Let's see, P.H.O.'s appearing in person at a meeting of twenty-thousand-dollar sellers. I think I can lift some tickets, but that doesn't mean you'll get to talk to him, and if you do, please don't mention my name. Keith would kill me."

I nodded. "Twenty-thousand-dollar sellers? You mean people have actually sold twenty thousand dollars' worth of soap?"

"No, franchises. Five thousand a piece. That gives you the right to sell more franchises and to take a percentage on each and on further soap and franchises that are sold by your clients. No one is really much into selling soap and bleach. Mostly just franchises. Sort of a pyramid thing."

"Weird. Is that legal?"

Portia shrugged. "Questionable. The state legal people are looking into it, but he'll have it made by the time they work it out."

Jo Anne had been writing furiously; we fell silent to give her a chance to catch up.

We thought, watched the cats, sipped coffee. "I guess that's all," I muttered.

Portia narrowed her eyes and stared into middle distance. "We'd better make a page on Hermoine."

"Her life, you mean? We don't know much."

"No," she drawled. "Her parts."

We waited.

"Like that foot. Why was it there last night? And why was the head on that TV program? Someone's going to an awful lot of trouble sending these parts all over. Why?"

"A madman."

"Maybe. Maybe not. Let's make it an assignment. Come next time with all the reasons you can think of for a head on TV or a foot in the fridge." We all nodded agreement. "OK, I guess that's all for me."

I struggled to sit up straight in Jo Anne's flowered, down-filled chair. "Wait, there's something else. I just thought of it. Cecile, I think you should read us what you've been writing in your notebook."

She scowled at me.

"After all, we're supposed to be doing this together."

"Those are my private notes. This is just more of your hostility!"

"No, Cecile, Mary's right. If we're doing this together, why would you need private notes?"

Inez giggled. "Yeah, let it all hang out."

Cecile stared mutinously about at the rest of us. "You are all against me."

We all sat looking at her, waiting. "Either you're with us or you're against us," Portia said. "I need to know before I steal the twenty-thousand-dollar tickets."

"Oh, all right," Cecile snarled, jerking the notebook from her back pocket and flipping it open. "But I resent this. I resent you invading my privacy. I resent—"

"Oh, just read for Christ's sake," Inez groaned.

Cecile glared for a moment, then read:

JILL:
1. Doesn't talk much.
2. Obsessive serving.

REMARKS: Classic schizophrenic pattern. Murder seems masculine. However, subject's obsessive feminity could be reaction formation masking deep-seated homosexual tendencies (witness effeminate boyfriend, possible lover). Perhaps subject had formed attachment to victim and committed crime in reaction to, rejection of, said attachment.

REMINDER: Interview subject privately. Check this out.

Definitely publishable material. Could easily become case famous as any of Freud's.

Cecile finished reading and then glared down at her notebook. The rest of us eyed her in silence, imagining that Jill stood just behind our shoulders like a specter. Suddenly, Jo Anne jumped to her feet, snatched up her platter of cookies, sniffed at Cecile, then flounced from the room.

14

Three days and no leads later, I woke early and decided to make muffins for breakfast in the hope that it might bolster my slipping housewife image. I flopped around the kitchen in my old fur slippers, sifting flour and ideas, measuring sugar and suspects. The stolen Channel 3 security pass. Was that really how the killer got in to plant the head? Likely. Still, there could have been other ways. Someone at "Heart's Desires" might have once worked at Channel 3. And if not, if the stolen pass had given the killer entrance, then he or she would have had to follow the technician, watched her, waited until her attention was diverted, and then taken the wallet from her purse. Smith said she'd seen no one, probably only noticed the wallet was gone when she finished her meal and went to pay the bill. That was creepy. A sort of ordered madness. Somehow I thought that was how it had happened. Still, I decided we should investigate the possibility of other methods of entrance. I oiled the muffin tins, slopped in the batter, threw the tins in the oven, and ran to call Cecile.

"The thing is, we really ought to check all this out," I finished, after a long and rather incoherent explanation.

"And how're we gonna do that?"

"Let's go down to the studio and just sort of casually wander about talking to people, then bring the conversation around to where they've worked and things like that." Even saying it I began to doubt.

"You been lifting handbags?"

"What?"

"You got a pass to the studio?"

"Oh."

"Oh, indeed."

"Harvey will have one. He'll get us in."

Cecile thought about it. "Well, call him," she said grudgingly. Then, as an afterthought, she asked, "Is Roger going?"

"Nope. He's still off kidnapping his daughter."

"Oh," she sighed.

Harvey did have a pass. He would indeed take us in. He would even pick us up in his princely gray Fiat. Such luxury. No buses.

I hung up the phone, took the burned muffins out of the oven, dumped them in the garbage, and started eggs as the kids drifted into the kitchen, sniffing the air, then settled at the table.

"Burn something?" Sid asked as he bustled in to pour coffee and grab a piece of toast.

I smiled sweetly.

Just then the door burst open, and Roger came in on a wave of fresh bay air.

Behind him came Storm.

The kitchen quieted, and even Sid—overcoated, briefcased, and on his way out the door—checked and stood staring.

We all gulped in our breath, which might account for the fact that the little kitchen was suddenly airless. Tim choked on his milk.

"This is Storm," Roger said.

"Storm," I croaked.

She was beautiful. A Marilyn Monroe body even at sixteen. Long, straight black hair; red, white, and blue eyeshadow; a sullen expression; and a mauve T-shirt with the word *Hustle* picked out in glitter across the front.

I think my family read the T-shirt as one, then all eyes jerked back to her face.

She watched us from smug, though patriotic, eyes. "Hi," she said, stuck her hands in her back pockets, glanced about the kitchen, and sniffed. I was unsure whether the sniff was disdain or burnt muffins.

"Kelly, Tim, and this is Carolee," I said. "You'll be sharing her room."

Storm narrowed her eyes and looked up and down Carolee's designer jeans and the forty-dollar, flower-printed sweater she just had to have. "Your mother make you wear those clothes?"

Carolee looked pained—like it was just possible I had.

"School time," Sid cried in that false hearty voice he uses when he wants subjects changed, scenes switched, life to move on. "Come on, everyone. Let's get going. I'll give you all rides. Get your things. Get moving."

He had them out the door in record time, which was nice for me but a touch futile since Storm would still be here when they got home.

"Breakfast?" I asked Storm.

She looked at me from haughty, star-spangled eyes and didn't bother to answer.

Roger raised his palms in the old I-can't-do-a-thing-with-her gesture.

Great, I thought. But he looked so helpless and wistful, I had to give it another shot. "Storm, would you—"

Just then a car horn sounded in the street outside. "Oh dear," I cried, trying to sound distressed when I was secretly relieved. "That's Harvey. He's taking us to the studio today. Help yourself to anything." I gestured about the kitchen, grabbed my jacket, and headed for the door.

"Wait," Roger cried. "I better go with you."

Well he *was* supposed to be helping, but I suspected he dreaded being left with Storm just as much as I did. So then why had he kidnapped her?

Cecile was already in the front seat, so Roger and I piled into the new-smelling, gray plush back.

"She's rebelling a little," Roger said as we drove away.

A little! I thought.

"I'm hoping maybe you can help me with her, Mary." He gave me that slow, sad smile, and I melted. I'd find a way. I'd solve the murder, make a million, solve Storm's problems—everything, anything, to ease those sad, sad eyes.

I smiled and blushed and felt my eyes fix on his.

Cecile flounced about in her seat. "Hi, Roger," she said in that fluttery, new Cecile voice.

I blushed deeper and looked out the side window.

"Did you get your daughter?" Cecile cooed.

"Yes," he said and sighed. She reached over the seat and touched his arm. "Anything the matter?"

"Well—" he began, but Harvey cut in abruptly.

"Mary says you've been in communes for the last twenty years."

"Not all the time," Roger answered gently, steepling his fingertips and smiling at Harvey's gray-suited shoulders.

"Well, I don't believe in all this new-fangled sexual promiscuity," Harvey snapped, turning to send a frown toward the back seat.

Roger nodded once. "Mary tells me that Hermoine was promiscuing with most everyone on your . . ." Roger hesitated just long enough to indicate a search for the right word, ". . . show."

Harvey reddened, and his little face swelled like a balloon. "Well, I didn't approve. I think we all should try to recapture a little old-fashioned decency. Value the family. Protect our women."

"How delightfully Neanderthal," Cecile murmured.

I agreed with her in theory, but Harvey's old-fashioned chivalry was rather endearing, and besides, it was his car and his card, so I kept quiet.

"I think," Roger said, his voice growing even quieter, "that we've been cramped and constipated by all the rules. If sex were accepted as a free and natural act, we probably wouldn't be on our way to investigate this particularly nasty killing."

Harvey huffed and stepped on the gas, scaring about three pedestrians.

I thought about Roger's words. Maybe he was right. Maybe if Sid and I felt free to see others, maybe if we weren't dependent on each other for so much—suddenly something else occurred to me.

"You don't mind if Storm . . ." I hesitated, searching for the right word.

"I encourage her," Roger said haughtily.

"Oh," I breathed.

I thought of Carolee then. No, I could never be that free.

"Sick," Harvey muttered.

Roger smiled patiently.

I could see it was going to be a great day. "Harvey," I said quickly, "do they film your commercials in this studio?"

"Yes," he muttered, obviously still upset. "Patrick Henry O'Brian owns it."

"I see."

There was a two-block silence, and then Harvey offered carefully, "They're writing me into 'Heart's Desires,' you know."

"No, I didn't," I said.

Roger rolled his eyes at me. "What part'll you play?" he asked in a bland voice.

"P.H.O.'s idea. A sort of product placement. You know how the raisin people payed all that money to get raisins in *Back to the Future*. Well, P.H.O. figures Harvey Folk and Sterex Bleach will be subliminally identified."

"Not too subliminal," Cecile muttered, and Roger laughed.

"I'll be a doctor. A sort of confidante and comforter to the female leads."

"That's really very clever," I said, glaring at Cecile. "Free advertising, really."

"P.H.O.'s nobody's fool, Mary. Don't ever underestimate him." There was something in Harvey's voice, and I wondered if he feared the millionaire entrepreneur.

"Do you think he could have killed Hermoine, Harvey?"

Harvey's little body shivered slightly. "He could kill. Believe me, Mary, that man is capable of most anything."

I thought about that until we turned into the block before the studio. Thousands of women were massed in the narrow street before the building. Some wore black, others just black armbands. Some carried placards.

"REST IN PEACE, MADALINE," Cecile read aloud. "AVENGE MADALINE. And look at that one. MADALINE. GOD'S OWN. Can you believe it? They're not even using her right name."

"But it's Madaline they're mourning," Harvey said softly. He drove two blocks before he found a parking space. We got out of the car and walked silently back to and then through the mourners. They seemed hushed and cowed, most standing quietly looking up at the blank, gray stucco face of the studio. Many of the women wept. One recognized Harvey as he passed and seized his arm. "I'm going to miss her," she cried. "I'm going to miss her so. I spent more time with her than I did with my friends."

Harvey nodded and patted her shoulder. Roger and Cecile giggled. Harvey moved on, stopping now and then to comfort the women who turned to him. Once he even held one of the weeping women. He really was a dear little man.

Once inside, we passed through several acres of plain white halls until we came to the set.

It was a gymnasium-sized space of half-rooms all opening onto a large middle clearing filled with cameras and hose-sized black cables, dozens of blue-jeaned technicians, much noise, and more confusion.

"They're blocking before the final shooting," Harvey said. "It looks like they're doing one of Polly's scenes. She's getting out of the mental institution today."

"That's nice," I said. "Losing the baby?"

Harvey frowned. "Still debating that."

Polly stood looking out of the barred window of a grim little half-room.

Brad entered from a side door.

"Adjust that light!" the director shouted, and a man with a long pole ran in and began poking at a strobe light overhead.

"Turn and walk back toward Brad," the director called, watching in a small monitor. "Boom shadow there. Get it out. Stop there." Polly froze. "Mark her."

A man with tiny pieces of colored tape stuck all over his shirt ran forward and put a red piece at Polly's feet. She looked at it for a moment and then said, "Have they found my mother yet?"

"No," Brad said.

"No, no, no!" the director screamed. "Four beats there! We want time to see the pain on your face. Give us pain! Give us pain!"

"I wonder if this is the something worthwhile my mother's always telling me I should come back and do?" Roger muttered.

"They still murdering Madaline?" I asked Harvey.

"Yeah." He smiled.

Brad, looking pained, tapped out four beats with his foot. "No," he said. "No, they haven't found Madaline yet. But she'll be all right, my dear. You must think of yourself now. We, all of us, experience hurt in this world. But in spite of it, we go on. We help, we give, and we grow better."

"Barf," Cecile said a little too loudly, and several people turned to frown at her.

"Now," the director said, "you reach out and touch his arm, Polly. You want comfort. Brad, give us an eight-beat look. You want to hold her, but, no, you're too attracted, and you're going to remain true to Madaline—alive or dead. Take her hand instead. That's it."

Brad was into about count five of his faithful look when Polly jerked her hand free and whirled toward the camera. "That's dumb!" she screeched. "Dumb. She was old. He wouldn't—"

"Polly!" the director screamed back.

She hesitated, and he continued in a softer voice. "Polly, dear, we'll talk to the writers. We'll have him mad for you later on. But just for today—just for me—do it my way, OK?"

Polly sniffed.

There was a stir behind us. Several people turned to look. "It's Patrick Henry O'Brian," Cecile whispered. "Come on. We've got to question him."

Harvey grabbed her arm and pulled her back. "They'll throw you out," he whispered. "He's got bodyguards."

Cecile huffed, batted her shoulders with irritation, but finally agreed to leave her interrogation until P.H.O. was less well-guarded.

Brad took something from his pocket and set it in the middle of the white hospital bed. "I wanted you to have these," he said, followed by a three-beat look. "I bought them for your mother, but I think she'd want you to have them for today. Wear them to remind you of her courage, her strength." Brad turned on his heel and strode from the room, the camera peering all the while into his grief-set face.

"Camera four, a close-up of Polly. Polly, walk toward the bed, reach out for the box. Camera three zoom in on those earrings."

"Wait!" someone said, and everyone froze.

Patrick Henry O'Brian and five bodyguards marched forward over hose-sized cables, through a forest of disco tables, and on into the small mental-ward room. "Theah," he said, and threw another box beside the first. It bounced twice. The technicians and actors erupted into a flurry of comment. Polly, an awed and quite real expression on her pretty face, reached out for the box and opened it. Even from where we stood, the new earrings caught and shot the harsh white light. "Adjust the lights," the director called. "Get out a press release," I heard him say in an aside to an aide. "Get an appraisal. And they look like that pair Hermoine wore to parties. Find out if they are."

"Oh, Patrick!" Polly squealed.

Without another word, a backward glance, or a beat, P.H.O.

and guards marched away through Madaline's kitchen, where a prop man frosting a cake watched with round eyes and dripping spatula.

Polly darted to a small mirror over a sink and tried on the new earrings.

"Fifty thousand if a penny," Harvey whispered. "Think of the starving children that'd feed."

I smiled.

"OK," the director said. "OK. Let's get back to work. Polly, take off the earrings and put them on again for the camera. Look sad. You're thinking of your mother. Get camera three in for a mirror shot. Good. Good. Now touch the packed bag. Now go to the closet for your new dress. Slowly. You're thinking about the new life that's beginning for you today. That's it. Good. That's it."

Polly reached out slowly for the closet door, turned the knob. Two cameras moved closer on their silent rubber wheels.

The earrings flashed at her ears.

She pulled open the door.

And screamed.

Then screamed again.

15

"What is this anyway?!" the director kept shouting.

He had it out of the closet and kept shaking it as if it were some wild animal. Polly sobbed. To me, it looked like an old, tattered garment. Luxurious at some time, perhaps, since it seemed to be silk—red silk. Now it leaped and trembled in the director's hand like a scarecrow in a windstorm. Polly wailed and hiccupped sobs; she fell to the floor, rolled, and bucked.

"What is this thing? Where are those prop people? Who put this here?"

Everyone else seemed oddly subdued. Frozen almost. Only the director and Polly moved or spoke.

And then a technician muttered something.

"What?" the director barked.

"It was Hermoine's."

The director lowered the garment and stared down at it.

Cecile and Harvey and Roger and I began to work our way closer. Now we could see it wasn't tattered but slashed.

"Bloodstains," Cecile whispered.

"Yeah," Roger agreed.

Polly pushed up onto her hands. "This isn't the first time," she screamed, her face mottled red and white, her eyes wild. "It's not the first time. I'm next. I know that's what it means. It's a warning! I'm next." People began to gather about her, slack-faced, hands hanging, looking totally helpless.

"Let me through," Roger said in a soft voice. "I'm a doctor. Let me through."

That's just what he said. A doctor! And everyone pulled back and even patted his shoulder as he passed.

"Doctor!" Harvey snorted.

"He's a healer," Cecile defended.

Roger knelt at Polly's side and began to murmur to her in a soft voice. "Listen, Polly. Listen. I'm holding your head now. Relax and just let it fall into my hands. Relax. Relax."

"Unfortunate choice of words," Harvey muttered.

I giggled, but Polly did seem to be quieting some.

"Clear your mind. That's it. That's it." He laid her head gently on the floor and then worked at her shoulders. He looked up at his circle of silent watchers and said, "Acupressure." They muttered and moved slightly. It was a strange scene—Roger in his jeans and embroidered shirt bent over

Polly, his beard and hair nearly engulfing her face, while Brad in white and stethoscope stood helplessly behind. Polly wept silently now. Roger put a hand on her forehead, another on her abdomen. "Feel the energy flowing between," he ordered. She turned her eyes toward him like a trusting child.

"They're trying to make me lose my baby," she whimpered. Everyone jerked back from her.

"Baby!" the director gasped. "Did she say baby?"

People near him nodded.

"Call the writers!" he gasped. "Call the God damn writers."

A young woman with a clipboard scurried from the room. Someone else went to call the police.

Roger picked Polly up off the floor, whispered something to her; she pointed, and he carried her away. They were looking at each other with these silly, ten-beat looks.

I watched for a minute, feeling old and sad and quite finished with life. Then I thought of Detective Smith speeding toward us. "We better leave," I whispered to Cecile and Harvey, "before the police get here."

"She's half his age and an airhead to boot," Cecile whispered back.

"Let's go," I said.

We crept away. Harvey led us out of a small back door behind Pauline's, Hermoine's soap sister's, hospital bed. She lay in it with full makeup, tubes, and IVs in place, reading a *Playgirl* magazine and awaiting her scene. She nodded as we passed and went on reading. We hurried down a short hall and back out into the street. But once there we slowed and wandered down sidewalks oddly pallid after the brightly lit studio. Cecile kept muttering, "That Roger is an idiot. She's young enough to be his daughter."

"Why was Hermoine's kimono there?" I said.

Cecile threw her arms wide and proclaimed to passersby, "All men are chauvinist pigs." Harvey patted at her broad shoulder.

"All that blood—the slashes. She must have been wearing it when she was killed."

"Makes sense," Harvey said.

"And she wouldn't have worn it out on the street. Doesn't that mean she had to be killed either at the studio or at home?"

"Or in some man's apartment," Harvey added.

"I bet for all his enlightenment, you're cooking for him and cleaning after him," Cecile snapped, two inches from my face.

I glanced uneasily at her wondering if I would find her so objectionable if she weren't so damned accurate. "If it was a man's apartment, Harvey, it would almost have to be someone connected with the show. There's a pass missing for the Channel 3 studio, but not for this one."

"I don't think I'll let him help with my thesis after all," Cecile muttered.

"And whoever substituted that kimono for Polly's getting-out-of-the-institution dress had to know the 'Heart's Desires' script and its props."

Harvey thought about this, his smooth little face wrinkling briefly, then he nodded. "You're right. It does almost have to be someone connected with the show."

"Which lets out Jill," I cried excitedly.

"Don't be silly," Cecile sneered. "She had constant access to Richard's scripts. Let's not split the reward with him, either."

Harvey and I both glowered at her. "He's already been promised," I snapped. "Besides, with Polly, well, he might turn out to be our best source of information." Housewifery does teach one to make the best of leftovers.

Cecile sniffed.

"Who has access to the props, Harvey?"

"Prop people, mainly. But this wasn't a prop. Someone took away the prop after it had been placed and left the kimono."

"Right. So when would the right dress have been placed?"

"Yesterday. Scenes are set the afternoon before, checked in the morning. But it's highly likely the prop people wouldn't bother to check a closet."

"So the substitution was made either during the night or sometime this morning when no one was about."

"Bet for last night," Harvey said. "The sets are never that empty during the days."

I stopped dead in my tracks and stared at the ordinary, everyday people rushing past. "We've got to go back," I whispered.

They both looked at me.

"She lived with P.H.O., Harvey. Bodyguards and all. It's possible that she was killed there, but it seems logical that she might have been killed in the studio. It would have been easier even if it was P.H.O. who was the killer. No one around to hear her screams. Richard, Tom, and Brad are all married. Awkward to kill her in any of their places."

"Brad's a good man. He wouldn't—"

"I know. I know. But most likely she was killed in that studio. We've got to search it."

"The police have already done just that, and probably will again," Harvey said.

"So will we," Cecile stated, then about-faced and marched back the way we'd come. Harvey and I hurried to catch up.

"Why pick on Polly Purger?" I asked as we walked.

Harvey glanced at me.

"And why Hermoine?"

He didn't answer.

I frowned, thinking. "There *is* a pattern. Of course Polly could be diverting suspicion from herself, but if not . . . well, look at it. The two of them. Two female leads. And both of them P.H.O.'s women. What does that suggest?"

"Jealousy?"

"I'd say. Professional or sexual. Did P.H.O. have any other women friends?"

"No one steady," said Harvey. I wondered what that meant exactly.

"Anyone else on the show? A woman?"

Harvey hesitated. "Well, there is Anna Lisa Sloat."

"Who's Anna Lisa Sloat?"

"The one in the bed. Pauline. Madaline's sister. She was the show's bad woman." Harvey's little blue eyes rolled up into their hairless lids as he sought old plot lines. "She kept taking Hermoine's men. Striking-looking woman. But the fans were getting outraged with her behavior, and Hermoine took a dislike to her and demanded her out of the show. The writers are in the process of killing her off."

I nodded. "The respirator."

"Yup."

"Can she be brought back?"

"Nope. She lapsed into a coma last week. She's a vegetable."

"Lucky for Polly."

Harvey thought about it, frowned. "Anna Lisa was P.H.O's main lady before Hermoine."

"Ah ha!"

Harvey frowned deeper, his little face crumpling now with trouble. "Still, for all that, she's a nice lady."

"Maybe it wasn't her," I said, patting his thin arm in its spotless sport coat. "But one of us better talk to her."

He nodded. "Do you want me to?"

"No, I will, Harvey. You're obviously fond of her."

He looked startled. "It's purely platonic."

"I understand," I said, and I did. No one could ever displace Jill from the niche in his heart, but he'd a lot of leftover caring.

We walked back into a suddenly transformed studio. The vast room was tomb-silent and tense. Cameramen raced back and forth pushing huge cameras on those quiet wheels, while technicians darted about lashing thick black cables out of the path.

"This is dress rehearsal," Harvey whispered. "Sammy, over there, said the police are questioning people up in the main office. I think we can avoid them."

"Great!" I whispered back.

"Do you want to watch for a minute?"

"Yeah," Cecile said. "Let's. We need to know as much as possible about all this silly shit."

Harvey reared back slightly and glared at her. She never even noticed and just kept peering about, looking for Roger, I suspected. After a minute, Harvey turned away and led us up into the control room where a number of men sat bathed in the light from a bank of flickering screens. The director sat front-row center, tapping different screens with a long stick. "Camera four. Zoom in on Aunt Kate. Camera four . . . now."

"Four," a man said and punched a button on the control board. Aunt Kate came at us smiling sadly. "Camera three . . . Brad . . . now." A huge, tearful Brad appeared, and then others. All wept or looked sad and spoke of their great love for Madaline, their great sorrow at her loss, their fear that she was dead. I reflected on how much more mourned Madaline was then Hermoine. Even P.H.O. was busy giving away her earrings. Feeling was probably something reserved for soaps, housewives, and the simple-minded, while the smart and powerful just used it to make money.

Harvey signaled us, and we crept silently out of the control room. "We can't go on the set now," he whispered, "but this *is* a good time to search the rest of the studio."

So off we went, sneaking into dressing rooms, opening drawers and closets, looking under beds. I felt guilty at first, but soon I was into it like some wicked child on Halloween night. After nearly an hour of searching, the only stains we'd found were the remains of a chocolate malt on the hand-braided rag rug in kindly old Aunt Kate's dressing room. It seemed that the only real clue to be found today was the one in the fake closet.

"No more dressing rooms now," Harvey said. "Dress rehearsal's about over. Someone could come back for something. Let's search the tape library and prop rooms."

The tape library was beyond a large glass window. As we entered, the earphoned music director glanced up from his sound consoles and sketched a wave. Harvey pantomimed that he was showing us around.

The director nodded and went back to his work. Cecile and I peered about. The floors were gleaming, spotless. Obviously no one had been murdered in here. Cecile leaned in to read the labels on the shelves of taped background music. "Look at this," she murmured. "This whole shelf is for 'turmoil.' And here's 'agitated.' 'Haunted.'"

I giggled. "Here's four shelves of 'love.' 'Love's awakening.' 'Love's flowering.' 'Love's consummation.'"

"Nothing here," Harvey said. "Let's go."

Roger caught up with us in the hall. His face called for a swelling orchestration of love's consumation while Cecile and I deserved a short chorus of pissed.

Next we did the prop room, looking under jukeboxes and peering into refrigerators, cupboards, and even a fake iron lung.

Nothing.

"Nothing," I sighed. "Damn. I would have sworn she had to have been killed here."

"There are any number of places she could have been killed that even a quick cleaning would have hidden," Cecile said.

"We haven't searched the sets," Harvey said.

"No, but they'd have had to notice anything suspicious there," I said. "As much traffic as it gets."

"Well then," Roger said, smoothing his beard in a large mirror, "let's get on home, Mary. You've got dinner to fix, and I've got to go out later on this evening."

Something tensed in my shoulders, and I clenched my teeth to keep back the words pressing to be said. That was certainly a short guruship, I thought.

"Why don't *you* fix dinner?" Cecile blurted. Right then, I loved her.

Roger looked infinitely soulful and hurt. "Well, of course. If that's what Mary wants."

I started to say no, then caught myself. "Sure. Why not?"

There was just a pinprick of light in Roger's eyes before he covered all and smiled gently. "Well then, I will," he said with wonderful red-hen stoicism.

"There's just one thing I've got to do before we leave," I said. "Wait for me here."

"No!" Harvey cried.

I ignored him and took off, remembering the way exactly.

He caught me halfway down the hall. Roger and Cecile were right behind. "You can't," Harvey whispered. "They'll have started taping. You can't go on the set while they're taping. Any foul-ups now and they have to freeze-frame and then re-tape. Tapes can't be cut. It costs them a lot of time and money to retape. You'll get me fired."

"No I won't, Harvey. I'll just slip in at that little back door. When her scene comes up, I'll slip back out. They'll never see me. I promise."

Harvey shook his head. "I don't like it."

"Trust me." I touched his arm. "Remember, it's for Jill."

He hesitated just an instant, then nodded and held Cecile and Roger back as I hurried away.

Anna Lisa was still there in full makeup and tubes, stretched out on her hospital bed, and still reading *Playgirl*. As I crept in, she pulled out the centerfold, studied it with scientific interest, sighed, tucked it back in, and turned the page. "Anna Lisa," I whispered.

She turned, stared, then spat the breathing tube from her mouth and whispered, "You can't be here now. They're getting close to my scene."

"Just a minute," I whispered back. "I just want to talk to you for a minute."

She considered it, brightening slightly despite her gray make-up. "You the press, honey?"

I hesitated, understanding that it would help considerably if I were. So, principles fading fast, I said that yes indeed I was.

"Well," she said, sniffed and began arranging the fake needles along her arm. Machines just beyond the bed huffed and spat a tiny line of green light. The floor held a piece of blue tape in front of the large electric plug by the door.

"Today's the day, huh?" I asked softly.

"Yeah. It's final payday for me."

"Sad," I said. "You were terrific in the part. I cried when you had your . . . accident."

"Really?"

"Oh yes," I said, nodding emphatically, glad I'd gotten the cause right.

She smiled and ran a smoothing hand over her pale hair, which was all tugged back in sick-bed fashion.

"I understand Hermoine Leanders had something to do with all this." I gestured at the bed.

She stared at me. "So you think I killed her?"

"No! No, of course not."

"Keep your voice down," she ordered, leaning forward to see beyond her little room. Satisfied that the filming crews were still some distance away, she leaned back and frowned at me. "Well, I didn't. But I sure as hell don't know why not." She laughed, then caught herself and quieted immediately. "Shoulda done. I tell you, honey, that Lady Bitch deserved it if anyone ever did."

She stopped. Obviously Anna Lisa Sloat had not loved Hermoine overly much. But then, who had? I wondered what to ask next, but not for long. Almost immediately, she was off again. Actually she wanted to tell her story badly, and probably did three times a day. It was an urge I recognized. I felt sorry for Anna Lisa, and already I liked her. Harvey was right. She was nice.

"We grew up together, you know?"

"You and Hermoine?"

"Oh, hell no, honey. Where you been? She was all finishing schools, Vassar, and white gloves for summer. Everything but money. Her mama got her all fixed to be some rich man's wife, but she just never made the grade. P.H.O. and me. We grew up together."

"I see," I murmured, and stole a quick glance beyond the wall to see where the cameras were. I wasn't about to mess up Harvey's career.

"We got a little time yet, dearie."

I nodded. She was into her story with gusto now, talking fast but so softly I had to lean in to hear. Just occasionally I caught faint echoes of the suffering going on beyond our three walls.

"We's both white trash. Dirt poor. Pat 'n' me. 'Bout all we had was each other. Kids laughed at us—we's so raggedy. 'N' Pat'd get this tight white ring round his mouth. 'It's gonna be different some day. You'll see,' he'd go, just all quiet 'n' hard like. 'You'll see,' and I guess I did. His folks did some migrant pickin'. Cotton mostly. Sometimes I went with 'em to make myself a little money. This one time, they took a kettle of hot soup for lunch. They's up at a house talkin' terms, 'n' we's s'posed to be watchin' his baby brother. But instead, we git to foolin' round—kissin' 'n' a bit more. That poor little kid falls right into the soup. Liked to a killed him. Pat's daddy beats him so bad he can't stand. Then he drives off and just leaves him lyin' there in that ol' dirt road. Weren't the first time, either. That old man was just plain mean. Well, when Pat can walk, he does. I went with him. We weren't but twelve 'n' fourteen then.

"I ain't gonna lie to you, honey. He had me on the street to get the money fer a start. 'N' he reads all these books about every business started by someone didn't have them a lot a money. *Dare to Be Great, Amway, Coscot,* even *EST.* Borrows from all of them, and he swears he's gonna beat 'em all. He's doin' so-so, 'n' I'm off the street for a good many years when he gets the idea for this Sunshine Soap and then the idea for how to sell it. Hell, how else do ya sell soap but with a soap opera. 'N' the soaps make the most money 'n' cost the least to produce of any TV programs. You know that, dearie?"

"No."

"Yeah. Well, neither did I. But Pat did. He's no dummy. 'N' ours cost less than the others. 'N' as our characters get known, they're all tied up with P.H.O.'s products. He's even gonna put that bleach guy right into the show. You know that?"

"Yes, I did."

"Anyway, he's going good, 'n' he's got Madaline hired. I was the sister that got kidnapped 'n' raised by hoods see?"

I nodded.

"Then Madaline's in his bed, 'n' I'm out. He's on his way up, 'n' I figure he needs him a high-class whore now." She grinned. "Of course I make the mistake of tellin' her that, so here I am." She spread her tubed arms wide. "Can you believe this? Can you believe after all that I did for him, he'd let her do this to me?"

I started to answer, then stopped at a noise in the hall.

"Oh God," Anna Lisa gasped. "That's Brad coming to unplug me." A camera poked its nose around the wall.

"Quick!" Anna Lisa gasped, shoving her *Playgirl* under the covers and snatching up her breathing tube, "git under the bed!"

Infected by her panic and my guilt, I didn't even think but just scrambled under the bed. Once there, I had to bite my hand hard to keep from giggling. This did seem a trace Victorian. I watched Brad's feet move slowly up to the patch of red tape at the bedside, listened as he began a long and tearful oration to the unconscious Pauline about how he knew his dear Madaline, wherever she was, didn't want her sister to suffer more, so now he was going to do this for her. Brad, it seemed, was all over the place today doing things for his dear lost love.

There was a pause; Brad was tapping out beats with one foot. I rolled onto my back and bit hard on my lip. Why did I find being stuck under a bed like some clandestine lover so damn funny? Well, I would surely watch "Heart's Desires" for the next few weeks and probably forever. Suddenly my eyes focused, and I saw where I was staring. "Oh my God," I whispered. Suddenly I was scratching and clawing at the slick floor, scrambling to my feet. Brad bent slowly toward the plug. "I found it!" I cried. "I found it!" He jerked up and looked back at me, his face blank with shock. "Get up!" I shrieked, pushing at Anna Lisa, tugging at her covers. "Get up!"

"Hey don't! You nuts or something?"

"What's going on?"

"Who's she?"

Cameramen and technicians began to come around the camera. Loudspeakers roared, "Get that woman off the set! Security, get that woman off the set!"

I jerked up the bottom sheet with Anna Lisa still on it, then the rubber sheet beneath. Men pushed and shoved their way into the little three-sided room. Several grabbed my arms.

"There!" I shouted, pointing. "There."

Silence. Somewhere in my head I heard the ominous music that should have been playing behind this. The bloodstain was so large that it covered even the small portion of the mattress I'd managed to uncover. Large enough that a small amount had seeped through the cheap mattress that had been put on the standard-issue hospital bed. Anna Lisa looked at it and then turned gray under her gray makeup, which is about the most gastly special effect I think I've ever seen. Slowly, she pushed back the white sheet and blankets and got out of bed. Slowly, several men advanced, and with tentative fingers gingerly reached and removed the undersheet, then the rubber sheet.

Anna Lisa fainted, scattering tubes and bottles across the waxed floor.

But right then, I felt pretty good.

16

Lieutenant Smith sat for the longest time, head bent, fingertips pressed to his eyes. "OK. Tell it to me just one more time. What were you doing under the bed?"

Obviously, neither Roger nor I was going to get home in time to fix Sid's dinner. Smith was truly an unimaginative man. "I found where she was killed, didn't I?"

He sighed deeply.

Two hours later, the four of us made our silent way home. "I'm really sorry, Harvey," I said finally. "I hope this doesn't get you fired."

He glanced toward the back seat. "Nah!" His little face shone like a Christmas ornament. "They're pleased, really. We're going to be on the six o'clock news."

"Wonderful," I muttered, my heart sinking. "My, isn't that nice."

And so there I was on the evening news.

Sid was not pleased. Actually, he was not pleased even before the news came on. Roger and I were so late getting home that Sid had already driven the kids through the golden arches, and they were all sprawled about the living room with their Big Macs watching TV when we walked in.

Sid looked at me and then back to the screen.

"Sid, I'm sorry I'm so late. Something came up. We . . ." I stopped. We what? My mind shorted with the effort of finding words to dress this particular explanation.

And then it wasn't necessary, for there I was on the TV, shooting out from under Pauline's bed, jerking at her sheets. Sid choked on a french fry.

"The police kept us," I whispered when it was all over.

"Hey, neat, Mom," Tim began, then caught a glimpse of his father's face and thought better of it.

Sid turned a red, swollen, pop-eyed face toward me. Maybe he'll have a stroke, I thought, and couldn't help noting uneasily that fear wasn't my only reaction to this thought.

Sid said nothing. But then Sid always says nothing. And yet his exact meaning came to me whole, like it was teleported from his head to mine. His mother rang up almost immediately to provide the voice-over for the look. "How could you, Mary? You're a Sable. We Sables . . ."

The Sables believe themselves a superior breed. I've never quite understood why. She'd quite a bit more to say, but I tuned her out. I've become quite good at tuning out.

"At least my mother cooks," Storm said somewhere in the middle of Mother Sable's speech. Another generation heard from.

But then Roger—God bless Roger—announced, grinning from ear to ear, "Hey, everybody, I've got a date with a star."

"Who, Uncle Roger?"

"Polly Purger. From the soap opera."

"Hey, hey," Sid leered, calling up easily his good-old-boy front. Often I'd seen that cold, saved-for-wives face disappear at the sound of a door bell or the sight of a child. I figured it was some sort of economic principle. Don't spend charm unwisely, and certainly never squander it on wives.

My children looked at their uncle with round eyes. "Can we meet her, Uncle Roger?"

He shrugged and spread his hands in a gesture that said maybe they could.

"My father, the stud," Storm muttered at the ceiling. Both men glanced uneasily at her.

And since everyone's eyes were on Roger or his daughter, I hung up on Mother Sable and then took the receiver off the hook before she could call back.

"Well, it's nice something good came out of this mess," Sid muttered.

"Did she tell you what she meant when she said the kimono wasn't the first time?" I asked, avoiding Sid's eyes, which frosted whenever he looked my way.

"Some nut's been sending her things. The murdered dame's ring. Stuff like that."

"Why?"

"She doesn't know."

"Not in front of the children," Sid muttered.

"Oh, sorry." I dropped the rings and the kimono into my mind to let them steep. Why?

"I bet you won't haul *her* off to your old commune," Storm muttered.

"Look, Storm, don't start."

"I bet she won't screw your friends just because it's supposed to be so beautiful!"

"Storm!"

"Big star like her ain't about to make it with some garlic-breathed turkey just because it's on the fair-and-share chart."

"Storm, that's enough. You never once tried to understand what we were trying to accomplish."

"Big fuckin' deal, Daddy!" she screamed. "You never tried to understand me!" She jumped to her feet and shot from the room. A moment later, we heard the door to Carolee's room slam.

There was a long silence during which we all carefully didn't look at each other.

"I don't quite understand, Roger," I asked in a wee voice, "if you don't mind her—uh, you know—how does she rebel?"

"She," Roger said with disgust, "smokes."

"Oh," I said. "Oh."

The next day, I slipped out as Jo Anne slipped in. I wanted to talk to Jill alone, without the help of the detection committee of Cecile, Harvey, and Roger. Jill was my friend, and this time I vowed there'd be no grilling, interrogating, or analyzing—just a simple talk and a few thousand calories. I skipped breakfast in preparation.

Though it was just past ten, Jill had already baked two kinds of cookies and was now busily frying up the last of a batch of homemade doughnuts. I couldn't decide whether to be impressed or depressed. Once settled with coffee, cookies, and hot doughnuts, I began. "You've no idea who made that phone call, Jill? Who it was that told you to watch 'Surprise of Your Life'?"

She blinked twice into her boiling oil. "I've no idea at all about who made the phone call or who told me to watch 'Surprise of Your Life.'"

I sighed and shook my head. I began reciting aloud the questions that kept rolling in my mind. "I just don't understand all this. Why the head on TV? Why the kimono in the closet?

And where's Hermoine's body? That's the big one. Or, to be exact, where's the rest of Hermoine's body?"

Jill sat down across from me, tipped her head to the side, and, still smiling, regarded me with bright, unblinking eyes. She considered. "Publicity?" she suggested finally.

"Surely no one would do all this just for publicity."

"It's in all the newspapers you know. Harvey says the ratings have shot sky-high and that the show has been offered a slot on the national network. All of them have had offers from the *National Inquirer*. And Harvey says that P.H.O.'s company's sales have tripled—both soap sales and distributorships. Besides which, Harvey says, he stands to make a lot just on the show alone. Harvey says all the writers and actors have offers from other shows." Jill leaned closer to murmur in an awed voice, "Polly even got one from 'Dynasty.'"

"No," I said.

"Yes."

"She going to take it?"

"Harvey didn't say."

We both sipped coffee and considered this for a moment.

"So in fact everyone's benefiting from this grizzly mess. Everyone's got a motive."

"Everyone but Hermoine."

"What?"

"I don't think she benefited, though Brad does say—"

"Can I have more coffee, Jill?"

"Oh? Oh, surely." She popped up to fill my cup.

"Still, it would take someone clever to figure out ahead of time that all this was going to happen. Someone like P.H.O., who's an expert, it seems, at forecasting. But would he kill his lover just to make money?"

"Not just. But Harvey says he's into pain."

"You mean sadism?"

"I think so." Jill sat back down.

I nodded, stunned. It was him. Surely P.H.O. had to be the murderer.

The doorbell rang, and Jill popped from her chair. I found myself suddenly remembering the jack-in-the-box we'd bought Kelly for Christmas some ten years before. I sighed and took another cookie. "That's Harvey," she cried happily. "He comes by every morning at ten for coffee." Which explained the cookies and doughnuts. The way to a man's heart, etc.

Jill led Harvey into the coppery kitchen, and immediately my head filled with all the questions for him.

"How is everything, Mary?" he asked, his bright blue eyes fixing on mine.

"Oh," I shrugged. "You know . . ."

He watched me for a moment and then piped, "No, I don't. What's wrong?"

"Oh, just home things. You know."

"No. Tell me."

And because he sounded like he cared, I really couldn't help myself. "Well, it's Roger."

"Yes?"

"Well, Storm, really."

"Storm?"

"Roger's daughter. Last night Carolee invited her to this Halloween party—asked her what she was going to dress as, and Storm said a whore. I thought that was what she was dressing as already."

Harvey shook his head and patted my arm.

"Not that I would care," I added quickly, "but the thing is, Carolee seems to admire the kid. This morning she wore one of Storm's blouses to school. It's probably OK, but I can't help but worry."

"It's not OK," Harvey squeaked stoutly. "Why don't you tell that man to get out of your house?"

I sighed and snatched up another cookie for comfort. "Sid wouldn't allow it. The Sables are a close family." I frowned. "Or they think they are. Can you be close to someone you never talk to about anything but the weather?"

Harvey frowned, his smooth little face reddening and rumpling. "That's terrible. A man should protect his women."

I smiled at him, understanding for the first time how Jill could be so fond of him. "Thanks, Harv," I murmured, "but look . . . here I am going on about me, and I really wanted to ask you some questions."

He smiled, leaned back, and began to sip the coffee Jill had brought him. "So ask away."

"Well first off—I'm dying to know. Is Polly going to take the job with 'Dynasty'?"

"Nope." He grinned wider. "She figures right now that the 'Heart's' gig is an even hotter item. And of course there's P.H.O. He's begun to take her out in public—which for him is an announcement that they're an item. He might even marry her."

"Of course there's the threatening messages."

"She's decided to move into P.H.O.'s house. Break off with all other men. He's going to keep a couple of his bodyguards with her at all times. She should be all right."

I shook my head and grabbed a doughnut. "But Jill says he's sadistic."

Harvey shrugged. "Likes whips and stuff like that."

"But think about it, Harvey. P.H.O.'s women cheat on him. Now one's dead, and the other's warned back into line. Besides that, he's profiting enormously. And he obviously has no conscience. Just look how he treated Anna Lisa."

Harvey nodded.

"I think he's guilty, Harvey."

His face stilled. I could see facts computing behind his eyes. "Could be," he said finally. "O'Brian's not a nice man."

"So Cecile's right. We've got to find some way to talk to him—question him. Do you think we'll get a chance at the twenty-thousand-dollar sellers' meeting?"

"No."

"No?"

"No. Bodyguards and assistants and all—you'll be lucky to get a handshake." Harvey ate two cookies and a doughnut, chewing

slowly all the while, his little face working with concentration.
Finally he shook his head. "I don't know how we'd ever manage it.
I've got a day pass because P.H.O. has some of the Sterex com-
mercials filmed on his estate. It's a selling point for his marketeers.
But I can't take anyone else inside the house on my pass."

I sighed. The more P.H.O. barricaded himself and the
harder it was for me to get to him, the more convinced I grew
that he was our killer. And the more remote he became, the
more determined I became to get to him. "Does he talk to the
twenty-thousand-dollar sellers personally at the meeting?"

"No," Harvey said. "But he does give out little blue passes—
invitations really—to the lavish party he gives afterward at his
home."

I looked at him round-eyed. "Well, that's it then!"

"Well . . . no . . . he only hands them to a special few that
happen to catch his attention. Generally beautiful women or
people that look like swingers."

"Hmm," I said. How did one catch the attention of a sadistic
killer? I shuddered at the thought. And at the next. "Are they
going to ask us anything about selling, Harvey? Like, how did
we sell twenty-thousand-dollars' worth?"

"Nah. Not everybody there will be twenty-thousand-dollar
sellers. Every seller can bring two guests. These are the only
times P.H.O. pitches personally anymore. And he *is* good.
Fame and charisma—they're hard to resist. Most guests end up
joining, which means next year the twenty thousanders will
probably be forty thousanders. Best kind of reward, really.
Amway just gives diamond pins."

I nodded, thinking that P.H.O. sounded like a formidable
opponent. I wondered at myself. I couldn't get Sid to pick up
his socks. I couldn't invite my brother-in-law out of my house.
And here I was planning to out-maneuver one of the world's
champion maneuverers.

And yet I felt suddenly strong, and clear, and cold. And sure
that somehow I could do it.

17

I spent the next four days in the library reading everything I could find about Patrick Henry O'Brian. The more I read, the more convinced I grew that he was our killer. He was a ruthless, conscienceless businessman who'd climbed to the top on the backs of a number of helpless poor he'd rooked out of their last dollar. I found myself thinking about him and how to get to him almost continually. The fourth day, I stayed at it so long that it was after six by the time I got home. That meant chicken for dinner. My life and thoughts often center on what's for dinner, but on good days, days that seduce my mind to bigger things, we have chicken. I took it from the fridge, the knife from the drawer. You save a lot of money by cutting up chicken yourself. Sometimes I tell myself that even if I'm not worth Loreal, surely I'm worth precut chicken. Still, the budget's tight, and maybe the cutting would get a kid to college or something important.

I put the knife to the leg joint and then just stood there staring at that yellow headless carcass. "Where is that damn body," I whispered to it. "Where?" It couldn't be in the studio. The police would have found it. Dumped in some alley in the city? Surely it would have turned up by now. So where?

I sliced off a leg and mentally turned the pages of the *Time* magazine I'd read that afternoon, looking again at pictures of P.H.O.'s estate.

"I wonder," I whispered.

Roger wandered into the kitchen.

"Have you ever seen Patrick Henry O'Brian's house?" I asked.

"Um, I drove Polly home the other night."

"Big?"

"It could house a village of starving Ethiopians."

"Fences?"

"Everywhere. Solid steel."

"Gardens?"

"Half the size of Yosemite."

I nodded to the chicken.

"Capitalist pig," Roger added, picking up the saltshaker and turning it in his hand. He looked sadder than usual, and I supposed that he was one of the men Polly had excised in her new austerity program. Roger sighed and set the saltshaker down. "You should use powdered kelp, you know."

I looked at him.

"Instead of salt. Blood pressure, heart attacks; salt's a killer. If old Sid dies at fifty, you'll know why."

I felt my eyes getting bigger, my mouth smaller. The chicken wings came away with two slashes. "I shall probably be caught standing over his body, smoking salt cellar in hand," I said through barely moving lips.

"Well, if you can't take a little helpful criticism, Mary . . ."

"Storm didn't go to school today."

Roger shrugged. "School is such a middle-class trip."

"So's work, I guess."

Roger laughed. "Mary, Mary. I thought you were bigger than this. It's all right for you not to work because you're a woman; is that it?"

"I work!" I shrieked. "I . . . I . . ."

Roger made a gesture with his hands. "I'm not going to argue with you now, Mary. You're getting all emotional." He turned and strolled from the room.

"Emotional!" I muttered. "Just look at the Sable popping out. Emotional!" I looked down at the chicken. It had somehow become minced. I couldn't really remember doing that. It would be chicken soup tonight. I smiled slightly. Sid hates chicken soup.

* * *

"It's not going to work having Storm and Roger here," I told Sid that night after the children had gone to their rooms.

He gave me a pained look and went on grading papers.

"Sid, she's not going to be good for our kids. Carolee looks up to her. And Storm is always saying things like if she has to do it, she's going to get paid for it."

Sid closed his eyes and pressed the bridge of his nose with his thumb and forefinger.

"Carolee's a child. I want her to go slowly and carefully into adulthood."

Sid put a red B on a paper and shuffled it to the bottom of his pile. "My mother, now Roger," he muttered. "It seems to me, Mary, that if you cared at all for me, you'd make an effort to get along with my family."

I stared at him, stung. "And if you cared for me, you'd make your mother stop criticizing me. And you'd make Roger stop . . . stop . . ." Stop what? My thoughts had stampeded. Sid watched me patiently, his composure overwhelming. Perilously close to tears, I fell silent, defeated again.

"Leave Carolee alone," Sid said. "Trust her. She's all right. She says you pick on her. Maybe she does these things because you tell her not to. You ever think of that?"

My mouth opened and closed like a dying fish, but my mind would provide no words.

"I really do have to finish these papers, Mary."

He went back to work, and I stood there twisting my hands. Did she? Was it my fault? I flung out a few wild protestations, denials, but they spattered, useless, against the walls of Sid's silence. Sid could have made a great politician. *When you can keep your head when all about you are losing theirs, then you'll be a man! Ha!*

So he should be free? Communicative? And understand that it is all right to feel? And take his children to communes to be garlicked?

Surely there was something in between.

Me probably.

*   *   *

The next morning, Sid coffeed early and left to attend a be-
fore-school faculty meeting. I was vaguely pleased. I would organize my day, get a lot accomplished, pay the bills, watch
"Heart's Desires," and call an architect friend of ours to see if
there was any way we could get copies of the plans of P.H.O.'s
estate. The *Time* article said P.H.O.'s estate was fenced on
three sides and overlooked the ocean on the third. I wondered if
Cecile and I could possibly row in from the ocean and climb the
cliff face. I supposed it wasn't very likely. O'Brian had security
with a capital S. Maybe we could get in through the sewer.
Maybe I was going mad.

Oatmeal for breakfast, I decided. Vegetarian and non could eat
that. Stirring flakes into boiling water, I reflected on how God in
his infinite wisdom had not created fertile and sterile oatmeal.

Roger came in wearing his cut-off jeans and two strings of
seed beads. He stared into the pan. "Oatmeal," he muttered
unhappily.

"Busy day," I chirped. He turned away, and I up-ended the
saltshaker over the pot.

Carolee slid in wearing a guilty look, bright red lipstick, half her
blouse buttons undone, old jeans she'd pruned into short-shorts,
and three-inch platform shoes she'd borrowed from Storm.

I looked at her; she glared back. It was not going to be a good
day. I studied the oatmeal, carefully stirring words into it.
"You can't wear that to school, Carolee."

She flung herself about the kitchen, something in the manner
of a Shakespearean tragedian or a dying grouse, crying, "Don't!
Don't start! Just don't start! I'm tired of you always telling me
what to do! It's my life! I'm going to live it like I want! Just
leave me alone!"

I checked in midstir, slowly took the spoon from the oatmeal,
then glanced at my daughter. Was it true? Was I always telling
her what to do? I didn't think so. I tried to think back.

How many times have I stood just so, panic-paralyzed, staring at my children, wondering what I'd done wrong or what to

do now? Sometimes I envy those earlier generations who did so much wrong but were so sure they were doing absolutely right.

"Really, Mary," Roger's soft voice chastened, "it's only a body."

Yes, and she'd probably be raped on the way to school, and even if she got there safely, they'd kick her out for breaking dress code, and that would be my fault too. If the children rob banks or the husband has ring-around-the-collar everyone knows it's the woman who is to blame. I stood there with the tip of the spoon breaking the thickening oatmeal. On the other hand, maybe Carolee wasn't even planning on going to school. Storm never did. She slept to ten or so, came in for breakfast, and then did God knows what. Maybe Carolee . . .

Dear God, handle this and I'll believe in you. I'll make all my trips to the supermarket on my knees. Right then, if I could have found a way into the sewers, I'd have been on my way.

Tim came galloping into the kitchen, caught sight of his sister, and stopped dead. "Hey," he whooped, "Get a load a' her." He circled her, sighting and snapping an invisible camera. "Listen, deary, I'll tell all the guys to start saving their allowances if you'll cut me in for ten percent."

"You are such a child, Tim," Carolee said coldly, tossing her head. "You know so pitifully little about life."

Silently I groaned.

The doorbell rang, and I heard Kelly go clattering through the living room. "I'll get it," she cried.

A moment later she led Richard into the kitchen. He wore a satin shirt and a ruby ring on his left little finger. He glanced about the kitchen, greeting each occupant with a slight twitch of one brow, then settled half-leaning, half-sitting on the edge of the counter. There is something Old World about Richard; he fairly cries out for a snuff box. "Mary," he said, and managed a faint smile.

I introduced him to Roger; they eyed each other across the kitchen, neither one speaking—two wrestlers costumed and charactered for a bout. King Richard vs. Simple Man.

The children stood in the middle of the floor and gaped at Richard as if he were Elton John or someone. "That was really something about that lady on your show," Tim blurted in an awed voice.

Richard dropped his eyes modestly and waved the rubied hand to signify it was nothing.

"Hermoine was one of the new women," Carolee said, stroking her long wavy hair.

Richard glanced toward her, then did a double take when he noticed her get-up. A real smile tugged at the corners of his mouth. He turned back to me. "Mary, I want to talk to you about the Brant's party."

Uneasy, I shut off the oatmeal and poured Richard coffee. "The party?"

He sipped delicately, watching me over the rim of the mug. "Yea, that foot thing."

I stiffened, glancing at my children.

"Ah yes, the foot," Roger said with a smug little smile.

Cavalierly—with graceful hand gestures, flowing satin sleeves, the ring sparking points of red light—Richard related the tale of the passed foot. The story, of course, had been in the paper but my name hadn't. My children listened round-eyed. I cringed inside.

Carolee stared scornfully at me. Mother, the passer of human feet, trying to dictate morality to *her*! She did have a point. I turned back to the stove so I wouldn't have to meet her look. "It was a mistake," I muttered. "I didn't know what it was."

"Jeez, Mom," Tim said sympathetically, whapping my shoulder, "that is one big grosso. It must have really laid you out. Did anybody eat any?"

"No," I mumbled. I felt Richard looking at me. Busily, I stirred the uncooking oatmeal. Tim managed a few more absolutely terrible comments about the foot; Roger asked Richard just how much *that ring* cost, and my stomach churned. Richard informed Roger grandly that the ring came in a Cracker Jack box, muttered a few pleasantries toward the children, then pushed himself away from the counter, set down the coffee mug, and said, "Well, I better be going. We're working night and day trying to patch the show back without Hermoine. Mary, would you mind seeing me to the door?"

I did mind, but it was easier to say I didn't and go with him.

At the front door, he drew me out on the porch and shut the door behind us. "Mary," he murmured, with his slightly mocking smile. "This is me, Richard. We've known each other a long time, long enough for me to know when you aren't being straight. Level, baby. You knew that foot was there all the time."

I picked at a fingernail.

"Mary?"

I shrugged.

"Why? That's all I want to know. Why?"

I glanced at him and then away. Should I tell him about the networking group thing? No! He would think it a good story and tell everybody. Worse, he would laugh.

"Why, Mary?" His voice now was low, puzzled, kind.

"I don't know, Richard. Revenge maybe. Anne asking me to serve. Years behind the tray . . . no one noticing or caring." Once started it did seem the reason. I found myself wanting to go on and on, list instances, rage, cry. I made myself stop.

Richard's eyes narrowed; he stared at me for a long moment then looked off down the street. "Maybe that's what it is with Jill," he muttered.

"Maybe," I said.

He reached out and took my hand, and we smiled at each other, really liking one another for that moment.

Then he turned and galloped down the steps, muttering about being late for a writers' meeting and how they had to decide on a killer today. I went back to the kitchen.

It was getting late. "Carolee," I said briskly, snatching up the oatmeal pan, "go and change."

She flounced down at the table and shot me a look that said, clearly, *Make me.*

I looked at her for a long moment.

"Come on, Mary," Roger said in a soft, coaxing voice.

Carefully, I took down bowls. Carefully, I filled one with oatmeal and set it before her.

She peered into it. "Jeez, do you really expect us to eat this shit?"

With all the interruptions it was now lumpy, overdone, probably too salty. I stood with the pan in one hand watching intently how the sun's rays clung in the waves of her fair hair.

"Mom?" Tim said.

I tried to make my mind move ahead into alternative breakfasts—eggs, sterile or fertile.

I heard a distinct snap. Then I watched with interest as the hand holding the saucepan whipped it over and slung the oatmeal hard at the floor. It landed with a plop, spreading out across the tan linoleum.

"Don't eat it! Don't eat it! I don't give a good God damn!" I lifted a foot and stamped on the round, gray glob. It squashed wonderfully. "Starve! See if I care!" I stamped harder. Oatmeal splatters climbed the stove and cupboards and chairs. *You'll just have to clean it up*, a voice somewhere within me said plainly. I stamped harder than ever.

Vaguely, I was aware of round eyes, round mouths, Kelly whispering, "Mommy!"

Then something else penetrated the haze. A *slop-slopping*. I half turned. Tim in his giant purple tennis shoes was clomping through oatmeal right behind me. He looked brightly about at the others. "Oatmeal wine," he explained cheerfully.

I burst into tears and fled, snatching up my purse and slamming out the front door weeping, angry, and deeply ashamed.

"Mama! Mama!" I turned. Kelly was tearing after me, her eyes wild with terror. "What's wrong?! Where are you going?! Are you coming back?! Are you leaving?!"

Frantically, I swallowed back tears and fury. I even managed a small false laugh. "Oh, Kelly, of course I'm coming back.

I . . ." I sniffed and fumbled in my purse for a handkerchief. "You know . . . I just got . . . mad."

She watched me with uneasy eyes.

"You do that sometimes. Get mad."

"You don't," she whispered.

I looped the strap of my bag over a shoulder and gave her a watery smile. "Well, today I did."

She nodded uncertainly. "About the oatmeal."

No, it didn't make sense. "Come on. You and I'll go have breakfast at a restaurant. No old oatmeal for us."

She managed a shaky smile. "I'll be late for school."

"I'll write you an excuse."

Now her smile was wider, surer. She nodded shyly and we walked down the street together, me sniffing, her holding tight to my hand.

Later, as I walked her to school, I saw Carolee ambling casually in a direction opposite the high school, and that familiar core of cold unease rose within me.

There was no help for it then. Busy day, oatmeal to clean, architects to call, sewers to find. Whatever, I would have to go talk to Portia.

18

"And Portia, it's getting worse," I said. "I blew up this morning and threw oatmeal all over the kitchen. I had to call Jo Anne and tell her not to come in. I couldn't let her clean up oatmeal I'd thrown."

Portia leaned back, crossed her long legs, and listened intently.

"I never lose my temper with the children. Poor Kelly was terrified."

Portia drew on her cigarette, exhaled, squinting at me through the smoke. "She was terrified because you never lose your temper."

I frowned. We had done this before in the group.

Portia refilled my cup and looked out the window at San Francisco falling back, silver and gray, to the gray-green ocean. She sighed and bent forward to retrieve her own coffee cup. "Bitches. Hostile and aggressive. How we women fear to be labeled or to appear so. It's one way they control us. But if you've grown up with it, it's so hard to change." She shrugged. "I know, believe me."

"But Portia, I really don't like people who are pushy or hostile or bossy. I like gentle people. Anger does so much damage."

Portia shrugged, then began giving me instructions for the twenty-thousand-dollar seller's meeting. Cecile and I would need male escorts since most attendees would be couples, and we shouldn't look conspicuous. We called Harvey, who agreed not only to go but to drive, and Roger, of course, expected to go.

Such problems settled, I leaned back and just let myself enjoy being there in Portia's living room. It was my ideal room, with its white walls, wooden floors dotted with Persian carpets, the bentwood rockers, the ferns on their high antique fern stands. And in the bay window there were the two heads Portia had modeled of her children, Laurie and Michael. Portia has tried to make a career of her sculpture but so far hasn't had any luck. Still she has a calmness the rest of us lack. She seems to have her life in control. She rarely complains at the women's meetings. Her children seem well-behaved, and Keith, her husband, still pulls chairs out for her and looks at her with special eyes. I envy her a little, but more, I admire her. She's sort of my ideal, a goal to be aimed at, proof that it can be done.

Portia looked across the room at me now and said, "You are going to have to get rid of him, you know."

"Him?"

"Him. The brother-in-law."

I frowned, sighed. "Yeah, well I tried. Sid says no. I don't

know, Portia. Maybe I'm exaggerating this. Kids go through
phases. I don't really want Carolee to save for marriage like we
did." I frowned. "But I don't want her to take up with just
anyone, either. I want her to be a child for a while, move carefully into adulthood, know what she's doing." I shoved back
my hair. "God, that sounds joyless. Maybe it's me, Portia. The
old church stuff. I still carry a lot of that. Maybe she's appren-
ticing for a happier, more carefree life. I do want that. Maybe
I'm binding her feet rather than protecting her."

"Maybe," Portia said, frowning thoughtfully at the end of
her cigarette. "Maybe God is a detergent bottle, and we both
should be doing dishes."

I looked at her for a moment and then nodded. "You're right,
I gotta get that bastard outta my house."

Portia grinned. "Kidnapped, huh?"

My mind was just a skip behind hers. Slowly I grinned back.
"Yep, kidnapped."

"Use my phone. You won't want it to appear on your bill."

"Well," I hesitated just an instant. "Well, only if you'll let me
pay you back."

She nodded.

Information, operators, and five minutes later, I was speaking
person-to-person with Ruth, Roger's ex-wife. She had a quick,
pleasant voice.

"Who?"

"Mary Sable. Mary Sable, your ex-sister-in-law."

"Oh yes. Yes, of course, Mrs. Sable." She waited.

"Roger's staying with us right now."

She gave a hard, high laugh. "Oh really? That must be fun."

Long distance, person-to-person, on Portia's phone, I found
myself doing Roger with Ruth. "Middle-class," she cried. "He
was always saying how middle-class I was. Well, I am! I am,
and I'm proud of it!"

"He wants a good mother," I said. "You take care of him, he
does anything he wants, and he gets to disapprove of you besides."

Portia lit another cigarette, raised her eyebrows, and grinned at me. "Don't forget Storm," she mouthed.

I smiled back. "Uh, Ruth, I . . . Storm is here. I felt it was my duty to inform you. I mean, I know how worried I'd be."

Portia rolled her eyes.

"Ha!" Ruth exploded. "He just had to take her to that commune of his. Save her from me! Well, she's never been the same since. I tried, Mrs. Sable. I did try. But that girl . . ." She stopped, calmed herself. "I'm remarried. We have a daughter, six. For Amy's sake, I think it best that Storm stay with her father."

"Oh?" I said weakly. I guessed I could relate to that. Lucky her, she had a choice.

"What?" Portia whispered. "What'd she say?"

Ruth muttered a few pleasantries, a few excuses, and then a quick good-bye.

I hung up the phone and told Portia about Amy, etcetera.

"Oh Christ," she said, pacing back and forth across her Persian carpet, thinking. "Money would solve it," she said. "Money solves most anything."

"Yeah. He said he'd get his own place if we should happen to get that reward. If not, well, maybe I could get a job. I'm not trained for much though."

"Maybe *he* could get a job."

I looked at her and laughed.

"Yeah," she said and shrugged. "So then you've got to solve this murder."

"Ha," I said. "Fat chance."

"You've already made a start. And remember what Cecile's always telling us."

"Victims make good observers," we quoted in unison and then broke into a fit of giggles.

Still, maybe it was a possibility. I reviewed my other options. Maybe it was the only possibility. Somehow I just *had* to get rid of Roger.

The architect couldn't help me, nor the library, nor the newspaper morgue.

It would have to be the twenty-thousand-dollar sellers' meeting.

A blue pass.

How to get a blue pass? Maybe if I wore manacles, maybe a dog collar and chain . . .

I caught myself actually considering it for a moment, which I suppose was a pretty accurate measure of my desperation.

19

The house was quiet, the children all at their homework. I did the dinner dishes and then wandered in to join Sid and Roger in the living room. Sid had mixed gin and tonics, and they sipped as they talked. I thought about just how much I'd like a gin and tonic right now. Best not, I decided. It was part of the Sable family ethos. Good women didn't drink, and right now I just didn't need any more black marks on my record. I listened for a while as they talked about old times. The girl Roger dated who always chewed gum; Lucky, the old family dog. Slowly my mind slid into its familiar track. Solve the crime. Write the book. Get rid of Roger. But how to solve the crime? How? The sellers' meeting? The blue pass? How? How? And Polly's pregnancy? Others knew of that now, but not who the father was. Now that I owned that fact, how did I spend it? Could she get me in to see P.H.O.? A thought. But even in fantasy I couldn't make it work. Brad? Find out if he was impotent, Cecile said. Ha! Just how did one go about *that*?

Something that Roger said drew me slowly forward.

"Rigid. A capitalist right down to her painted toenails. And she always wore these long, false fingernails." I listened, now knowing he was talking about Ruth. "She painted these stiff, little pictures of daisies and tulips and told people she was an artist." Roger snorted. "She was a hobby painter like Mary is a hobby writer." They smiled together in easy understanding and sipped their drinks.

I felt a surge of anger so strong it jerked my fingers into rigid claws. Somehow I got myself off the couch and out of the room, walking oddly, hoping they wouldn't notice.

How dare he? How dare he?! Maybe I would be a writer if I wasn't so damn busy buying and boiling his fertile eggs and worrying about the effect his daughter was having on mine. Well to hell with him. I'd show him. I'd salt his fertile eggs and slip Lipton's into his camomile tea and . . .

No! I made myself stop. Forced myself to calm. This wouldn't help. Think. Think. I snapped on the TV and then lay on the bed willing myself to relax, my heart and head to stop pounding, my fists to unclench.

And on came "Scarecrow and Mrs. King." I waited for the familiar slide into the story, the comforting fading away of Roger and crimes and cereal bowls.

In this episode, Mrs. King was under suspicion of being a double agent.

"*Amanda King?*" a female agency operative squeaked. "*Why, she's just a housewife. She isn't smart enough to be a double agent.*"

I shot up and glared at the TV.

Dumb? Doesn't work? Hobby writer? They didn't give us any fields to play in, did they? We worked damn hard. We just didn't get payed for it. Which I guess is pretty dumb when you think about it.

Sid and his fellow teachers are always saying how little they can do with difficult kids, that it's the home that makes all the difference. All teachers say that. So do those high-status, hundred-dollar-an-hour psychiatrists who are supposed to correct the mistakes of us zero-dollar-an-hour, low-status, untrained mothers.

And Cecile is always saying in our group, "How can you stand not to work? Not to earn your own money?" Cecile, who loves to come to our houses and eat and never ever asks us back. Margaret Mead, who tossed her kid off on some other woman to raise, wrote in *Redbook* how women are beginning to take responsibility for their own support. Ha!

How can it be everything and nothing?

I hate Margaret Mead, and I hate the damned phony tinsel, plastic-plated, success-mad world, and . . . I want in. Oh God, how I want in.

I really do think mothering is the world's most important work. But it really doesn't feel that way. Sid never thinks to look at a newly scrubbed floor and say, "Mary, that's good." The Downy ad promises they'll notice, but they don't, and the Ajax ad says you'll get a feeling of power, but you don't.

I watched Mrs. King's bumbling and grew sadder and sadder. It was a stupid plot. There was no reason on earth for all the elaborate plans to bring in defectors, who had somehow already escaped their governments and made it to this country. Why didn't the good guys just meet the bus? Then the stupid plans wouldn't have to be typed in the first place. "I'll bet a man wrote it," I muttered, and then froze, vaguely watching the ashamed-to-show-it sock commercial but seeing instead the plan that was rising from the mists of my own mind.

"No." I shook my head. "I couldn't."

But for some reason I was grinning.

"No."

Suddenly I bounced off the bed, found the card Lieutenant Smith had given me, and quickly, before I had time to think, dialed his home phone.

"Yeah? Smith here."

"I need to talk to you," I whispered.

"Who's this?"

"Mary Sable," I whispered, even quieter.

"So what's the problem, Ms. Sable?"

"I need to talk to you. I have some information about the killing."

"OK. Good." Excitement crept into his voice. "I'll come by your place first thing in the morning."

"No!" I cried. "No. Not here. I don't want anyone to know."

"You OK? I can get a car there in minutes."

"No. Only you. Meet me. The Exploratorium. Ten o'clock."

"Exploratorium? You mean that science museum for kids out at the Palace of Fine Arts?"

"We'll need a password."

"A password? Now look, lady—"

"Formica. Yes, that's good. Formica."

He sighed wearily. "You've seen too many—"

"If you're not followed, spell it out in Morse code on the electronic tree and them come to the center of the Feelatron."

"Now look—"

I hung up the phone. It rang almost immediately. I lifted it from the hook and set it on the bedside table, then went to take a long bath.

It was silly, I grant that. I even felt ashamed, but it was also infinitely soul satisfying to watch Smith in his shiny blue suit and blunt black shoes, standing out there dot-dashing *Formica* to that tree wired to flash at the sound of the human voice.

I waited and watched high in the dark mouth of the Feelatron. I'd loved this particular exhibit ever since I'd brought Kelly here three years ago. I return often. It's an assemblage of curling, climbing, dipping tunnels, completely dark, hung with webs and feathers and other tactile sensations. It felt right that I should meet Smith here. On my territory, so to speak. That bright, hard world out there—that was his. But this was mine.

The lieutenant had acquired quite a circle of pop-eyed school kids by the time he'd finished *Formica*, and he looked red-faced, hot, and cross. He said something, and a dozen kids turned and pointed to the Feelatron. He came on, stopping at the ticket booth, digging out his wallet. I squirmed away, up and then down the dark, soft, wriggling tunnels, through trailing webs and rumpled foams, finally whooshing down into the vat of wheat in the center of it all. I rolled to the side as I'd learned to do and then just lay there, listening and waiting. There were no images here. Just a blackness and a silence that expands the longer you hold it, swelling out and out until you are just lying there—one small and still particle in a gentle infinity.

After a time, I heard the tunnels overhead creaking, and then Smith cursing. Soon with a shout, he came tumbling into the wheat.

There was a silence.

"Were you followed?" I whispered, but my voice was serene. Steeping there in the slow darkness, I found I'd lost my enthusiasm for chicanery.

He swore again, then said, "This better be good, Sable." He began to thrash about, trying to move in all that wheat, and it does take practice. "This better be God damn good."

"I want to trade information," I said.

He grew still. We stayed that way for a while. I was aware of the space about us growing again.

"Just what you got to trade?"

"Something. Do you agree?"

A silence. "No."

"Then good-bye."

"Listen! Withholding evidence . . ."

I slid up into the exit tunnel.

"Wait!" he shouted.

I stayed where I was, going neither forward nor backward.

"Look, be reasonable."

I crawled two feet.

"I'm a police officer."

I crawled through a patch of silk strips. Some people reserved the Feelatron on off-hours and went through nude. Never us, of course. Still the idea appealed to something in me.

"All right!" Smith shouted. "All right."

I stopped and smiled into the softness for a moment, then squirmed backward and dropped into the wheat.

"If I possibly can—if it won't screw up our case—then I'll tell you what you want to know."

Somehow I sensed I'd have to be content with that. "Polly Purger's pregnant," I said. It sounded like a tongue twister. "O'Brian's the father. Hermoine was keeping them from getting married."

Smith was still for a moment, then he said, "OK, I admit it. That is interesting. Now what do ya want from me?"

I moved a little, and wheat spilled away in slow, small eddies. I stared for a time into the darkness wondering how best to word it.

"We want to know about Brad Preston."

"Know what?"

"Well . . ."

"Come on, come on. I ain't got all day." He struggled and wheat pitched all over the vat.

"We need to know if he's impotent."

Silence. Not a grain moved.

"What?"

"We need—"

"Impotent!" he shouted. "Impotent!" He began to laugh a great barking laugh that bounced back from the leather walls. He must have been kicking or pounding with his fists because wheat began to trickle out over the sides. "Impotent! Oh, God, the great lady detective strikes again. Did he or did he not raise his mighty weapon 'n' strike the fatal blow?" Smith laughed harder. The sound filled the cavern, suddenly defining its smallness. I began to feel suffocated and miserable. My life surrounded me. I reached out and kicked him. Hard.

He roared and sort of rose up, scattering wheat every which way, coming at me, a vast, dark wall emitting heat, spatters of grain, the smell of male, curses.

He grabbed and shoved me back, and I sank deep into the wheat. I struggled, and so did he. Both of us were furious, thrashing, cursing. And then suddenly, as one, we stilled. I sensed him there above me, staring down. I heard his heavy breathing. The darkness grew again, and reddened, and warmed. I felt him coming closer, felt his lips cover mine. "Let's get out of here," he said. "Let's go to my place."

I thought about it uneasily. Frightened really. Something was wrong. I had to have known he wouldn't have that information about Brad. Had this been the purpose of the exercise from the beginning? No. I'd have known. Wouldn't I?

Go, a voice inside whispered. But it was dumb—dangerous even. What if Sid found out?

And now somehow that seemed the point, the purpose of the exercise. Not that he should find out. Never that. For the sake of the children, he couldn't know. But I'd know.

"All right," I whispered. "Let's go to your place."

His place was done in a sort of early Salvation Army with fingerprints on the walls and dirty shirts, socks, and dishes everywhere else. Before I could stop myself, I'd folded two T-shirts and a jacket from the back of the couch.

"Needs a woman's touch," he said, and immediately I stopped touching.

He led me into the bedroom. In the middle of the unmade bed was an aging, half-eaten baloney sandwich. No way was I going to lose control again. I undressed and got right into bed with it. Smith joined us.

I ended up with my back oiled and breaded. Not a totally unpleasant sensation. It was perhaps the freshest aspect of the incident. Otherwise, if I'd closed my eyes, I'd have thought it was Sid. The same silent, busy competence. Afterward, Smith dozed, and I lay there thinking about how men and women probably suffered from incompatible allegories, men viewing sex as a chugging cylinder that runs the rest of the engine, women thinking of it more as a meeting and gradual merging of two fronts ending only eventually in thunder and lightning. I imagined laying my problems before various experts.

"Dr. Ruth, the brightest point of my week was a stale baloney sandwich."

She would tell me to go out and find exciting sex.

Kindly old Aunt Kate tells me to endure and get on with my life.

My networking group is always telling me that I should get rid of Sid.

Advice is always so simple while life itself is so complex. The children loved Sid. Their life would be worse. Somehow I couldn't choose for me. I never seem able to choose for me.

No, there was just one answer. Get rid of Roger. I sat bolt upright in the baloney. "What about alibis?!"

"What?" Smith jerked awake, looking startled.

"Alibis. Who had alibis for when Hermoine was killed?"

He groaned. "Hey, lady, is it my body or my body of evidence you lust for?"

I grinned. "Who had alibis?"

"Who knows when she was killed?"

"What?"

"Stomach contents. Settling of blood. Rigor mortis. None of the above can be determined from a head . . . or a foot. Our guys have tried, but they can't determine the exact time of death."

"I see."

"So, let's talk about something else," he said, slowly brushing crumbs from my back.

"So we've got to find the body, right?"

"*We* don't got to do nothing."

"What about P.H.O.'s place?"

"Nice architecture."

"You know what I mean. Have you searched there?"

"I have not."

"Why not?"

"Why?"

"The body could be there, Sam."

"And it could also be in the bottom drawer of the mayor's desk. It is, however, smart on my part if I don't go looking without some damn good reason."

I nodded. I saw that. Still, the body was there. At P.H.O.'s. I knew it. And I was going to find it. I watched with fascination as P.H.O., dressed all in black and Count Dracula cape, flapped forward from some luminescent point in my mind.

"This was nice," Smith said, still brushing. "What say we do it again soon?"

"I can't, Sam. I shouldn't have today. I . . . I am married, you know."

"So? He doesn't have to know."

"I don't think," I offered uncertainly, "that I love you."

He snorted with laughter. "What's that got to do with anything? We can still enjoy afternoons like this. Maybe even collaborate on a couple of articles—maybe a book."

I sat there for a while making patterns in the crumbs with a finger and thinking. Probably it was me who was wrong. I kept loving people and caring for them and thinking that somewhere, sometime, they'd return the favor. While for the rest of the world it seemed rather like business negotiations—give this, get that. Maybe it was time I entered the twentieth century. He'd asked for what he wanted, so now it was my turn. So what did I want? For a moment I drew a blank, then one of those strange disembodied voices whispered in my head, *"What you don't have. Ask for what you don't have."*

That would most likely be love, but that seemed a bit ambitious. "Would you say good things about me and give me presents at Christmas?"

"You husband doesn't do those things?"

"He doesn't."

Smith frowned. "I ain't too good at choosing pretty words or gifts."

"Well, just try. And keep in mind, no brooms or toasters."

"OK. I'll do my best," he said with an earnest little-boy expression, and right then I thought maybe I could learn to love him. I sat there in the rumpled sheets and the crumbs and thought about Sid, about how enraged he'd be if he knew about this—and then about how enraged his mother would be. And about how the very next time Sid just stared at me when I was trying to talk to him, how I'd just stare back and think about today or Smith or baloney sandwiches and just maybe be able to stand there feeling smug inside—instead of so damn hollow.

The thought was strangely aphrodisiacal, and I began to rather lust after Smith. Still, it was my market, and I wasn't about to sell cheap.

"So," I said brightly. "So, listen, have you any idea how that foot got in the Brants' fridge?"

Smith lay there looking at me for a moment, and then he grinned and reached to brush my nipple with a hairy nuckle. He knew love words when he heard them. "The Brants were at the Taylors' making up some more of those tear-milking, breast-beating stories. They had caterers coming, a cleaning service, deliveries. So they left the back door open. Dumb. Seems like we'll never get the word out to the public not to do that. They made a lot of calls about the party from the studio, ordering booze, setting up all them services, and of course telling everyone that that door would be open. A whole lot of people overheard them. It's a wonder that they didn't lose some of that wormy furniture or some of them ugly little statues." I gazed at Smith in wonder. Definitely there was some basis for a relationship. "We questioned caterers, cleaners, neighbors. Nobody saw nothin'. We figure the killer probably dressed up like a delivery person or a caterer, and nobody looked twice."

"Unless the Brants put it in their own refrigerator and then left the door open to cover themselves."

"Hard to figure why they'd do that."

"Hard to figure why anyone would do it."

"True. True."

We were silent for a moment, and I found myself thinking of Sid's mother prowling through my house, looking as if she sniffed for the cat box or the fried-fish-last-night-dear smells, as if she wished for a white glove to test my dusting. I pictured just how her carefully pruned and painted face would look if she could see me now, and I grabbed Sam's hand and held it hard against my breast.

He lunged. "Sam?" I said against his neck. "Sam?"

"What?" he groaned.

"How'd the killer get the head out of the studio and onto the game show?"

"Forget it," he growled, his hands slipping in mayonnaise.

"No!" I gasped, though it wasn't easy. "No, I need to know."

"You don't either!"

"Yes."

He huffed—irritated—but lay back, drawing me with him, and muttered, "Heads aren't that big. Could a' stuck it in his lunch pail for that matter."

"You don't know?"

He sighed. "First of all, the killing had to be at night when the studio was empty."

"Yes, I see that."

"Then he put the head in a hatbox and took it to the studio. We found it—blood-soaked towels in the bottom—just stuck there, in among the other prize boxes. The killer'd even put a set of electric rollers in it. Hey! Electric rollers any good for Christmas?"

I smiled to myself, touched. "Surprise me," I said. "Who's box was it, do you know?"

"The Leanders dame. She kept it there in her studio dressing room."

I nodded, shivering a little. Smith seemed to enjoy the shiver.

"No fingerprints on any of the boxes that shouldn't have been there. We figure the killer wore gloves."

I nodded, watching in my head as a faceless murderer trucked across town carrying that gastly head in a hatbox, watched as he or she crept into the game show studio and opened boxes until he found the one with the hat, watched as the head was moved and hot rollers substituted. And as I watched, some terrible cold unease began to creep around my shoulders and up my neck. It seemed to me as if the hands that moved in the dark of my mind were familiar, as if somehow I should recognize them. It's P.H.O., I told myself, and then I watched myself walking steadily toward him, watched as his hands reached out for me.

I was trembling in earnest now and making strange noises.
Sam abruptly turned me under him. Who can say? Fear? Sid
and Mama? But whatever, I had quite the loveliest time I'd had
in ages.

20

After I left Smith, I took a bus over to Marin, and then hired a
cab to drive me past the O'Brian estate, which took quite a bite
out of the week's food budget. We would all eat lentils, which
should please Roger. Still, I vastly enjoyed the ride. I sat there
deep inside myself, smiling vaguely out the window, half
watching the bright green world fly by the window, half watching Smith and myself.

And then suddenly from nowhere came a new image: Sid
standing at the door, pointing dramatically out into a raging
snowstorm—which was odd since it never snows in the Bay
area—and saying 'Go!' or 'never darken my door again' or other
things equally melodramatic.

He could take my children, I thought, and I was suddenly
deathly still inside. And even if some judge did give them to
me, I would, like so many other women, carry them away into
poverty or at least a poorer way of life.

The smile was gone now. I was deeply sad inside, but I saw
clearly what I must do. I could live without Christmas presents
and kind words. "So that's it then," I whispered. "Over before
it started."

"This is it," the driver said, pulling the cab over to the side of
the road.

I got out and stumbled up to the fence. "It'd been 'You're an

OK broad' and plastic roses," I whispered to myself, but still it was a moment or two before my eyes cleared enough for me to see the O'Brian mansion.

P.H.O.'s house was on a hill high above the Marin headlands, the ocean on one side, a black, steel-barred fence on the other three. It was at least eight feet high and wired at the top, and even as I looked a pack of growling Doberman pinschers tore across the acres of lawns toward me. Black-garbed guards followed at a slower pace.

I got back into the cab, and we drove away. P.H.O. could have thrown Hermoine's body in the ocean. But I thought not. It could wash up someplace. So many gardens and gullies there behind those fences. Probably even if you were searching, you'd never find it, but I was determined to search.

"Then it'll have to be the twenty-thousand-dollar sellers' meeting," I muttered, ignoring those hands reaching again there behind my eyes.

"What?" the driver said.

"Nothing."

We were going to have to get one of the blue party passes. Someway. Somehow. But how? A new dress, I decided. Black and low-cut. Something that would disguise thickening hips. And I'd have my hair rinsed and done. I'd borrow the money from Portia, pay her back a few dollars a week. Desperate circumstances called for desperate measures. And something about this afternoon had made me suddenly more desperate.

"Sure," Portia said. "No problem. But what about the other suspects? Brad, for instance."

"Oh him." I made a gesture with one hand. "I just have a feeling, Portia, that it's O'Brian."

"And Cecile's sure it's Brad. We ought to go at this scientifically—not like some popularity contest."

"Well," I said sullenly, "I did ask Smith. What more can I do?"

"Asked him what?"

"If Brad's impotent."

"You didn't." Portia giggled.

I shrugged.

"What'd he say?"

I sniffed. "He laughed."

Portia did too, which didn't endear her to me just then. "Still," she said when she finally quieted, "still, there must be a way."

"Well, I can't think of one. It's Cecile's theory. Let her do it."

"No." Portia thought about it for a moment. "Maybe Wendy would be the one to ask."

"Oh, Portia," I groaned. "You've got to be kidding. 'Hi, Wendy. How you doing? How's the kids? How's your sex life? Can Brad . . .'"

Portia grinned. "We'll have her for lunch. A few gin and tonics and then we start talking about our sex lives. Have you ever known a woman who could resist chiming in?"

I thought about it. It was P.H.O. I was sure it was P.H.O. But Portia was right. We needed to investigate all suspects thoroughly. "Do you know her well enough to ask her for lunch?"

"Sure. Tuesday OK?"

Tuesday was beautiful. Full sun and just a faint breeze carrying in the smell of the sea. We lunched on Portia's deck, which overlooked her postage-stamp garden set on the brow of a steep hill. Beyond, the city sank back to the blue bay, where an occasional sailboat tacked beneath the orange bridges.

Wendy was dressed in a black crepe dress with huge shoulder pads. Her blond hair was carefully curled, and she wore sheer white, ruffled gloves. She had the look of a lady missionary, and I began to seriously doubt the success of our project. Still, I was determined to try.

"Brad will be by at four to pick me up," Wendy said as she settled at the glass-topped table.

Portia nodded. "There's a memorial for Hermoine today," she explained to me.

My ears perked. "Will P.H.O. be there?"

"No. Just the people from 'Heart's Desires' and the press. You can read all about it in tomorrow's paper."

"You going?"

"Certainly not. I hated the broad."

"Oh, Portia," Wendy murmured, "forgive past slights. Fill your heart with love. Forgiveness will heal your soul."

Portia shrugged and grinned. "Sure, but on the other hand maybe a good case of pissed would heal the world."

Wendy sighed and fell silent.

I sipped a gin and tonic, trying to estimate how much would make me loose enough to execute the plan but not too loose to do dinner after.

Portia served seafood salads and chatted and conscientiously kept gin glasses filled, particularly Wendy's.

"Keith and I are fighting," Portia confided with dessert—no coffee. "We haven't made love in a week." She swatted the air with the back of one long hand.

I didn't believe a word of it. Somehow I just knew Keith and Portia's love life was perfect. Hence, it was clearly up to me to pick up the ball and run with it.

"Fights never stop Sid." I laughed. "If he's in the mood, he'll come at me even if we've just been damning each other to hell forever. I lay there and just want to slug him." It occurred to me that I was saying too much, probably drinking too much. I resolved to slow both.

Portia and I looked brightly at Wendy.

She smiled sympathetically and fluffed the ruffles at her wrist.

I tried details, fer-instances. "If I say 'no' he comes back every thirty minutes to ask if I'm over my bad mood yet. It's never his indifference; it's always me, my mood."

Wendy clucked sympathy.

"I guess sex and feelings are two different things for men," I speculated, frowning.

"Maybe that's what that Ann Landers' survey was about," Portia said, looking out into the bay.

Wendy just kept smiling.

"You know the one where women said they'd rather be cuddled than have sex. I mean we get sex, but not much cuddling. No Christmas presents. No nice words." Definitely I was talking too much. I glanced about to see if anybody noticed.

Wendy just kept smiling.

"Love," I said. "Not much love. Did I ever tell you I keep having this dream where I'm married to a refrigerator."

"Refrigerator?" Portia giggled, refilling my glass. "Refrigerator?"

Wendy smiled on.

"Yeah, you know, dependable but cold."

"Hollow," Portia added.

"Square." Me.

"Smooth."

"Reliable."

"Sleek."

"Ponderous."

"Pee's ice cubes."

We went on, giggling and listing qualities. We'd not forgotten our mission exactly, but this was certainly more fun.

Finally, I turned and, choking back a giggle, asked Wendy point blank, "Is Brad like that?"

Wendy blinked, and her smile grew dreamy. "Well, he used to be, I guess." She shrugged shyly. "A little."

"Before the walk-in," Portia said.

Wendy nodded. "But now, anymore, we just hold each other for hours. We feel such depth of closeness that, well, sex is unimportant."

Portia and I stared. I was horrified to feel tears begin to slip down my face. "It just sounds so wonderful," I sniffed. "Brad really is a sweet man."

Wendy's smile grew; she reached across the table and took my hand in her gloved one. "You're not really happy are you, Mary?"

"Oh, off and on. I love my kids. Lots. There's good times. Like everybody else, I guess."

"But have you thought about . . . what we talked about?"

"Walking out?" Portia said. "You know, she keeps trying, but not one of them damn spirit-dudes will agree to take her gig."

We all laughed, even Wendy. Then Portia refilled all our glasses.

"I shouldn't," I said.

"Ah, live it up," Portia said. "Sid can take them all to McDonald's tonight."

I giggled and drank. "He'll be so mad. Besides, do they have fertile Big Macs?"

"It's un-American to even question it," Portia said, toasting.

We had a wonderful afternoon, giggling, drinking. I was floating in a rosy glow. Once when Wendy went to the rest room, Portia leaned to whisper in my ear, "It's been fun, but you know, we still don't know. Is he or isn't he?"

I sobered for a moment. But right then, I just didn't much care.

Sometime later the doorbell rang, and the three of us half listened as Portia's maid clicked across the hardwood floor to answer it. A moment later, several of the "Heart's Desires" cast stood in the doorway—Brad; Polly, dramatic in black; Anna Lisa in a frazzled poncho and loud velvet skirt; Harvey, wearing an immaculate gray suit, holding an expensive gray hat with both his small, pink hands, and looking a bit like the white mouse the children once had as a pet.

"Harvey's driving us," Brad said, moving out onto the patio. "Sure you won't go, Portia?"

"Love to," Portia said, waving her glass, "but I must drink. You all want one?"

"No time," Brad said.

He came toward us, and the others faded into the background. He was in tweed and leather patches again, and his eyes were electric. He touched Wendy's shoulder, Portia's, then mine. I looked up at him hard, trying to decide. His eyes smiled down into mine. Cecile was wrong. It just wasn't possible. He was too vibrant, too alive.

He began now to frown slightly. "Mary," he said to my watching eyes, "I sense that you're seeking something. I'm not sure what." He waited a moment. "An answer perhaps."

I blushed furiously. "Yeah." No way was I going to ask him the question.

He nodded, hesitated, then put his long, slender hands on either side of my head. "It's all in here, you know."

"It is?"

"Our subconsciousnesses are all plugged into the universal mind. We all receive—much like individual sets pick up TV stations. Some have better reception than others."

Obviously my reception wasn't so hot. Unless, could my feeling about P.H.O. be more than just feeling?

"It's there," Brad murmured. "You've only to believe. To try. People scoff. But the Soviet Union spent twenty-one million dollars researching E.S.P. The C.I.A. is investigating it. It is a force that can be harnessed—for good or for evil. Believe in its power." The purr of his voice seemed to further dissolve the edges of my mind. My eyelids sagged and then popped open.

The others came out onto the patio and spread out about us. "Brad, don't get started on that stuff. We gotta go," Richard moaned.

"One moment," Brad said in his best competent-soap-doctor manner. "This is important. She's a good subject. I feel it. I knew it the first time we met. Everyone be quiet. Please! Give her a chance."

After a moment, the others quieted.

"Now," Brad whispered, "close your eyes." I did so gratefully. His fingers moved over my temples and ears. "Make your mind a blank screen, Mary. A blank screen. Relax. Relax."

The gin kept rolling up and fogging my screen, but the relaxing part was so easy I almost fell off my chair.

"Now picture a ninety-petaled lotus revolving, revolving slowly. Slowly. Count the petals as they go by. Count."

The lotus turned slowly in the mists. I counted.

"A blue-violet lotus."

I colored it.

"Do you have it? Do you see it?"

"Yes."

"Now ask your question. Or make a telepathic command. Either. Do it several times, then wait. Wait for answers. Wait."

I debated telepathically commanding Roger out of the house or asking about Brad's sex life, but then decided what the hell. It wasn't going to work anyway; I might as well go for the big one. *Who killed Hermoine?* I asked the lotus. It turned on. *Who killed Hermoine?* I was at forty-seven petals and almost asleep. The gin mist kept rising and rolling over. I swayed in my chair. Someone outside moved slightly.

Then suddenly the mist split apart, and I saw clearly—a hand—a knife. And the knife kept throwing lights—blue and red lights. Like a miniature police car. I wondered what it meant. And then the hand jerked up. I saw a face, and then a red veil covered everything, and I knew somehow that it was blood.

I screamed.

Then my eyes were open, and I was crying, and everyone was exclaiming and holding me and shaking at me.

"What's the matter?"

"She's had too much to drink, that's what's the matter."

"What'd you see?"

There was a silence then. I looked about at them. Everything seemed so bright and unreal. Everyone was leaning in toward me, their eyes huge. "What did you see?" Polly whispered.

"A hand. I saw a hand."

"So?" There was a little flurry of movement.

"It was holding a knife."

Polly gave a strange little sigh.

"And the knife shot blue and red lights. I don't know why. But there were red and blue lights."

"K-lights?" Brad murmured.

"They wouldn't be red and blue," Richard snapped.

"And then the knife struck and there was blood—lots and lots of blood."

A long silence, and then Polly's hand fastened on my arm. She made an odd noise in her throat. "Who was it this time?"

I hesitated, looking about at them.

"Who was it?" Polly shrieked, her nails sinking into my arm.

I sighed. "My brother-in-law."

Portia laughed.

"Ah shit, Mary," Richard said. Everyone straightened and drew back.

"No," Brad said in his soft, firm voice. "No. I don't know what it means, but she has seen the hand of the killer."

"'N' I'm Herman Melville," Richard muttered. "Let's get going. We're going to be late."

They left then, and shortly after I did, too.

I knew they all thought my vision, or whatever it was, was just some hostility thing for Roger. And it probably was. After all, what could Hermoine's killer possibly want with Roger? Still, it had seemed so real.

For the first time since we'd started all this, I was truly frightened.

Maybe it was just the gin.

Or maybe it was the thought of going home and facing Sid.

21

The twenty-thousand-dollar seller's meeting was held in the ballroom of the Drake Hotel. Roger, Cecile, Harvey, and I followed the massive curving staircase past elaborate weavings and large jade statues, feeling rather awed and silenced. We presented our tickets at a small table covered with a gleaming white cloth outside the ballroom. The man behind the table looked at us sternly, as well he might, what with Roger's hair and the nice middle-class outfit Cecile had found at the Goodwill, which consisted of a matted green sweater, a plaid pleated skirt, and a string of discolored pearls. Still, we had our tickets, and the man immediately recognized impeccably dressed little Harvey as Mr. Sterex Bleach so he passed us along into the inner sanctum. Most of the sellers and guests had already arrived. They were a polished, clipped group, liberally sprinkled with furs, pearls, beehive hairdos, and double-knit suits. A veritable Midwestern Sunday school convention. They stood about or sat along the rows of metal chairs in clumps—smiling, talking, smiling, shaking hands, smiling.

After a time a young, tanned, blond man, who looked as if he should have had a tennis racket in hand, leapt onto the makeshift stage and proceeded to "warm up" the audience, much as I imagine happens on quiz shows ten minutes before air time.

The sellers laughed at his jokes, cheered when he said cheer, clapped when he said clap, but it was obvious everyone was waiting for the main event, the big man, Patrick Henry O'Brian.

"Now," the young man said, and his voice hushed, grew reverent. "Now, I have been given the supreme honor of introducing to all you fine people tonight the founder of our Spine and Sunshine Corporation. A man who . . ." He went off into a long biographical sketch, which I truly would have liked to listen to but a lady seated on my left suddenly reached over and laid a white-gloved hand on my knee.

"Isn't this exciting," she warbled.

I smiled at her. She was about four feet tall, dressed all in lavender, including a lavender tint in her precise curls, and wearing (I swear) lavender scent.

"Imagine," she went on in her wee-honey voice, "seeing Patrick Henry in person."

The announcer continued, ". . . a poor boy who grew up to head one of the world's biggest . . ."

"I just can't tell you what a difference he has made in our lives, Mr. Muncie and I." The little hand tapped me again. "Why, we were hardly even alive, just working away, Mr.

Muncie and I. We run a little mortuary down in Pleasant City.
But now, my dear, we have sold four dealerships already. And
who knows what may happen next! We sell soap and cosmetics
right out of our little shop."

"In your mortuary?"

"Oh yes, dear. Yes."

My mind scrabbled, trying to picture just how that might
work.

". . . And here he is, ladies and gentlemen!" The M.C. was
suddenly bellowing, "The one, the only, the great Patrick
Henry O'Brian. Let's get him up here with our traditional win-
ner's chant."

The back door burst open, and a phalanx of brown-suited
men strode in, followed by P.H.O. himself.

"Go! Go! Go!" the audience chanted.

Tense, purposeful, P.H.O. strode forward like a national
president. The guards fell back, looking suspiciously right then
left. How would we ever get close enough to talk to him? As-
sassinating him would have been distinctly easier.

"Go! Go! Go!" The M.C. increased the tempo. Patrick
Henry stepped faster. "Go!" the lavender lady screamed at the
top of her tiny voice.

"Go! Go!"

Patrick Henry came toward the stage at a full run and lept
high over the foot lights, landing in the midst of hysterical
cheers and applause. He grinned, waved. The cheering increased. P.H.O. waited, smiling. He looked as good as science
and industry could manage: the expensive black suit exaggerating broad shoulders and minimizing the small pot belly, the
luxuriant black hair (I knew it was false only because Portia had
so informed me), the expensive black shoes that very nearly
concealed the fact that his left leg was two inches shorter than
the right.

He lifted his hands and signaled for silence.

The cheering grew louder.

He smiled tolerantly and waited again.

The lavender lady was slamming her gloved palms against each other; tears ran down her cheeks.

P.H.O. leaned in to the mike. "Please."

The cheering quieted slightly.

"Ladies and gentlemen."

At last he managed to quiet the room. He stood there in the silence and looked around at us with intense eyes. The silence grew deeper.

"Brothers and sisters . . ."

Again he looked around, waiting.

The lavender lady squirmed with excitement.

"Ladies and gentlemen. Brothers and sisters." He paused for effect, then hollered, "God loves ya!"

Cheers bounced from the lemon walls, slowly dying back to another breathless silence.

"'Course," P.H.O. continued, "loves somaya mor'n the others."

His audience was off again. Cecile and I exchanged glances.

Now P.H.O. wheeled from the mike and began stamping up and down the stage, lifting first one foot and shaking it before him, then the other. "See them shoes?" he bellowed. "Ya all see them shoes?"

"Yeah!"

"Yeah what?"

"Yeah, we see them shoes."

He whipped to the mike. "Well, if ya see them shoes then maybe ya see that they ain't no ordinary shoes. No ordinary shoes at all, folks. Ah paid me close to five hundred solid American buckeroos fer them lil' ol' shoes 'n' ah got me a good many more like 'em at home too." He paused again to let his listeners scream shoe approval.

"All God's chillen got shoes, raht?"

"Right!"

"When we get to heaven we're goin ta put on them shoes an walk all over God's heaven, raht?"

"Right!"

"But let me tell ya raht now, brothers 'n' sisters; you go up to heaven in some funky ol' ten-ninety-five discount special ox-fords, you gonna feel right shamed when the Lord comes round lookin' you over. You gonna scrunch down and just wish you could stick them ol' feet in some cloud, 'n' the Lord he's just gonna walk right on by you til he sees me, 'n' then he's gonna start hollerin', 'Now raht there's my boy Patrick in them fahn shoes a his. Jes' get yerself on over here boy 'n' jaw awhile.'"

The audience laughed wildly. I felt oddly deflated. He should have been taller somehow—and meaner. Or at least more dramatic. This was a little like Red Buttons playing Frankenstein.

"Now then brothers 'n' sisters, it ain't that the Lord loves shoes so much. Naw, you know that ain't it." He paused. As one, the audience leaned toward him waiting to hear what 'it' was. "It's jes' that he loves tryers so much!"

Clapping, yelling. The lavender lady bounced up and down on her chair crying, "Amen! Amen!"

"Now ah guess you all noted sompin' else about them shoes. Ah guess you all noticed that lil' ol' left shoe a mine is a just raisin' himself up in the world. Lord God, when he's makin' me says, 'Man, that there boy's so fi-i-i-ine! Ah'm jus gonna keep me a couple a inches to remember him by.'"

His audience roared.

Maybe he wasn't the killer. I reviewed possibilities again. Brad. Richard. Polly. And then slowly, shyly, Jill crept into my mind.

"Now some a' you out there might be thinkin' 'poor him.' But probably not. Probably you're too busy thinkin' 'poor me.' Let me tell you somethin', folks. Ninety-five percent of the people you know have nothin' to look forward to."

He paused to let that sink in. I found myself feeling vaguely uneasy.

"Ni-i-i-inety fa-a-a-ve percent. Not one thing, folks. Not one teeny-weeny thing!" He fell silent and stared out over the audience. There was a stirring, murmuring.

"And yet folks . . ." P.H.O. shrugged, shook his head. "Life is just what ya make it. Yea, ah know. You think when ah was a boy growin' up down there in De Queen, Arkansas, ma Daddy tryin to make a livin' fixin' shoes when all them folk down there then was too poor to even wear shoes; you think ah didn' say poor me?

"You think when all them kids are makin' fun a this heah leg 'n' all them tattered clothes ah didn' say poor me?

"Well ah'm here to tell ya, ah 'poor me'd' all over that county. Not enough ah'm trippin' over this bum leg, ah'm trippin' over that lower lip too. Ah got so low ah could hardly milk mah Daddy's poor ol' cow. But she's a good ol' thing 'n' she looks round 'n' she sees how bad ah'm feelin' and damned if she didn't jes' up and take pity on me.

"'Patrick,' she says, 'you jes' grab hold 'n' hang on 'n' ah'll jump up and down.' So's ah did 'n' she did 'n' ah'm here to tell you ah learned somethin' from that. So you out there that's guests let me tell y'all what the rest these fine folks know. Ah want ya to jes' grab hold 'n' do some hangin' an ah'm gonna do some jumpin' 'n' we'll both get us some go-o-o-o-od cream."

Everyone laughed. The lavender lady pounded on me. "Isn't he just too wonderful for words?" Cecile seemed to be swearing.

Suddenly Patrick Henry pointed a finger at the audience and roared, "Do you like money?!"

"Yes!"

"Yes what?"

"Yes, we like money!"

"Then let's hear it!"

"M-m-m-m-m-m-m-m-m-m-m-m-money!" Their cheer rolled about the vast room.

"Guests raise up yer hands."

A number of hands went up. We glanced at each other, then decided to keep ours down.

"You theah, the lady and gent in front. Y'all stand up."

Blushing, smiling, a middle-aged couple stood.

"What's yer name, honey?"

"Sara."

"'N' yer hubby's?"

"Jerry."

"All raht folks, let me ask y'all somethin. Would you, Jerry, want Sara to come into this here program if she could make herself fifty thousand dollars a year?"

"Yessir!" Jerry hollered.

"Would you, Sara, want Jerry to come into the program if he could make him fifty thousand dollars a year?"

"Sure would!" Sara said softly, blushing.

"Ah now pronounce ya smart man and wife."

He began skipping over the auditorium asking guest after guest this question. Every yes was cheered wildly, and the yesses grew steadily more fevered, the cheering more hysterical. Then P.H.O. asked people to tell how the Spine and Sunshine Corporation had changed their lives. Person after person jumped to his feet to relate how loneliness, poverty, and boredom had vanished from their lives. All over the room people began to weep. The lavender lady kept moaning, "Oh oh oh." Suddenly a man was on his feet shouting, "I want to join! Right here and now! I got the check! I wanna do it!"

"Plant," Cecile muttered. "Seed the crowd."

Several people followed his example. Men with clipboards strode from the back of the room to collect checks even as the testimonials went on. Then just as the fever seemed to be slacking, P.H.O. had everyone stand and chant together, "I am great. I am great!" In unison with each "great" the crowd thrust first the left then the right fist into the air. I looked about. We were the only four people in the whole room not participating. We stuck out like sore thumbs. Like an out-of-step rockette I watched to catch the left-fist "great."

"I am great," I bellowed.

"What are you doing?" Cecile hissed.

"I am great!" Right fist. "Joining in," I whispered back quickly so as not to loose step. "I am great." Oddly, I *was* beginning to feel rather good somehow.

"Well stop it, Mary!"

I glanced sidelong at her. "I am great."

"Stop it! You're embarrassing me!"

Now that did stop me for a moment. I looked about at all the other chanters. Surely her reaction was distinctly peculiar. "I am great."

"OK, folks," P.H.O. exclaimed over the noise of the crowd. "I guess that's it fer tonight. Jus wanna say that after tonight there's gonna be a hell of a lot more tryers fer the Lord to love an' a hell of a lot more comfortable feet. Yer on yer way now," he shouted. "Yer aimed fer fame. Y'all jus fight for yer right to riches, ya heah? Keep after it! Keep steppin' and tomorrow yu'll be wearin' ya them Guccis jus like the swells!"

So saying he leaped from the stage, and the crowd boiled up and out to the center aisle waving paper or twenty-dollar bills for him to autograph or just reaching to touch the great man.

"We've got to get one of those blue cards," I whispered to the others. "We've got to."

"Right, we'll never get to talk to him here," Cecile said. "Go for it."

We pushed and shoved to the front of the crowd as ruthlessly as any teenybopper at a Springsteen concert. P.H.O. was coming slowly down a narrow aisle his guards were forcing through his adoring followers. He kept pausing to shake hands, sign autographs, and kiss pretty girls. Here and there I saw one of his cards go out: one to a tiny blond with watermelon breasts, one to a tall brunette, then a slick young man. It was hopeless. Still I fluffed the new dress, held out a hand, and looked pleading. He shook my hand and passed on, laughing, calling out, grabbing a hand here, one there, acknowledging other calls with brisk waves or quick smiles.

"Mr. O'Brian, Mr. O'Brian," Harvey was hollering, trying to trade on past acquaintance. O'Brian slapped his shoulder and passed on by.

I sent a desperate look at Cecile. She pushed forward, leaned out into the aisle, and began batting her sparse eyelashes at him as he approached. He glanced at her, gave her an odd look, then veered away, walking a little faster.

Hopeless, I thought. Only Roger was left. I could see him down almost at the door, hanging out from the crowd in an odd sort of skier's stance, glaring intently into P.H.O.'s oncoming eyes. P.H.O. hesitated, broke stride briefly, then pressed to the far side of the aisle. Several of his bodyguards started toward Roger. The crowd caught their tension and quieted, so I heard quite clearly as Roger shouted at the passing man, "You suffer from migraine headache, red spots before the eyes, and constipation." He straightened then, threw out his chest, and waited triumphantly. A bodyguard still moved in on him. P.H.O. walked faster. A murmur of comment rose about me, then suddenly died.

P.H.O. had stopped just beyond Roger. Slowly he swung about and stared. The room grew absolutely silent. P.H.O. came back down the aisle on his gleaming shoes. "How'd ya know that?"

"I'm a healer," Roger answered proudly. "I can help you."

P.H.O. narrowed his eyes and studied Roger, who looked back calmly. P.H.O. sniffed, looked about, then suddenly snatched a blue card from his breast pocket and shoved it into Roger's hand. "Ah'll talk to ya," he said, then whirled and proceeded on up the aisle and out the door.

The crowd broke now and began to file toward the door. Cecile and I, squealing, hugged each other and jumped up and down. "We did it!" Cecile cried.

I hesitated and then said, "Roger did it." It hurt to have to give him credit, but fair was fair.

"Yeah," Cecile said and turned to Roger, who'd just made his way to us. "I guess you'll get to see *her* tonight, huh?"

Roger grew wistful. "I hope so," he whispered, and I remembered suddenly my odd vision there on Portia's patio. I ought to warn him, I thought, but somehow I just couldn't get the words out.

*   *   *

Harvey drove us over the Golden Gate Bridge to Patrick Henry's Marin estate. It was even more impressive at night, a vast edifice of cement squares and triangles looming black against the midnight-blue sky, surrounded by that high fence. Inside the fence, we could see the watchmen with flashlights and the Dobermen pinschers on leashes now criss-crossing the lawn and gardens.

Two armed guards, dressed much like the guards at Buckingham Palace, took Roger's blue card and gazed into the car. With expressionless faces they said, "Thar's too many a you in thar. Mr. Folk, you kin go in too, but not them women."

Roger told them most firmly that Mr. O'Brian wanted and needed to see *him,* and *he* certainly wasn't going in without *all* his friends. I was grateful, if a little surprised, at this sudden display of loyalty. He isn't all bad, I told myself, but I didn't really believe it.

A little more argument, a call to the main house, and finally a guard pushed a button, the gates slid open, the drawbridge slapped down, and we drove in. A curving road of crushed white stone, glowing in the moonlight, led up to the main house. We drove it slowly, all of us quiet, overwhelmed, and perhaps scared. "Tonight, you meet him," I whispered to myself. "Tonight."

A man took the car at the door, another ushered us into an elevator and pressed a button. The door whooshed shut, and a taped female voice, soft and warm, filled the padded red velvet car. "Welcome, ladies and gentlemen. Zero minus three, zero minus two, zero minus one. Blastoff!" With that, the car shot upward, and we just sort of looked at each other. The elevator opened on the main floor, where P.H.O. waited to take all the guests on a guided tour of his holdings.

And how to describe those holdings? Inside, everything was primary colors, circles and triangles, lines slanting away into the distance like some set for a science fiction movie. Yet the gardens were formal English, right down to sculpted bushes and a maze. There was a foot-shaped pool and foot-shaped desk in P.H.O.'s private office. On the desk was a ceramic-shoe music box. When you pulled one lace it played "The Impossible Dream," the other "Santa Claus Is Coming to Town."

After the tour, people stood around and drank champagne and gobbled up quarts of caviar. Roger went to give Patrick Henry a deep foot massage, and Cecile, Harvey, and I slipped away to look for clues.

I was, I must admit, intimidated by the sheer size and splendor of our surroundings. I felt like a child lost in Disneyland. "How will we ever find anything here?" I whispered. "It's huge . . . and guarded. Look. There are security cameras in the halls."

"Dogs and watchmen too," Cecile said. "This place is paranoia personified. It does give some support to your theory, Mary, that P.H.O. is the killer."

I looked at her, pleased that for once she was admitting that she might be wrong.

"Though," she added, "it is highly unlikely. He's got too much obvious power. He can destroy without resorting to overt violence. My money's still on Brad." She turned to Harvey. "Can you get us into P.H.O.'s office?"

"That's easy," Harvey said. "But he keeps all his records and papers in a small locked office off a back hall. Does most of his business there. That's where he interviewed me for the bleach job."

"Great. Get us in there."

"I can try," Harvey said doubtfully. "This way."

We wandered down the vast halls floored in black marble and hung with Picassos and Degases and Dalis. Real ones, not prints. Despite the priceless decor, the guests were allowed remarkable freedom. We passed room after room in which people sniffed coke or made love while doors stood open. Everything but theft seemed allowed and perhaps encouraged.

It was certainly a new world for me, and I found I'd hunched into myself and was tiptoeing by the time we turned into a smaller hall and stopped before a door. Overhead, a camera turned steadily this way and that; Cecile, nevertheless, tried the door. "It's locked all right," she whispered. "Can either of you pick locks?"

"No, Cecile," I sighed. "I can't. Besides, there's that camera."

"I might know a way in," Harvey muttered. "Wait 'til the camera turns away. Now. Run."

We darted after Harvey through a huge metal door and out into a small enclosed garden.

I peered up at the building through the thick darkness there in the bottom of the tiny square. "Harvey," I whispered, "the windows are all six feet above ground. We'll never get in."

"They are," he said, "but maybe we could climb that." He gestured, and Cecile and I leaned to see through the cool blackness. Harvey snapped on a penlight, and the faint light climbed six feet of steel hair and glittered on long ivory teeth. I squeaked. For a moment, it looked like some monster straight from a grade B Japanese horror movie.

"It's only a statue," Cecile said.

"I see that now."

"Of his dog," Harvey murmured. "P.H.O.'s. From when he was a kid." Harvey moved the penlight down to a bronze plaque set in the base.

"BUDDY," I read aloud. "A TRUE FRIEND."

"He had the dog's bones dug up and flown in from Arkansas. They're buried underneath."

"Jesus," Cecile muttered. "You know, he could be it."

Dog bones? Killer? There had to be a jump in her logic that I'd missed somewhere. But then there usually was.

"The window's open," Harvey whispered. "P.H.O. likes fresh air. Usually leaves it open. Feels secure with the cameras. But his guards play a lot of poker when they should be working. Hold the light. Let's see if I can climb Buddy."

Up he went, clutching Buddy's nose and then his ears, finding footholds in sculpted fur. "I'm in," he whispered a moment later. "You coming?"

"Yes." I gave the light to Cecile and copied Harvey exactly.

Soon the three of us were inside P.H.O.'s office. It was dark and still and smelled of good leather, lemon polish, and mint mouthwash. We stood for a moment, listening. My heart was beating so hard I was sure the sound must be ringing down all those long marble halls.

Harvey snapped on a desk lamp. Footsteps sounded in the hall outside. He snapped the light off fast, and we stood listening as someone tried the door, then went on by.

"Watchman," Harvey whispered. "Wait 'til he goes back by."

We waited. I wondered just what P.H.O. might do to us if he caught us. Not the police, I thought in sudden horror. Not Smith. Torture was infinitely preferable. Death? No, I didn't think I'd go that far. "And how did you three get in here, Ms. Sable?" "By the doggie in the window." Maybe death. No. I had to think of the children.

"He's gone," Harvey whispered, and turned the light back on. He and Cecile began to pull open drawers and filing cabinets, riffling papers. After a moment, I started to help, hoping no one would notice how badly I was shaking.

"Look here," Cecile whispered triumphantly, jerking out a paper from a file drawer. "O'Brian has been indicted in Texas, Arkansas, Oklahoma, and Tennessee."

"For what?" I asked.

"Fraud."

"Pyramiding," Harvey added. "The California attorney general is after him, too, but so far the lawyers have gotten around an indictment."

"Maybe she knew too much," Cecile said. "Maybe he did kill her."

Too much what? I wondered, sliding open another desk drawer and listening hard for sounds from the hall outside.

Something glinted up at me. I bent closer and then jerked back. Blue and red. The words as well as the colors exploded in my head, and sweat began to slide down my ribs, probably ruining my new dress. Blue and red lights. Somehow I couldn't seem to catch my breath. Red and blue lights flashing from a jeweled knife handle. The blade was long and curved. Antique probably. The kind you could even imagine the Borgias carrying. I shook my head, trying to clear it of the vision of this very knife at Roger's throat. There was something encrusted in the jewels. I made myself lean closer. I touched it with one finger at the very instant I realized it was blood. I jerked back as if burned and saw the one, long, red hair stuck to the blade. "Oh, God," I whimpered, remembering suddenly Brad saying, "She has seen the hand of the killer." I heard some odd gurgling noise, and after a moment, realized it was coming from my own throat.

Both Harvey and Cecile straightened and turned to look at me. I kept pointing, and after what seemed like forever, they walked over in slow motion and looked down into the drawer.

"I saw it," I whispered.

"I remember," Harvey murmured.

Then we all stood staring into the drawer.

"We better call the police," I said finally. No one moved. I reached for the phone.

Cecile grabbed my hand. "No."

"Cecile!"

"No. We're in here now. Call the police and this is all we're going to get."

All? In my opinion it was too much.

"We've got to keep searching. And we've got to question O'Brian if we can."

"But Cecile . . ."

"Pick up the knife by the tip and put it in your purse."

Now I could only stare in horror.

"You can always give it to Smith tomorrow. Tell him where you found it. We'll back you up."

"Call Smith?" I gasped. "I can't call Smith. Besides, that's obstructing justice, or something like that. Anyway, it's against the law!"

"Smith thinks you're wiggy anyway. You'd get off on insanity."

"He does not! He thinks I'm—" I stopped myself just in time. "I won't! If you want it out, you do it."

"All right, all right. Don't get in a snit. We'll call Smith tomorrow and tell him it's here. But for now we've got to question P.H.O."

"Someone's coming," Harvey whispered and snapped off the light. I had the strangest feeling in my head, and there again against the blackness, I watched as the jeweled knife slid across Roger's throat. "We've got to check on Roger," I whispered.

"Right," Harvey said. "We should get out of here anyway."

Like a robot, I followed him and Cecile out the window and down Buddy. I was halfway down when I slipped and grabbed out at his tail. My purse swung and then clanked loudly against the metal dog. I froze there, clinging to his cold, slick hide. I didn't have to look; I knew. "Cecile," I whispered, "you put it in my purse!"

"We couldn't just leave it there, Mary. He could move it before the police ever got inside. And I don't have a purse. Don't be such a baby."

A baby! I wondered if temporary insanity would get me off should I just happen to use the damn knife on her? No, justifiable homicide was the appropriate defense.

"It's clear," Harvey whispered. "Come on."

"Cecile's put the knife in my purse, Harvey."

"Well toss it or bring it, but let's move. We've got to get out of here."

I jumped down into the patch of violets that surrounded Buddy, stumbled, and fell into the soft dirt. I could bury it here. Who'd know? It was too dark for Cecile to see. But I'd know. I'd sworn to do this, and I would, even if it killed me, which seemed a possibility. Harvey held the door to the small hall open a crack, waited until the camera turned its head, then called, "Move it!" And we all raced back through and into the vast, echoing marble halls. There Cecile began to stroll nonchanlantly along, looking at pictures and nodding at other guests. Harvey followed.

I watched for a moment and then shot forward. "Let's get out of here," I whispered. "Let's get the car. Let's go home."

"No way," Cecile snapped. "We'd never get back in. And stop that shaking. It makes you look suspicious."

Harvey put his arm about me. "Don't be frightened, Mary. It'll be OK."

I calmed a little.

"Where's Hermoine's room?" Cecile said. "We'll search there next."

One of P.H.O.'s black-garbed guards passed. I swear that he stared at my purse, that he and I watched that thin curved blade glittering there in the darkness of my purse and my mind.

"I've no idea," Harvey said. "I'm often in O'Brian's office on business, but"— he laughed—"never Hermoine's room."

The guard went slowly on by.

I breathed again.

"Damn," Cecile snorted. "Well, we've got to find out somehow."

We went up and down the halls, Cecile peering into rooms and muttering, "Not this one. No, too small. Too dull."

I carried my purse.

"Ms. Sable," a voice called from behind me. I spun around.

It took a moment to recognize Polly Purger. She was smiling. Besides I could hardly see through the blue and red sheen of rococo knives.

"Ms. Sable, you were right," she cried, running a little to catch up to us. She flashed a thimble-sized diamond in my face. I watched blankly as it shot the harsh white hall light. "Like he did it. He really did it."

"I thought he did," I mumbled.

"He's really into being a daddy."

"Oh." I shook my head, beginning to understand. "Oh good," I managed to croak. "Great." I found myself suddenly afraid for Polly. "Great."

Polly turned her hand to Cecile.

"Very pretty," Cecile said. "Do you know where Hermoine's room is?"

Polly looked quizzically at me.

"We . . . we thought we'd like to see it," I muttered.

She shrugged. "Well, sure. I mean if you're into that kind of thing. Bummer, if you ask me. But I owe you, Ms. Sable. Patrick, he goes to me, 'Polly move out her stuff, move in yours.' But no way. It's got bad vibes. I don't want it. No way! Bummer!"

Polly led us off down the hall.

Suddenly, from nowhere, Brad came at me. "Mary," he said, and his eyes kept boring into me as he came on. He reached out, hesitated, and then with just two fingers touched my purse.

"Hi, Brad," Polly said.

He just stood smiling slightly and touching the purse just over where the knife was.

I looked into those eyes and considered the fact that anyone could have climbed Buddy and put that knife in the drawer. I couldn't move; I was as mesmerized by those eyes as a rabbit by the blazing beams of oncoming headlights.

"Brad?" Polly said again. "Hey, man, you're bein' weird again."

He turned abruptly and strode away.

Polly sniffed once and gestured us on down the hall. "This is it." She threw open a door, and we all filed in. Hermoine's room was about the size of an airline terminal, all done in white satin and fur, and dominated by a bed unimaginable outside the pages of a Barbara Cartland novel. It was pink and white with ribbons, net poufs, and curtains, and a vast headboard curving into a ceiling covered with angels and cupids, love birds and swans.

At the sight of it, knives and killers, everything, slipped from my mind; I could only stare speechless.

"Dig this," Polly said, moving to the bedside control board and punching a button. A ceiling angel with golden curls and a face of incredible purity began to descend slowly, truly the blue fairy straight out of Pinocchio. She stretched out one fragile, fiberglass hand toward the white satin pillow, fingers uncurling to reveal a quantity of white powder in the palm.

"Coke," Polly explained. "Cocaine. I don't do it cause of the baby. But help yourselves."

The angel smiled beatifically.

Polly pressed another button and a swan about-faced and began to defecate yellow joints onto the pink satin comforter. With the press of another button, the cupids and angels and love birds all began to cavort obscenely. Another, then another, drawers popped out revealing love letters, vibrators, all the paraphernalia of passion.

Another and the whole bed vibrated.

Another and it all began to rock back and forth, all its creatures still jerking through their routines, a grotesque ship of fools afloat on the sea of love, a Disneyland of beds.

By the time the pink and white had stilled and docked, the three of us were laughing wildly; Polly watched, looking puzzled.

"Just imagine her fantasy," I gasped.

"Father fixation," Cecile returned.

I choked back laughter and studied the giant, obscene candy box. I tried to understand how one got a father fixation out of it. I tried to imagine the life of its former occupant.

"She wasn't a very good woman," Harvey said softly.

"Father fixation," Cecile repeated, cross with our lack of understanding.

"Didn't P.H.O. mind all the other men?" I asked, thinking again of Roger.

"Nah." Polly gestured to a large mirror on the wall behind the bed. "One-way glass. He's into watching."

I stared into the glass for a moment, my mind boggling.

"I'd like to read those love letters," Cecile said.

"Why?" Polly asked.

"That's what I'm into."

"I can dig it." Polly punched a button that sprang the letter drawer. "Do your thing."

Cecile, Harvey, and I started toward the bed. The door behind us opened quietly. We swung around.

One of P.H.O.'s guards dressed all in black loomed above us.

Polly took a large step away from the control board, and we all stood in deepening silence looking like children caught at the cookie jar.

"You shouldn't be in here."

"Oh, Pat won't mind," Polly gurgled.

"He said nobody while her stuff's still here."

Polly nodded and drooped. A chill ran over me. The man had strange flat eyes nearly as dark as his clothing. I had no doubt that he, like the dogs outside, would kill if Patrick Henry O'Brian gave the order.

"Mr. O'Brian wants all the guests in the projection room for the movies." The guard made an abrupt gesture for us to pass before him. I grabbed my purse hard against me.

We filed by, our eyes fixed on our feet, and headed down the stairs. He watched us all the way into the projection room. Kill yes, I thought, but the question was, did he cut up and deliver?

The rest of the guests were in the projection room when we arrived. Roger had saved us three seats near the middle. We slid into the chairs just as the lights dimmed. I told myself how glad I was to see Roger in one piece, and I even tried to believe myself. I gradually relaxed. Surely we were safe here in the midst of several hundred people. And after this, we were going home. I was determined. I'd find some way to talk to P.H.O. when I didn't have his knife in my purse. That way, I'd at least get to keep my head.

The movies! All I can say is that they were orgy movies. Piles and piles of people stacked every which way, all white and wiggly, like a glob of maggots or an overturned bowl of worms. One pile even had a goat's head sticking out of the middle. I remember thinking at the time that it was a joke, that P.H.O.'s saving grace might well be his sense of humor. Everyone in the movies was totally naked except that everyone wore shoes. Cecile leaned toward me and whispered something about a foot fetish and how that might be signifigant in light of the foot in the frig.

All in all, it seemed rather sad. I mean, P.H.O. growing up lonely and scorned and having this dream about being handsome and having matched legs and stacks of women over him. And now here it was all come true, sort of, and it must still be lonely as hell.

During the movie, P.H.O. carried on a running commentary. "This heah's the Kansas City convention swingers. Here's the state a Texas where everthin's bigger."

And I watched and felt rather sickened and disappointed. Was this the wealth and power I thought I wanted so badly? But then, what did I want? Conversation? I might not have stacks or singles, but "What's on for Friday night?" and "Where's my red tie?" wasn't the world's best conversation either.

I was into this so deeply the films were just blurs moving before my eyes, when suddenly I felt a vicious pinch on my left arm. I jumped a mile, and Cecile gestured toward the screen.

This movie *was* different. It even seemed to have a plot of sorts. The camera was panning through a number of potted plants in front of a green velvet drop resembling a woods. A plump, little cupid with a tiny bow and arrow came skipping in from stage left. He wore only golden shoes and a wig of golden curls. He turned and waved and gestured toward the camera, his small round body glowing soft, hairless, and pink as a baby's against the deep green backdrop. His wee tube was totally unadorned. Even in the golden wig it was obviously Harvey. I sat rigid and red-faced in my seat, willing myself not to glance sidelong at him. I sensed Roger and even Cecile doing the same.

Cupid hid behind a potted Boston fern.

"Now ah know y'all recognize this little lady," Patrick Henry called through the darkness. Hermoine wearing crystal heels slithered in. Several men audibly caught their breath. She was truly spectacular. "This heah is the little lady some dastard did in. Ya ask me, ah say it was them attorney generals. Only way they could get at me. Ya know, folks, ya gotta wonder just who it is in our government is so scared of a little Christian free enterprise, and just why thah're so scared. Sometimes it seems like the only thing left for me to do is run mahself fer president and look into that. Course they know ah been thinkin' about that too. Got 'em plenty worried. Folks say as how it was the

F.B.I. that killed Marilyn Monroe. Well, ah say it was them attorney generals killed mah little Hermoine."

"Typical paranoid fantasy," Cecile whispered.

P.H.O. went on a bit about his qualifications to lead this great country, the evils of attorney generals, and the sweet Christian purity of his poor little lady cavorting there against the green backdrop. Then Cupid fired one of his tiny golden arrows at her and P.H.O. stilled to watch. Hermoine jumped as the arrow struck home; she looked about lasciviously. A tall, dark man wandered in from stage right.

I stiffened.

Hermoine leapt on the man, twining her full arms and legs about him. He resisted until Cupid let fire again, and then the two sank together to the Astroturf.

"Cecile," I whispered. "Cecile, that's Keith. That's Portia's husband."

"No!" Cecile said. "Are you sure?"

"Of course I'm sure."

The couple rolled there before us.

"Jeez," Cecile muttered.

That would be one more problem. Did a support and honesty group tell the wronged wife or keep it from her? I frowned, trying to decide. It was kinder somehow to keep quiet, but on the other hand . . .

The camera zoomed in on sandal-clad feet, followed them across a stretch of false grass until they stood beside the couple. Now the camera moved up slowly over a body as slim and graceful as Hermoine's was full and lusty, crept over folded arms below small breasts, and finally rose to a fine-featured, brown-eyed face.

Both Cecile and I came from our chairs shrilling, "Portia!"

"Shush," the audience hissed. "Siddown!" Harvey and Roger pulled at our arms, jerked us down into our chairs.

"I'm sorry," Harvey whispered. "I thought you knew. P.H.O. and Hermoine pretty much made it an occupational requirement. Still, he pays well."

We glanced at him, then back at the film. Portia gazed benignly at the couple copulating on her sandals. Well, I thought, there's one problem solved. I remembered Portia saying she hated "the broad." Cupid shot Portia and she dropped to join the others. More people skipped in in various shoes and were shot until again there was quite a pile.

I watched in stunned numbness. Portia had never mentioned this. Not once in over a year of truth and honesty sessions. Not once in a year of close friendship. And this whole murder-solving bit had been her idea. I had thought we were friends; instead I was just a damn pawn to be pushed about on her chessboard.

"Was Keith one of Hermoine's lovers?" I muttered, still staring at the movie.

Beside me Harvey sighed. "Yes."

"She never told me," I whispered.

"It isn't the sort of thing you tell," Harvey said. "I wouldn't have."

"Yes, but Portia and I were such close friends. I thought I knew her so well. Now—I don't know. She feels like a stranger."

Before me, Harvey still gamboled and gestured and leered. I watched with growing empathy. Poor pawns. Obviously, in this film *he* was the goat. I decided that P.H.O.'s sense of humor was not his saving grace after all.

I glanced at Harvey through the flickering light. He stared straight ahead, his small, round face pinker than usual and etched with misery. I laid a hand on his knee.

He glanced down then at me, and his face grew even rosier. "My condition got me the job as Sterex bleach, you know."

I nodded.

"And I really needed it."

"Listen!" Roger said, leaning excitedly across Cecile and my laps. "Listen, Harv, I can fix you up. Why, I can pull them ol' nuts right out like a squirrel from a hidy hole. Just you say the word 'n' I'll have you fixed up 'til you'll be as hairy 'n' horny as ol' King Kong himself."

For an instant Harvey's face glowed with hope, then it faded. "No," he said. "No, I better not. After all, my whole career is based on my . . . condition." The cupid face settled into an expression of resigned sadness.

We all thought about it for a moment.

"Harvey," I said. "God must have seen what a good job he did on you and kept a couple of inches to remember you by, too."

His doll lips quirked, then we all turned back to the movies. And then at last it was over. The guards herded us from the projection room and on out the front door. Over, I thought, but I carried away the knife in my purse, Portia's movie in my head, and gloom in my heart. The others talked out there, but I couldn't seem to grasp the words. I just kept putting one foot before the other, willing myself forward, much as one does when one has drunk too much and must make her way home.

And then, suddenly, there he was coming at me, looming larger and larger. The grayness within me sucked back, leaving only stark black hair and dark suit against the white white walls. P.H.O. and the knife burning away there in my purse became the whole world.

His hand reached out. I gasped, jerked my bag against my chest, wrapped my arms about it. From the corners of my eyes, I could see at least three guards. And Cecile. She got this kind of walleyed, wild look and darted away down the hall and out the door. So much for her planned interrogation. Little Harvey put a protective arm about me.

"Roger, thanks," P.H.O. said and went on by me, hand still extended but looking back now, watching me with estimating eyes. I knew I'd made him suspicious, practically signaling that something was in my purse. He probably thought I was carrying away the Dali melting watches or some such treasure. And if he decided to look! The rest of the guests kept eddying about us, each turning to look a last time at the great man.

"Ah'll need you again on Tuesday, Roger. Can you make Tuesday?"

I couldn't take my eyes off his, and my heart kept skipping, and I couldn't swallow.

His near-black eyes were still fixed on mine as he talked to Roger, and after a moment a light began to burn there. "And what's this little lady's name?"

"Mary Sable," Harvey said.

My hand, the one holding my purse and the knife, went suddenly numb. I knew I was going to drop it, that everything would spill right there at his feet. The other guests were almost all out now.

"His fingers closed over mine on the slick plastic. "Why don't you stay?" he whispered.

"She can't," Harvey said quickly. "Her husband's murderously jealous. And he's a policeman."

"He hurt yah, lil lady?" P.H.O. asked softly.

I hesitated, then just nodded since I wasn't sure I could speak. My answer pleased him.

"Bring her with ya on Tuesday," he said to Roger. "I'll leave ya name at the gate," he said to me. "Y'all come, heah?"

I nodded again.

He smiled, then turned and strode off down the hall.

We watched him for a moment, then stumbled on out to the car in silence. Cecile was already there, crouched on the floor with all the doors locked. Finally, we convinced her to let us in.

"I wasn't scared," she said. "But I thought one of us should be free to go for the police if necessary."

"I was," I whispered. "I was scared. Do you think he suspected, Harvey?"

"No." Harvey smiled at me through the rearview mirror. "But he did pick up on your fear. He likes fear."

The hair on my arms prickled. I watched as P.H.O.— dressed in black, knife in hand, all those jewels glittering red and blue—advanced on Hermoine. The hand lifts. Red and blue shadows dart across her pale skin. She cries out. A camera zooms in to capture the swift stroke, the dribble and then pump of blood, the fear fading slowly from the big green eyes.

"Snuff films," I blurted. "Could he be making snuff films?"

Harvey shrugged. "Anything's possible with him."

"All those cans and cans of home pornography," I whispered, and then another thought hit me. I leaned forward to look into Harvey's face. "What would happen to your job, Harvey, if P.H.O. was arrested?"

"The corporation would keep on." Harvey smiled. "He *does* organize well."

"Even if there was a death film—there, with all those others," I said, "we'd never find it."

"Well, we should try," Cecile said. "We need to get back inside."

"He wanted me to come back Tuesday," I whispered.

"Mary! Great! Now all you've got to do is find a way to search."

"I don't think I can go, Cecile. You don't understand what he wants. Besides his eyes are so . . . awful. And what if he notices the knife is missing. What if he suspects that we took it? I don't think I can."

"Don't be dumb. Why should he suspect us? There must have been a hundred people there tonight."

"Well, I'd suspect someone who went out clutching her purse and looking terrified, and whose friend cut and ran."

"She can't go back," Harvey said. "The man's a monster. He's got a room full of torture instruments."

"Really?" Roger said. "Far out."

"He's a sadist, Cecile," I said.

"Great. So you're a masochist. So the two of you were meant for each other."

"I am not!"

"Sure you are. You've stayed with Sid all these years, and the man treats you with positive contempt."

"He does not."

"Roger? I ask you. Does he or doesn't he?"

"Habit, probably. Dad treats my mother the same. Of course she is contemptible"

I rocked slightly in the dark backseat, feeling small and shamed, my whole life reduced to one-word diagnoses. "I stay with Sid . . ." I protested, my voice sounding suddenly high and whiney. I waited a moment and then tried again. "I stay with Sid because of my kids, Cecile. I want them to have decent lives. I stay because I'm trying to do the right thing for them."

"Yeah. So Freud called that moral masochism. But underneath, he says, it's all sexual. So go for it. Maybe you need a good active sadist for a change, instead of Sid the passive."

"You said Freud said all women are supposed to be masochists."

Cecile shrugged. "The man was a chauvinist pig, strung-out, nut case."

I looked at the back of her head, stunned. Her ability to pick and choose theory to suit her whim amazed me. "What kind of world would we have if people didn't try to do the right thing?" I whispered, and almost immediately thought, Maybe this kind?

"So do the right thing," Cecile said. "Go Tuesday and get this monster off the streets." Cecile was no masochist. She could send me to my death and not suffer one tiny twinge of conscience. I wondered if I should envy her?

I'm not going, I thought, and Roger moved in the darkness beside me.

Well, I think I'm not going.

22

The next day, I got the family off, fixed Roger three fertile eggs, lent him ten dollars from the cookie jar, and then got my purse from the back of the closet where I'd hidden it. I put it on the kitchen table and sat down to stare at it. This was Cecile's big fat idea. Why did I have to be the one to call Smith? I thought about the last time we'd met and actually blushed. I have to tell him it's over, I thought. But somehow, I just couldn't. Not yet anyway. Then, too, it didn't feel like it mattered all that much. Nothing did. Portia's movie kept rerunning behind my eyes, and I couldn't seem to stop watching. My closest friend was a stranger. I was not well meaning but a masochist. How much else of the world I thought I knew was illusion? I felt weak and scared, and I had a killer's knife in my bag, and I had to call my brief lover to tell him so.

I sighed and dialed the phone.

Smith walked through the door, said, "I've been callin' you," and grabbed for me.

I jumped away.

"Whatta ya say? Let's fool around."

"Not here," I gasped, ducking under his arm, and putting the kitchen table between us. "Not now! Someone could come in!"

"Who's here?" he said, coming around the table.

"Don't be stupid. Look at us. Like some old cartoon—the boss chasing the secretary around the desk. Now quit. I need to talk to you."

He kept on coming. Just then Roger walked into the kitchen. I thought he'd left. We all froze in place like wooden clock figures about to pipe the time. I looked away from the awareness dawning in Roger's eyes.

"You wanted to see me, Ms. Sable," Smith said in a suddenly professional voice.

I was awash in panic and confusion. All the things I'd thought of since that afternoon with Smith were suddenly there in the room with me: discovery, the children in custody court, the Sables sewing a scarlet letter on the front of my worn sweater. You're overreacting, I tried to tell myself, but I didn't believe myself. I shot a glance at Roger from under my lashes. Watching me steadily, he came and sat at the table with an odd smirk on his lips.

"Hey, Sarge," he said.

"Lieutenant."

"Whatever. You ever hear the joke about the ninety-five-year-old couple that went before a judge for a divorce?"

"No," Smith growled.

"Well, the judge asks them, see, 'Why *now*, after seventy-five years of marriage?' 'Oh,' they say, 'we were waiting for the kids to die.'"

"Very funny," Smith muttered.

Roger looked at me and smiled wider. I felt my heart drop into my shoes. He knew.

"Yes, well . . ." Smith snapped, "what was it you wanted to see me about, Ms. Sable?"

I looked at him blankly.

"The knife," Roger said, pushing my bag toward me. "Remember, Mary? The knife?"

"Oh yes. The knife." My face and fingers were stiff as I opened the bag and took out the knife. Cecile had wrapped it in a Kleenex—a dirty one at that.

"I had nothing whatsoever to do with this," Roger said complacently.

Ha! Big free-thinking, liberal rat-fink.

"What is it?" Smith said.

"We . . . we found it in Patrick Henry O'Brian's desk drawer. Last night." I whispered. "We—"

"You what?!" he roared.

"We—"

"You mean you took it?! You moved it?"

"Well—"

"That looks like blood there on the handle," Roger said.

Smith glared at him. "What the hell were you doing at O'Brian's anyway?"

"We—"

"This is tampering with evidence, you know. You could blow the whole case."

"You weren't going to find it anyway! Not going to search there or the mayor's drawer, remember?!"

"If I'd been with them, I would certainly have advised against it," Roger purred.

I stared at him, seeing again that knife at his throat and realizing the hand I'd seen might well have been my own.

Just then the doorbell rang. Grateful for escape, I lurched to my feet and darted to answer it.

It was Cecile. How else to round out such a perfect morning? She trudged past me toward the kitchen.

"Cecile," I whispered. "Wait."

"Did you hear? They got the killer. You got any coffee?" She stopped abruptly in the doorway. "Oh. Hello. I thought you were alone."

"Hello, Cecile," I said, pushing past her. She wasn't about to get a drop of coffee or anything else from me.

"Whatta ya mean they got the killer?!" Smith snorted.

"Yeah," Roger said. "Who got 'em? Who gets the reward?"

"Yeah," I echoed weakly. If they had him then it was over. My one chance and it was over. "Over," I whispered.

"On 'Heart's Desires,'" Cecile sighed. "On the soap. They're going to find Madaline's killer on Friday. It was in all the papers. Don't you people ever read the papers?"

"I've been very busy turning in murder weapons," I said, turning away to empty the coffee pot into the sink.

"That damn soap," Smith snorted. "What do you know about this?" He pointed at the knife.

Cecile sniffed. "We gotta call the group, Mary."

"What?"

"Listen . . ." Smith said.

"Hey, Mary, I wanted some of that coffee."

"Oh, Cecile, I *am* sorry. I guess I just wasn't thinking."

"You got any instant? The thing is we should get the group together to watch on Friday."

"Listen!" Smith said again. He seemed to be getting bigger and redder by the moment. "About this knife . . ."

"No instant," I said, then, "Why should we get the group together? Did you know all the big things on the soaps happen on Fridays or Mondays?"

Smith hissed as if he'd been punctured. I smiled at him.

"The rest of the week they talk about what happened on Monday and Friday. That way it doesn't matter too much if you miss a day or two."

"Jesus, Mary, the clutter you got in your head. Any tea?"

"No, Cecile. Sorry."

"Sure you do," Roger said, jumping up to pull open a cupboard. "This stuff 'll kill you, Cecile."

"Yeah," she said and turned the fire on under the tea pot.

Smith looked at each of us in turn with unbelieving eyes.

"Whatever." I shrugged. "So why should we get the group together Friday, Cecile?"

"I oughta run the whole mess of you in."

"Well, see," Cecile said, getting a cup and returning to the table, "people on that show know things about that killing. Maybe only subconsciously. Maybe they don't know they know. But they know. Truth will leak from their collective unconscious. We need to be ready to catch it."

"Great idea!" Smith said, and he and Roger exchanged smirks. Cecile went on with an elaborate explanation of how our collective consciousnesses would psych out the soap stars' collective unconsciousnesses. Smith took the knife by the tip and stuffed it into a baggie he had in his pocket. I watched a fly creep inexorably toward the butter.

"It will probably even be the person who plays the killer. People come to believe they are the roles they play." Now that seemed confusing to me since the killer would have to believe he was the role he played before he played it. But then everything seemed bewildering today. The fly reached the butter, climbed up; its wings began to tremble with pleasure.

"Enjoy," I muttered.

"What?" Cecile said.

"We can meet here. You call everyone."

"I'm really busy, Mare. Classes. Papers. Couldn't you call?"

"No."

"She's busy, too," Smith growled.

Roger looked up with peaked brows. "Doing what?"

It was not going to be a good day. "You want a meeting, you call," I said, and took my purse off the sideboard and walked out the back door to an outraged chorus of, "Mary! Mary! Mary!"

23

I walked.

The first block, I wondered if Smith might put out an all-points bulletin on me.

The second, I thought how peaceful it might be if he did. Just sitting there in that cell, reading—whatever. Passersby might frown in, but at least they wouldn't expect me to wash their socks.

The next block, sanity and Roger returned.

That was a ten-block problem. Would he tell? Nah, I kept telling myself. He doesn't know, just suspects. But I was uncertain, frightened. How could he resist, the way he felt about Sid's life-style? No. Now, more than ever I needed to get Roger out of the house.

Two blocks later I came across one of the old-fashioned, closing-door phone booths. Ah, the good old days. Harvey picked up the phone on the second ring.

"Do you think it's possible that Patrick Henry O'Brian might hire Roger as his personal healer?"

"Mary? Is that you?"

"Yes."

There was silence. "No."

"No?"

"No. He might be intrigued briefly, but he never hires anyone who doesn't make him money."

"Then I guess I've got to go back on Tuesday." I stood there, phone in hand, the bright, warm day stretching on and on, thinking about my assignation with a man who was attracted not by my face or figure or personality but by my fear. And *that* attraction was growing steadily. "Roger did this to me," I whispered.

"What?" Harvey asked.

"Nothing." You did it to yourself, the voice in my head insisted.

"You can't go Mary, it's not safe."

"I've got to get rid of Roger, Harv. I really do."

Harvey sighed. "Do you know what you're getting yourself into? O'Brian is not a nice man."

"I don't want to go, Harv. Believe me, I don't. I'm terrified. But I have to. We can't go on this way."

Harvey sighed again. "I'll do what I can to help."

"Will you, Harv?"

"I'll use my day pass. Roger'll already be there. We'll try to see that no harm comes to you. We'll stay nearby. You can scream if you need us."

I hung up the phone feeling comforted and resumed walking.

Sometime later, I came to a cemetery and stood just looking out over the graves and holding carefully the odd calm within me. Then some partially submerged thought began to nag. "Grass is the beautiful uncut hair of graves," I whispered. Now where had that come from? Whitman, of course, but why now? And then it hit me.

Hermoine. Her body. What better place for it than a grave? I felt again the soft dirt, the violets there beneath Buddy's monument. It would have been hard to bury a body in the patrolled grounds, but simple there in that private little yard. Besides, it fit with O'Brian's grotesque sense of humor—or whatever one might want to label that twisted little elf running around in there.

Tuesday, I'd find some way to look, to rob Buddy's grave, to search for snuff films. "This will end it . . . or me," I whispered, and then recited for one full block, "I can do it. I can. I can." Then it hit me, and I moaned aloud. First, I had to do the group-watching of Friday's "Heart's Desires." First, I had to face Portia.

Somehow I preferred O'Brian.

24

I hadn't seen Portia since movie night. I'd decided to play the game cool, her way, the winners' way. I wouldn't even mention that I'd seen the movie. I'd just smile and go on as if I knew nothing. I'd watch *her* dancing on *my* strings for a while. Maybe she had snuffed Hermoine. After all, Portia did have a motive she had just happened to forget to mention. Poetic justice if her little Machiavellian schemes should end up trapping her. Yes, I shall just smile and pretend.

I needed the extra moral support of having the meeting here, of being in my own playing field. Besides, after the Portia movie and the Smith/Roger bit, I was so depressed that there was nothing for it but to clean house. I even polished the pipes under all the sinks. A paradox—usually cleaning depresses me, but when I'm depressed cleaning can cheer me. I get a sense of things getting better, of returning order. But now, even as I walked through the gleaming rooms, I was not comforted.

And worse, I'd started to eat compulsively.

With Jo Anne and me both working on it, the house was so spotless it would have been a shame to waste it. The meeting began just as I'd planned. I stood in the middle of my gleaming living room eating peanuts and greeting arrivers with a brilliant smile.

Cecile came in. "Ten minutes," she said tensely, glancing at her watch, then the TV. She and I skirmished briefly for control of the peanuts.

Then Portia arrived. "Hi," she said, glancing at the bowl in my hands, then around at the spotless living room. "What's wrong? More trouble with your brother-in-law?"

I smiled wider, shoving the peanuts into Cecile's hands. I shrugged casually. "So-so."

She looked at me rather oddly and went to sit on the couch. Inez and Jo Anne came in together. Cecile looked at her watch and informed us we had eight minutes. We settled about the room.

"We were all going to think about why the foot was in the refrigerator," Portia said. "Did anyone come up with anything?"

"Who made you boss?" I muttered.

"What?" Portia said.

"Oh, nothing." I smiled warmly, sincerely, at the lamp just behind her shoulder.

She waited, studying me. I kept smiling at the lamp. She finally turned away, her voice less sure now. "What did you come up with?"

There was a silence.

"Well," Jo Anne ventured, looking about at us with timid eyes. Jo Anne always tries to please. "Maybe the foot was in the refrigerator to preserve it?" She glanced about hopefully.

We all just looked at her.

"Maybe," Inez said in her machine-gun style, "maybe the murder was done there in that apartment, and that's how they hid the body. There could be pieces all over the place. That's possible, you know. I mean legs in the clothes hampers, arms under the beds, liver in the bread box."

We all just looked at her.

"No," Cecile said firmly, looking at her watch and eating peanuts. "No, you're all wrong." She swallowed and glanced toward the blank screen. "Male sexual inadequacy. The foot and the head were both forms of demonstrating adequacy. Exhibitionism so to speak. I really think it's Brad."

"P.H.O.," I murmured. "After all, we found the knife in his drawer, and he's sadistic besides."

"It's possible," Cecile said. "I have thought about it. But it just seems too obvious. Besides, he's externalizing his anger. Anyone could have gotten into that office just like we did. Hidden the knife. Why would P.H.O. hide it in his own desk drawer? He's not stupid."

"He felt safe," I said, staring at her, trying to catch something. "Is that why you moved it?"

"What?"

"Because it disagreed with your pet theory."

"Really, Mary. This is all really just another example of your Jesus ego models."

Now I really did stare.

"Studies have shown that most women have Jesus ego models while most men have Alexander the Great ego models. That's why so many women are losers. Admit it. You admire Jesus more than Alexander the Great."

My chin dropped to my chest. It was true. I did. The thing is, until that moment I hadn't realized everyone didn't. No wonder I was losing. The other side was playing with totally different rules.

"That's what's hanging you up here, you know. You want the killer to be a bad guy. Someone you dislike. Life doesn't work that way."

"That's just not so," I shouted. Was it? I looked about for the peanuts.

"Cecile?" Inez said. "Exhibitionism? You mean that foot is a . . ."

"Symbol."

Inez giggled wildly. "Oh, I don't believe that. A foot . . ." She giggled harder. "Well, I mean, I do remember my mama always telling us to wear our rubbers, but . . ." She dissolved in laughter.

Cecile gazed at her with tolerant distaste. "Time," she said, jumping up and going over to snap on the TV. "Everyone watch closely. I'll pass out paper and pencils. Don't get emotionally involved now. Especially you, Mary. You need to work on that. Analyze objectively every single line for subconscious messages. I know when this program's over we're going to have an important clue to the killer." She went about passing out paper and pencils.

I doodled on my paper and watched the end of "As The World Turns," caught up as I always am.

"As The World Turns" is a kitchen soap. Much of the action takes place at the kitchen table—the women sit sipping coffee and discussing family problems. Every soap has a kindly middle-aged or older woman, a Miss Ellie–type character, who supports and mothers and counsels other characters. "Heart's Desires" has Aunt Kate, who keeps house for Madaline and makes and presses cookies spiced with good advice upon anyone who enters her kitchen.

This particular day, the show started with Kate in the kitchen stirring something in a bowl and listening to a niece debate whether she should give herself to her boyfriend before marriage.

I watched wishing for an Aunt Kate of my own—for someone to tell me what to do about Roger, about Portia, about P.H.O., about Carolee, about well, about everything.

"That's a decision only you can make," Aunt Kate said, smiling kindly upon her niece's bent head and setting a plate of cookies before her.

Jo Anne bent and wrote dutifully. We all peeked at her from the corners of our eyes.

"Standards are within your heart, dear," Kate went on. *"Only your heart can tell you what to do."*

"Ah shit," Cecile spat. "This is from another century." Now that analysis didn't sound too objective.

"Why dear, your old Aunt Kate would be the last person in the world to try to tell you what to do," Kate said, going to the cupboard and taking out a platter.

"Bullshit," Cecile shot back. Jo Anne was still writing.

Aunt Kate set the platter on the table, and both she and the niece stared at it thinking about Kate's words.

"It will have to be Sibel, the maid who stole the bracelet," Inez said. "I mean they've killed or jailed all their other bad women—unless . . . unless some way, they could get Rena out of jail. Do you think Rena's out of jail? I mean she could escape."

"Who's Rena?" Cecile asked crossly.

"The woman who was with Polly's lover when he hit her father. It was Rena who made him run because she was engaged to this rich man, see, and Rena shot Mr. Mopes, the witness, and the lover was tried for it, but then Madaline found out the truth just in time to save him. It was really dramatic. All there in this courtroom, just like Perry Mason. Richard and them really did a good job on that. But anyway, the thing is they've done away with all their bad characters. I'm sure they're ready to introduce more, but what a pity they didn't have a real good bad one for Madaline. Don't you think?"

We all thought about it.

Aunt Kate was arranging hors d'oeuvres on the platter.

"*I really want Joe sometimes,*" Niece was murmuring. "*And yet—oh—I do, Aunt Kate, I do always remember the standards you—and Dad and Mom, when they were alive—taught me. I guess I wouldn't like myself if . . .*"

"Drivel!" Cecile screamed.

Niece went on working out why she would wait for marriage, Aunt Kate arranged her platter, and I stopped worrying about Portia and began worrying about Carolee.

Niece kissed Aunt Kate's cheek and wandered out.

"*There,*" Aunt Kate muttered, fussily putting a final touch on her platter. "*Now doesn't that look nice?*" She looked up at the camera and smiled.

The smile slipped, shifted slightly, and the voice-over that represented thought began softly, "*Not that they'll notice. Oh, no. Do they ever notice? I'm always serving, caring. And does anyone serve back? Care back? Oh no! Twenty years behind this tray . . .*" I stiffened. Kate looked out at the camera, and her kindly face began to twitch and twist. I had a sensation of my own face twitching and twisting. *"No one ever saying, 'What can we do for you, Kate?'"* Her eyes began to glitter. *"Who cares what Kate wants . . . needs . . ."* Her lips peeled back from her teeth. Well, at least they had a good actress. Jo Anne stopped writing, her eyes riveted to the screen. In my mind I saw Richard standing on my front porch smiling his warm smile.

"It's the selfish ones who get it all. Attention, freedom, love. Madaline. She's had it all! Yes-s-s-s-s," Kate hissed evilly into the camera. *"She's had it all! And I've worked in her kitchen. All these years! All these years I've served her. Now we'll see!"* Kate burst into wild laughter. *"Yes, you'll see, Madaline!"* She leered aloud now. *"Today, Madaline, I get my own back!"* Kate whirled and snatched something from the refrigerator, slamming it down onto her platter. She snickered, *"Today, Madaline, I serve you for the last time!"*

The camera dollied in to reveal, there in the center of the hors d'oeuvres, a human foot. *"Yes, today I serve you for the last time."* Her mad laughter floated out over the fade music.

Then Harvey was jigging away on our little screen.

> All good housewives, hear my song.
> Choose me, and you won't go wrong.
> Use me for I've got the might—

Here Harvey took a great stick and chased away evil dirt— three huge, sullen men in smeared T-shirts.

> Make me bleach your whites so bright.
> Stick with me, I'll treat you right.

The three men reappeared clean and cowed. Harvey danced exuberantly. A naked shadow cupid danced behind him. Yes, and today I was the goat. The world was so wrong.

"Today's the last time I serve you," Portia said, trying to

lighten things. "Best line Richard's ever done. Didn't think he had it in him."

"Mary." Jo Anne touched my hand. I managed a half smile. Inez and Cecile muttered a few things, but mostly we sat silent through a few more commercials. Then Aunt Kate was back, in Madaline's living room now, serving the other "Heart's Desires" characters from her foot tray and none of them noticing.

"What do you know about this Kate person?" Cecile demanded. "Could she have killed Hermoine?"

No one answered.

I wrestled the peanuts from Cecile and ate handful after handful, though they tasted like cardboard.

Kate was actually slathering like a thirties' villainess, dribbling into her hors d'oeuvres, passing her tray in monstrous parody of her former good womanliness.

"It wasn't like that," I heard myself whimper.

"Of course not." Portia jumped to her feet and went over to snap off the TV. "Stupid fool Richard," she snarled. "Is there anything he wouldn't do for money?"

"Is there anything you wouldn't?" I shot back. Well, so much for cool, clever strategy.

She looked at me quickly, then walked back and sat down, snapping open her bag and taking out a pack of cigarettes. "Well," she said lighting one, "I have a feeling you saw my movie at P.H.O.'s the other night."

My ears began to ring as blood rushed to my head.

"Yea," Cecile said. "We did. Hey, Portia, you know this Kate character?"

I leaned toward Portia, fighting an overwhelming desire to weep. "You had motive," I whispered. "And you never mentioned it when you assigned us this little task."

"Hey," Cecile squealed. "I never thought of that!"

Portia inhaled smoke and looked at the wall. She exhaled slowly in my direction. "Yeah, I did." She managed a wry grin. "I did not like the woman."

"You used us," I burst out bitterly. "You manipulated us. You've told us just exactly what you wanted us to know."

Portia crossed her legs, inhaled again. "Well, hell." She gave a twisted smile. "I thought that was the point of these networking groups."

We all stared at her.

"To get us power."

"Portia!" Jo Anne gasped.

She shut her eyes and sighed. "OK, so I'm sorry."

"Why didn't you tell us what was going on at P.H.O.'s?" I demanded. "I thought you were my friend. I told you everything."

She looked at me through narrowed eyes. "You looked up to me." She gestured with her cigarette about the room. "You all did. Admired me. You know how little, middle-aged women get off on that. Can you really blame me for trying to hang on to it?"

We all still stared, and then when no one spoke, one by one our eyes fell away. "I *was* trying to help," Portia said.

"We'd have understood," I muttered. "You could have told us."

"Oh, Mary! You of all people! You've got all that old church crap. I think you believe that soap shit. I think you believe that there are such things as good women and bad women."

"Yes!" I screamed. "Yes, I do. I believe there are some things better than others. Honesty is better than self-interest. And I think it's damned bad to sell your body for a good job!"

She looked at me for a long time. Jo Anne began to sob. "Well at least, Mary, I don't have to do my own housework," Portia said.

I sat silent then, not hearing anything the others said. Soon everyone was making excuses, leaving, knowing that this was the end of our woman's group.

Funny how the world is a certain way, and then with a snap, a slide, everything shifts and is off focus, wrong; shadows that were soft grow hard and menacing; everyday things move from the background to loom at you and twang unease.

Your best friend is false, and you are not as you've always seen yourself—reasonable, kind—but rather a slathering madwoman passing a human foot.

You fear that if it doesn't snap and fall back to the old and known that you too must snap, and yet there is nothing you can do.

And on top of that there isn't anything for the vegetarians for dinner.

25

Life goes on, and after a while I went on too—to the health food store for five pounds of organic split peas.

When I returned, I could hear Roger and Jo Anne in the kitchen. I could hear the clink of dishes. Jo Anne, of course, had come to clean. It is the sort of offering she makes to comfort.

"We're out of fertile eggs again." Roger's sad voice. The sound of the refrigerator opening and closing. Cupboards opening and closing. "Mary just isn't very efficient when it comes to running a house."

"She's got a lot of other things on her mind," Jo Anne soothed.

"Yeah."

"I could fix you some of these squash with cheese," she offered.

"I don't want to put you out," Roger said in that weary, soft way he has. The hell he didn't.

"No, no. No trouble."

There was a silence then, broken by occasional kitchen sounds. Oil sputter. The clink of dishes.

Then Roger was asking hesitantly, "Do you think Mary is all right?"

Another pause, then Jo Anne, surprised. "All right?"

"You know . . . mentally?" His voice dripped concern.

"Of course. Why ever would you ask that?"

"Um." The scrape of a chair. "She does odd things, Jo Anne. I heard about that foot. And the other morning she threw oatmeal all over the floor, then stomped in it."

"Really?" Jo Anne squeaked. "My, that doesn't sound like her."

Roger was going on, doing me. He had tapped into the house-bound woman's isolation, her love to hear and speculate about people. It had become his rate of exchange. A little story for a little snack—organic, of course.

I stood motionless, listening to him do me as reward for Jo Anne's squash and cheese, just as he had done Mother Sable for my three-minute fertile eggs. I found I was sweating and nauseated and I couldn't seem to catch my breath. Funny how I had never seen myself as being a Mother Sable—as ever being a foolish, old woman who could be done.

I moved to the doorway.

"I think you'd better go," I said quietly. "Pack your bags and get out of this house."

For an instant fear brightened those pale eyes. "Where do you expect us to go. I've gone to all this trouble to get Storm. . . ." His voice faded, his eyes looked helplessly at me.

I looked back. Where could he go? Could I just turn him and Storm out into the cold? I suspected I could.

His eyes glinted, and he looked quickly away. "Don't you get all upset, Mary," he murmured. "You talk all this over with Sid. He would want that, you know. And that nice policeman. Talk it over with him too. Let me know what you decide."

I heard him clearly. I understood him perfectly. But I was so swollen inside I couldn't think or speak. I clutched my hands together to keep them from flying at Roger's throat. I turned around, and walked out.

26

I don't seem to be myself.

I don't sleep.

If I do sleep, I dream and wake, dream and wake. Vivid red dreams escape my head, spilling over and filling the room until I wake sweating and frightened, to lie and stare at their after-images moving on the face of the darkness.

A pattern of dreams. The same three over and over, and always followed by a long period of wakefulness.

I dream that Maverick—not James Garner, but Maverick, that ever-cool, never emotional cowboy with the constant faint grin—comes nightly to do my housework, much like those elves that used to come to spin straw into gold so that the maid might become a queen.

I dream I am driving a car, and a child darts in front and the car strikes her. I sit behind the wheel staring into the blackness beyond the windshield. A dream, I tell myself even in the dream. But the telling does not defuse my horror. When I get out, there will be nothing there, I say. I will it to be so. And then I get out and walk forward in that forever dream way. Carolee lies there on the pavement, and blood seeps from a wound somewhere, seeps across her chest; the trickle slowly writes a large red sticky word, *Hustle.*

Then, last, I dream of Hermoine. She stands in a spotlight, and someone in shadow moves toward her. I know it is the killer, and I strain to see his face. I must see his face. He comes slowly, slowly, toward me, until I hear myself saying, "Yes, of course it is you."

I wake and lie thinking that perhaps I do know who Hermoine's killer is. I am almost sure I do. My mind, my eyes, pry at the darkness trying to extract that embedded face, name. But nothing will come. "It's P.H.O.," I whisper, but the face slips back, away, and I am less certain than in full daylight.

Then as I lie there unable to fall back to sleep, my mind slides into a familiar groove. How am I to get rid of Roger and Storm?

Only Roger really.

For were he gone I could send Storm back to her mother, or to her grandmother. Everyone would expect that. Wouldn't that be funny? Mrs. Sable and Storm.

But how Roger?

After an hour or so I get up and turn on the desk lamp and sit staring into the small circle of light. I tell myself that I will just tell Roger he has to leave—let him do what he will. I will just take the consequences.

Last night the desk lamp began to flicker, and in the area just between light and dark, images moved: parents, church, a plaster Jesus.

The lamplight died suddenly, leaving me sitting, staring into some endless black hole of space within my own soul.

No, I just wasn't going to be able to do it.

Then it all hung on Tuesday.

If I couldn't order Roger out, then I had to get him out.

Monday night, I called Harvey and reminded him of his promise.

"I won't forget," he said, sounding affronted. Then he laughed. "Stick with me, I'll treat you right."

"Sure," I said. "I know." I hung up the phone.

27

It's Tuesday.

Bright. Clear. Warm. The sea breeze a caress.

Everything seems to be easing, clearing. Last night I went right to sleep and never woke once. Perhaps it's only that now at least everything is decided. One way or another. I remember reading once that suicides were cheerful and calm right before they committed the act. But whatever the reason, today, faced with the reality of meeting P.H.O. face to face and alone, I'm suddenly calm, almost cheerful.

Last night I dreamed only one dream, a new and different dream filled with shadowed dark blues and reds, like some ancient tapestry. Beautiful.

I felt oddly happy when I woke. It was as if I had been doing some of the restorative dreaming Roger recommends. Yet that's not possible. I didn't even understand what the dream meant, much less direct it.

Sid woke me from the dream because I was laughing aloud. We made love, and it was good for the first time in weeks.

Later, when Storm informed me she had a job starring in a movie, I just smiled, though I knew damn well just what kind of movie it was. I didn't even cringe when I overheard her telling Carolee that she too could be a star.

Then Roger sought me out and was terribly warm and friendly. He asked me about my writing, told me a few more Mother Sable stories. He smiled his sad smile and watched me closely with his weepy blue eyes. At first I thought he was only trying to reingratiate himself, but then I realized that he wanted something more. I waited, guarded and smiling. And indeed he was soon asking to borrow ten dollars. I understood that I wasn't allowed to say no. He said not to worry, that he and Harvey would both be there if I needed them.

"I'm not worried," I said.

Ten dollars for five minutes of 'concerned' conversation. He charged higher than a shrink. I found my purse and gave him two fives. "Good-bye, Roger," I said softly, gently.

Later, I found myself feeding all his fertile eggs to the dog. Odd.

My mother said that if you were good, people would love you; the lady on TV said if you used Downy people would notice. What I think is that they both lied.

I dressed slowly, carefully, floating in calm certainty, sure that somehow my problems were to be solved. And yet—why?

It must be the dream.

In the dream I am at the Last Supper. Serving actually. Organic lentils. The twelve and Jesus all in pale robes are behind the long white-draped table just like in the picture, but their faces are in heavy shadow. Jesus' is as still and tranquil as if it were carved from wood, but when he moves I am sure I catch the flash of eyeglasses. I look closer and one of the twelve turns to me and smiles. "You thought Roger was Christ," he says, "but have you ever thought that perhaps Christ is Roger?" He begins giggling wildly, and spittle spangles his long white beard. I watch him from a great distance, and I am filled with terrible sadness at his Alice-in-Wonderland words.

The Savior looks up then, and everyone falls silent, waiting. He clears his throat and says in his soft, sad voice that one of those here, one of the disciples, will this night betray him with a kiss.

All cry out, protest, then ask, "Will it be me? Me?"

And Jesus replies, "He who next dips into the salt."

And then the dream seems to shift slightly. It turns into a TV rendering of the Last Supper. The sets are now a little more elaborate, the costumes more studiedly shabby. The camera dollies in for a long and meaningful close-up of an old pewter bowl filled with salt. The camera lifts, moves to each of the faces of the disciples, but they are no longer disciples exactly. They are actors—actors from "Heart's Desires." The camera hesitates on each of their tense, attentive faces. Pretty, sultry Polly. Is it she? Big-shouldered Brad? He? Anna Lisa, looking bored and chewing gum? P.H.O.? Richard? Kindly old Aunt Kate. There is a long ticking wait. Now we will know the killer, I think in the dream. The camera pans salt bowl, faces. We are all silent—waiting for someone to move. And then someone does.

Brad! He smiles slightly, then in slow motion his strong, square hand reaches down the table. Someone gasps aloud. His hand hovers over the salt bowl.

So then it is him after all, I think. Cecile is right.

But suddenly, he jerks his hand back. He laughs. Polly moans.

Again we wait and watch. Who? Who?

And then in the dream I find myself watching my own hand move down the table. It hesitates above the salt. I feel its rough texture as my finger curls around a great fistful. But it can't be me, I think. And yet there I stand with the salt clutched to my breast, and everyone staring accusingly at me.

I set down my tray and bend to kiss the cheek of the Savior. Immediately the dream shifts.

I am outside in the darkness in some sort of grape arbor. The grapes hang all about me—lush, purple and black, frosted with luminescent dew and dust. I realize that I hold some coins in my hand. I look down at them, and I see that the head of Alexander the Great is printed on the silver faces.

I begin to caress them with my thumbs and to laugh, and just then the sun rises, and a cock crows three times. I seize him, his feathers fly off, and he comes to pieces in my hands. I throw the pieces into a pan and begin frying him, all the while shaking that fistfull of salt over him and laughing louder and wilder . . . kind of an . . . Aunt Kate laugh.

Here, Sid woke me.

An omen? A sign?

Who knows?

But I have felt strange all day—light, disconnected, a thistle on the wind. I turned on "Heart's Desires." Aunt Kate was still slathering about with her tray. I watched for a while with interest. In a philosophy class I took once, the professor theorized that what we see is just the shadows of reality flickering on the cave walls of our minds. I remembered that as I watched Aunt Kate and her tray.

Then I turned off the set and went to get ready to go to P.H.O.'s.

I decided to wear the new black dress that makes me look thinner and even the uncomfortable heels that I hadn't worn since our anniversary. I put on more makeup than I'd worn in years. A new Mary Sable left the house dressed to kill.

And I took a cab.

It seemed a day for luxury.

28

When I arrived, O'Brian was shut away with Roger—having his feet massaged. The guard showed me into a small side room and told me to wait. I waited until he was out of sight, then popped up and hurried to the door. The hall was empty, the security camera clicking back and forth. I debated and then sallied forth, looking about in what I hoped was a good imitation of a woman looking for the powder room. When the camera turned away, I darted into the projection room. I walked slowly down the thick red-carpeted aisle, letting one hand bounce along the velvet backs of the seats. P.H.O.'s projection room had the feel of a brothel, which was fitting somehow. I stood before the twelve-foot wall covered with shelves of home movies, touched one of the silver cans with a cold finger, and waited for the fear I was sure must be lurking down there somewhere. Nothing rose. I felt almost jaunty, and yet the other night with crowds about I'd been terrified. Odd.

"Oh, there you are," a voice boomed. I spun about. O'Brian stood grinning at me, a grin halfway between a halloween jack-o-lantern's and Jack Nicholson's in *The Shining*. My fear came rattling back.

"No movies today," O'Brian said and giggled. "No, no, not today. There's somethin' better I want to show you. Y'all come heah with me now." He turned and walked out with stiff, jerky little steps. I wondered how anyone so ridiculous could be so frightening. I started after him, thinking that it wasn't too late, that I could still turn and run out the front door. His guards might stop me, but surely they wouldn't hold me against my will. Would they? Somehow I thought they might. Besides, it would be so embarrassing, running shrieking from his house that way. Harvey was here, and Roger. "I can do it," I whispered. "I can."

I saw Harvey and Roger then, lurking in a doorway far down the hall. Harvey signaled me with thumb and forefinger that everything was OK, then mouthed, "Yell, if you need us." I nodded and trailed after P.H.O.

"Heah," O'Brian said. He opened an ornately carved door and actually shivered with excitement. "Heah," he said again.

I stepped inside. It was dark. As my eyes slowly adjusted, words began to whisper within me. "Then all smiles stopped together. There she stands as if alive."

Browning? I wondered. *The Last Duchess?* Now? Here? It was as if I'd walked into a Renaissance castle. Reds and velvets.

Overdecorated and suffocating. I had a quick impression that the walls were covered with Last Duchesses.

P.H.O. hit a switch, and several small, faint lamps flicked on, shooting glints of color from the priceless Tiffany shades that hooded them. The effect was muted and beautiful until my eyes adjusted enough to see what the priceless lamps lifted from the darkness. Duchesses indeed, but these didn't smile. The walls were covered with paintings and tapestries in old-fashioned sepias, rich reds and blues, sweet flesh tones, and every one of them depicted some form of torture. Screaming mouths and wild eyes spilled from the frames, filling the room with a muted agony. Beneath the paintings, rows of glass-fronted cases held whips and manacles and other less easily identifiable objects. My stomach turned. Win or lose, I was sorry I'd come. I didn't like or want to know this world.

"Y'all gotta see this," P.H.O. said proudly and strode to a six-foot long metal frame with three wooden rollers set inside. "This heah is part of an official rack from the Tower of London." He ran loving hands over the aged, well-worn wood. "Theah's some as say it came originally from the Spanish Armada. Y'all wouldn't believe what ah had to pay for it."

I swallowed and then swallowed again. He'd never believe how little I cared what it cost. "How nice," I managed.

"Touch it," he ordered. Still swallowing, I moved to obey. My fingers burned at the touch of the silvery wood.

"Cain't ya just see them was here before ya?" he murmured with a velvet voice, his dark eyes glinting blues and greens from the Tiffany lamps. Here in this room, he had gained in strength and stature. Something in me fluttered, and I remembered Cecile saying I was a masochist. I supposed this was the day I found out for sure. My hands began to shake, causing the rack to rattle and raising a slight cloud of exotic-smelling dust. "Cain't ya imagine the stories, the scenes, the screams as a fahn young man or fair maiden is slowly pulled—"

"Yes!" I snapped and jerked my hands back. I could easily. The inside of my head replicated the inside of this room. My heart began to pound.

O'Brian took his hands from the rack and put them on me; they felt as fat and slick as summer-fed toads.

"They say as how sensual pleasure is achieved by arousing the strongest possible feelin's," he whispered, moving his fingers up my arms and along my shoulders. "And how of all them feelin's—" he leaned in so his breath brushed my cheek— "pain is the strongest."

I turned a little so I could see him. My eyes felt like they filled half my face, and I couldn't seem to make them blink. Pain, I thought. All this time, they've been trying to pleasure us, and here I'd thought they were just mean clods. I considered telling him, I'd just as soon give the pleasure for a change, but I didn't. He was wrong. Pain wasn't the strongest of emotions. Terror was. I wondered where Harvey was? I wondered if he'd hear if I yelled. I wondered if it was time to yell?

"What if you slip?" I whispered. "What if you go too far, and someone's hurt?"

He watched me with bright, happy eyes.

"Or killed?" I added in a faint voice.

He laughed, and his hands slid up around my throat. "That's it, ain't it? Y'all think I killed her, doncha?"

"No! Oh no! I just said what if! I just wondered what if!" Definitely it was time to scream. I opened my mouth but only this choked little squeak came out.

His hands began to tremble. I could tell he was inordinately pleased with me. "That excites ya, don't it? It turns ya on? The blood! The knife slippin' in. The ultimate climax . . ." He leaned around until he could press his lips to mine. He smelled of Sen-sen. Surely not, I thought. Wherever would you get Sen-sen nowadays? And who gave a damn anyway? My mind kept spinning and turning out these weird, unrelated items.

"The ultimate climax," he whispered again against my lips.

"No!" I gasped. "No. People do get hurt." My mind scrabbled. "Anna Lisa told me about your father. That couldn't have been pleasant. You didn't enjoy that."

"My daddy," he said, and his fingers dug in hard. "Him." His eyes glazed, emptied. "That bastard." His thumbs sunk deeper.

I couldn't breathe. My mind furred red. I tore at his hands. "You . . . stop . . . hurting me!" I managed to gasp out.

His eyes were awful, vacant.

"Stop!"

He came back into his eyes slowly.

"Please . . ."

He moved his hands from my throat then and turned his back on me. "Raht. Ma daddy was a mean old buggah. But he was bigah see—so he hurt me. Bigah is as bigah does." O'Brian laughed, but this time the sound was angry, ugly, and held no excitement. "But now there ain't nobody bigah than ah am, see?" He moved away and flicked on a video player. Scene after scene of women bound and manacled and debased flashed before us. O'Brian's mood slowly improved. He began to giggle and then to dance a little on his expensive, mismatched shoes. Once, he even jiggled back to give me a good, hard pinch.

I wanted out of there. But more I wanted O'Brian. Cecile was wrong. It wasn't sexual. I'd never been more turned off. Never had I disliked anyone more. Desperately, I wanted to tear O'Brian from his throne and make him hurt as he'd hurt others.

"I saw the statue of Buddy," I blurted. If I got him, it didn't look like it would be from cunning.

He looked at me.

"Your dog."

"Buddy . . ." he said, and his eyes jerked from the woman hanging upside down before him. "Buddy was a good friend." O'Brian snapped off the set, which was a relief. "Mah best friend. Ah truly miss him. We'ah going to name our baby Buddy," he added softly.

I stared. "You're going to name . . ." I stopped myself, jumped up, and began to prowl the room. They were going to name the baby after the dog. All I am, all I've ever been taught, has never really prepared me for how to deal with all these new things. Rooms with racks. T-shirts that say "hustle." Naming babies after dogs. Lists formed and rolled in my head. And worse—there'd been not even one little flinch at the mention of the statue. Either O'Brian was a consummate actor or the damn body wasn't there after all.

I circled the cases wondering what to do next, glancing vaguely at the thumbscrews, the six-inch needles. The corpse beheaded that way? It had to be him. Didn't it?

And then I saw it. Pushed back behind a set of stocks so it was hardly visible. I blessed my twenty-twenty vision. An elaborately jeweled and embroidered belt. I stood on tip-toe and peered over and then around the stock. There was one, no, two sheaths attached, the kind that might well have held antique, jeweled knives just like the one we'd found. But both sheaths were empty. So where was the second knife? Perhaps it had been lost centuries before, buried to the hilt in the back of some Renaissance scoundrel. Then again, perhaps not. I glanced at O'Brian from the corners of my eyes. He grinned at me, pleased with my perusal of his exhibits.

I turned slowly, pressing my back and arms against the cold case. I was closer to the door than he. I thought probably I could make it if he charged. Harvey would be outside. "Where are they?" I whispered. I studied O'Brian's meticulous dark suit. He could have the second knife on him. He could have it on him right now. My breath came in strange little whimpers. I thought of my children, and how, if anything happened to me, Sid would remarry immediately and order everyone to be sensible and forget all about me. Probably this time, he'd get it right—choose someone with less pounds and less brains—not necessarily in that order.

"What?" O'Brian said.

"The knives."

"What knives?" He grinned wider.

I slid a little on the glass toward the door.

"Those," I squeaked and then forced my voice lower. "The

ones that belong there." I pointed behind me without turning to look. "There in that belt. Where are they?"

He came at me fast.

I screamed.

He shoved me hard, and I slid along the glass and landed in a pile. I scrambled to my feet and managed two steps on my rubber legs. Somehow I managed to get an iron maiden between us.

But O'Brian was just standing there, hands and nose pressed against the glass, staring into the case. "Those're fourteenth-century antiques," he wailed. "They's priceless. Priceless. And now somebody's robbed them. Somebody's robbed mah knives. It's them damn guards again. They're playin' poker again. Someone's stole 'em, and they're playin' poker. Wait heah!" He shot toward the door, wringing his hands and muttering, "Ah pay those guards a fortune. An' for what?" His steps grew shorter and faster. He looked and sounded not unlike Alice's "I'm late" rabbit. "For what? Poker, tha's what. They play poker 'n' let mah knifes be stolen. Priceless." The door clicked shut behind him.

I listened to the silence for a time and then whispered, "Shit."

I listened again, thinking hard now. "If not him, then who?" I muttered.

The iron maiden and wretched painted women watched in silence. "He's so perfect for the role," I wailed. I could hear Cecile saying that that was a perfectly predictable response from me.

I turned back to stare at the two empty sheaves. Where was that second knife? If there'd been a second. O'Brian had been fussing about knives as he went out the door. So there must have been a second. Where was it?

And then suddenly, as if by magic, the tumblers fell into place, a door within my head swung open, and the truth sprang out at me.

"No," I gasped. I took maybe thirty seconds to consider the possibility that maybe I'd known all along. And then I ran.

29

Ran for my life. I knew it was for my life. Not his—mine. I slid around the doorframe and out into the marble halls. P.H.O.'s voice trembled out over a loudspeaker. "Y'all get yerselves down to the main dining room, heah? Ah been robbed. Ah been robbed."

As I passed it, I snatched up a Picasso statue from a table. It was one of Picasso's series of heads of women. This one was grotesque, a nose like a knuckle, no forehead. I waved it over my head as I ran by the cameras. Let someone be watching, I prayed. Please be watching. Probably they were all down in the damn dining room by now. "Look, I'm stealing your priceless statue," I cried. "Look." The empty halls rang with my footsteps.

A photograph had been fastened before the camera in the small hall office. I knocked it away with the Picasso nose and saw, as it fell, that it was a picture of this same hall, empty. Clever, should any of the guards happen to be watching, which I prayed they were. I hit the door to the enclosed yard and skidded to a stop.

He smiled at me.

I swallowed twice and pushed the statue behind my back.

"You're heart's desire isn't really a dishwasher," Harvey said.

Roger was sprawled on the ground, his long hair tangled in the violets that encircled Buddy.

"What have you done to him?" I whispered. "Is he dead?"

"Not yet," he said and smiled that sweet baby's smile. I gazed into his cupid's face, at the pudgy, clean little hand that held an ornate knife, an exact match to the one I'd carried away in my purse. And it was at Roger's throat. Just as I'd seen it. Harvey moved slightly, and the knife shot blue and red lights across the high, white walls. I shook my head and moaned slightly.

"I understood what you were telling me," he whispered.

"Harvey! No! Look . . . I didn't even know about the knives . . . or about the blue and red stones then."

"The knives are such a nice touch, don't you think," he continued in that soft voice. "P.H.O. really is careless about his possessions. His security's got great holes." Harvey's little body jiggled. The red and blue lights danced. He was immensely pleased with himself.

"What did you do to Roger?" I whispered.

"Doper's are easy to drug."

"Hermoine too?"

"Oh yes. Easy. Bad, that one. She'd take anything . . . do anything."

"I don't really want this, Harvey." Tears began to run down my face. "I don't want to hurt anyone. I don't."

"I know. And you won't have to. You and Jill are good women. You never hurt people's feelings. But you must be protected."

He came toward me, his feet crunching in the gravel, his eyes glinting in the light filtering into the small yard.

"They'll know," I whispered.

"No, no. P.H.O.'s going to be blamed for Roger. Hermoine too. I took the cocaine from Hermoine's angel. I'll spread it around afterwards. A drug deal gone sour." He grinned. "Justice, don't you think?"

"Hermoine?" I whispered. "She's in the violets, isn't she? Under Buddy?"

"Well, part of her is. I brought her here inside my bleach bottle. Who'd ever suspect that?"

"Or you?" I whispered.

He grinned. "You're very good at this, Mary. You figured it all out."

"Not soon enough."

"Oh, come now. You've known for some time. Now, haven't you?"

"No," I cried. But had I? Somewhere? Sometime? "No," I whimpered.

"I don't want this, Harvey. Please."

"Go home," he said. "I'll take care of everything. You don't have to know, you know. Jill doesn't. Not really."

I stared.

After a moment, he turned away and trotted back to Roger. "Mary . . . Mary Sable," he intoned in a deep dream voice. "Mary Sable, I'm going to give you your heart's desire."

He lifted the knife high. Colored lights ran up and down the walls again.

I couldn't move. Like Salome, I was to receive that hairy head on a tray. But I'd never danced. I didn't want it. But that was a lie. I did. It *was* my heart's desire. No!

Harvey bent slowly, brushed the beard up from Roger's neck.

I did want it.

The blade tip touched Roger's neck.

I wanted it so much.

"You can have a dishwasher too," Harvey whispered.

"No."

"Jill got her vacuum cleaner, you know."

I hear the high unearthly moaning before I realize that it is coming from my own throat. The air about me seems to be hushing, thickening, sliding. The slight patch of sunlight at my feet tears, pales. The world has switched to moonlight. It occurs to me that I may be about to faint.

The knife pricks Roger's skin. A single drop of bright blood trails across his neck and begins to drip from hair to hair to hair, finally coming to rest, whole, like a bright red bead on one of the violet petals.

"Go home," Harvey says. "You don't want to watch this."

I don't. I start to turn away. The knife will sink deep and

214

impale me forever to the tray. Oh come, someone, I think. And then somehow I realize that I'm moving, flying practically.

Harvey turns in surprise and half lifts the knife. I bring the huge knuckle nose down hard on his skull. He crumples.

I stagger back, slowly focusing on my handiwork. Harvey's body is twisted over Roger's, and both of them are bleeding.

I collapse against Buddy and weep into his cold steel fur.

30

So the ladies solved it after all.

With but one deft stroke of a Picasso nose, I became a heroine and changed my life forever. Patrick Henry O'Brian purchased national air time for the occasion—a dramatic ceremony in which he presented Cecile, Roger, and me with the twenty-thousand-dollar reward. And then he turned to me and boomed, "Mary Sable!" I started and then managed not to shudder as he touched me with one of those slick hands. "Mary Sable, for your courage, little lady, we'ah proud to give ya this little token a' our esteem." Grinning now, he shoved a round box into my arms.

Now I did shudder. It was so like my dishwasher dream and like that "Surprise of Your Life" program, too, where Hermoine's head was found. I think *that* similarity was deliberate. O'Brian was nothing if not a showman.

So, with a certain amount of dread, I opened the box and pulled out the Picasso head, still with her bloody nose. Perhaps P.H.O. couldn't be bothered with cleaning it, but I suspect it was more for the dramatic effect. So I was standing there staring into its rather ugly face and thinking of Harvey, who was in a hospital with a concussion and set for a mental hospital after his release from the physical one, and I was trying to look composed—or at least not burst into tears—so I didn't even notice the paper in the bottom of the box.

"Tha's more!" O'Brian shouted. "Look heah, sugah." He snatched out the paper and began to prance a little on his uneven feet. "This heah's a contract. We'ah makin' you our Spine and Sunshine Lady. You'ah going to represent our products on TV and on personal appearance tours throughout this great land a' ours."

The audience, mostly O'Brian's cronies, went wild, and O'Brian passed me the contract. My eyes picked out the hundred-thousand-dollar-a-year salary, and I signed it right there on TV.

So now I generally spend my days at the studio, washing clothes or washing dishes for the cameras, or waiting, about to wash clothes or dishes. They wrote me into the soap, too. I'm the new kindly aunt who listens to everyone's problems.

I don't have much time now to listen to or wash for my own children, but that isn't really a problem. Sid quit his job to be home with them. His mother comes by and checks his housekeeping now. Sid isn't nearly as fond of her as he once was.

It's all a little strange. Now that my work doesn't feel quite real, people continually compliment me on really working for a change. I feel as though my mind is slightly askew, my life a little hollow, but then the outside is certainly better decorated. I have a big car and a big wardrobe and all kinds of people praise me, telling me I'm beautiful or good or smart. Sometimes they give me little gifts. They want me to put in a good word for them with O'Brian, and I do. I guess it's all part of the game, part of developing good old healthy Alexander the Great ego models.

Roger's gone, of course. He took his share of the reward and set himself up as a full-time healer and part-time dealer over in Berkeley. Storm stayed, and, strangely, I didn't mind. After I became the new "Heart's Desires" aunt, she started hanging around the set a lot. I became quite fond of her. She took the place a little of my own children, whom I saw so much less of, now that I worked such long hours.

After a while, P.H.O. began to notice Storm. She's there now. In the mansion. I see her rarely, and if I think about Storm now, I get this stiff, sick feeling all over.

Cecile says it's really dumb to blame myself for Storm.

Smith says the kid was bad to start with.

But I don't know.

I see quite a lot of Sam now. For a while we tried to collaborate on the Hermoine story, but we couldn't make it work. Sam kept trying to write me as the heroine, which was endearing of him, but it somehow didn't feel quite right. So I'd stop the writing and try to talk about Harvey and about how maybe I'd known all along.

Sam always snorted and said, "Ah, the guy was a kook—a killer."

Cecile says it's dumb to blame myself for Harvey.

Jill bakes cakes and cookies and takes them to Harvey. Sometimes I go with her. He smiles and pats my arms with those soft, little hands and says he forgives me—that he understands I had to do what I thought was right.

Still, I keep having this dream. I'm on the set, all done up in my fluffy skirts and ruffled apron. I grab a bleach bottle and, smiling for the cameras, turn it up. It gurgles twice, and only then do I realize that it's Harvey and that I have poured him down the drain. I feel terrible in the dream, but I have to keep smiling for the cameras.

Smith did give me a Christmas present. A book. *Famous Murderesses of the Twentieth Century*. Better he should have stuck to hot rollers.

But what happened to Harvey wasn't my fault. I didn't know! I had a vision! I had a vision of someone trying to kill Roger. That's all it was. And yet, I do keep remembering Portia saying, "Is it outside or inside?"

But then there *were* those red and blue lights.

It's haunting.

I thought once about talking to a shrink about it, but then I thought how I might get someone like Cecile.

So mostly I just keep busy and don't think about it.

But sometimes, just before the K-lights flare or just before I fall into uneasy, bleached sleep, I think how maybe I don't like the world or myself as much as I once did.

But then it likes me better.

So I guess it all balances out.

Doesn't it?